In Time of Harvest

John L. Sinclair

# In Time of Harvest

*Introduction by Frank Waters*

*A Zia Book*

**UNIVERSITY OF NEW MEXICO PRESS**

Albuquerque

**Library of Congress Cataloging in Publication Data**

Sinclair, John L.    1902–
  In time of harvest.

  (A Zia book)
  Reprint, with new introd., of the 1943 ed. published by
Macmillan, New York.
    I.  Title.
PZ3.S61543In    1979    [PS3537.I846]    813'.5'2    78-21434
ISBN 0-8263-0505-9

But he said, Nay; lest while ye gather up the tares, ye root up also the wheat with them. Let both grow together until the harvest; and in the time of harvest I will say to the reapers, Gather ye together first the tares, and bind them in bundles to burn them: but gather the wheat into my barn.

St. Matthew 13 : 29–30

If the Muse had ever bestowed upon me the gift of writing poetry, I would have dedicated my noblest ode, my most inspired sonnet, to that divine fruit of our native soil—the Pinto Bean.

The absence of a poetic tribute from me is not noticed. Nor do I lament my inability to achieve one. For John L. Sinclair, my friend for many years, has sung in his own way the saga of the eternal Bean in this bean-roots novel, *In Time of Harvest*.

I add the adjectives "divine" and "eternal" advisedly. For the bean, with corn, squash, and tobacco, has been one of the four sacred plants and staples of all Indian America since prehistoric times. In ancient Aztec Mexico, beans were the national dish, and they still are a favorite with most of us in New Mexico—Indian, Spanish, and Anglo alike. What would we do without frijoles, with or without an accompanying dash or dish of red or green chile? They are so ever-present that we take them for granted.

My old copy of the *New Mexico Guide Book* doesn't even list "beans," "frijoles," or "pinto" in its index. It seems more concerned with pointing out the locations of ghost towns and their mineral strikes in this widely advertised Land of Enchantment. Yet the humble bean has outlasted the crumbling camps and their worked-out gold and silver veins.

During the 1920s and 1930s the Estancia Valley in central New Mexico was the producing center of the pinto bean. This unusual background and the little-known people of the time are developed in *In Time of Harvest,* a novel unique and earthy as the Bean itself.

The story is unfolded through the lives of a family of nesters (homesteaders) who came from Oklahoma to this barren plain. Tod McClung, his wife, five children, and his father-in-law put up a one-room shack and begin to plow their homestead claim. All labor, parents and children, with "work corns on their hands, hope in their hearts." They are poor and illiterate, but their faith and heartbreaking toil are rewarded by successive crops of frijoles. Tod can say proudly that no matter how many blessings and hardships come their way, he can point out his 640 acres and his ten-by-twelve-foot shack, and ask, "What more can a man want?"

The novel is no trite, sentimental narrative of a family of "brave pioneers" clearing a wilderness, fighting off Indians, establishing a cultural center, founding a McClung dynasty. All the members of the family and most of the small community are grubby dirt farmers, bean growers, from first to last. Every character exhibits a crude realism, an earthy, unconventional response to every hardship. Their vernacular, to my knowledge, has never been recorded in print before and it carries a veracity that can't be questioned.

Their poverty and backbreaking work become too much for the children. They grow up dreaming of a romantic life beyond their bean-row horizon. Sudie runs off with T.J., a man afflicted with "chronic inertia," supporting him as a hasher in small-town restaurants. When he finally abandons her, she becomes a prostitute.

The day comes when Tewp throws down his hoe in the field and says, "The hell with it!" Scatterwhiskers, a cowpuncher, gets him a job on Dan Blakey's ranch where Tewp can become an honest-to-God cowboy and be free of bean chopping for the rest of his life. But on the ranch Tewp is caught assisting Scatterwhiskers in the theft of one of Blakey's yearling Herefords, and is sent to the state pen for five years. Says Tod, "If my boy played that coyote's trick on the man he drew wages from, he deserves a life sentence, and that's all there is to it." To his wife, Faybelle, he adds, "Another failure in the kid harvest, Hon. Another pesky tare in a sparse crop. . . . Why-all cain't I raise kids like I raise beans? Lord, Lord! It takes more than plain dirt farmin' to raise kids."

Roddy, another son, promptly skips out when he learns that he has made pregnant Earlene Smeet, a neighbor girl. "Now Roddy was not the loving kind; he was not the kissing kind, nor was he the marrying kind." He is seventeen years old and a free man to whom the rattle and roar of a freight train seem to call, "Come on, Roddy, hook me in the middle and I'll give you a free ride." So he becomes a railroad tramp until he suddenly drops dead during his travels.

Young Earlene is forced to confess her pregnancy to her parents,

Marvin and Virgie Smeet. The characters of these sanctimonious, narrow-minded, God-fearing Christians have been developed almost to the point of caricature. But at this crisis their basic human warmth redeems and transforms the caricatures into realistic characters devoid of hypocrisy. The Smeets induce Preacher Flowers, penniless save for scant hat offerings, to marry Earlene. So the fifty-eight-year-old preacher acquires a sixteen-year-old wife, a baby son, a comfortable home on the Smeet farm, and three square meals a day. Praise the Lord!

Such incidents reflect the author's compassion and his understanding of his characters' human frailties. We laugh and sympathize with them instead of judging them.

The novel abounds with irresistible humor. The country hoedown is unforgettably hilarious. Gathering together and counterpointing all members of the community, it is a high point too fully developed to be glossed over here; it must be read.

*In Time of Harvest* contains no gimmicks, no intricate plot structure. It is built on a sound knowledge of the people and the country. Mr. Sinclair worked for fourteen years as a cowboy on cattle and sheep ranches in the area. Here, while riding over the range, he learned to know the nesters intimately.

Yet firsthand knowledge alone cannot produce such a narrative. A sound craftsmanship and inborn artistry are required to mold such raw material into finished form. Mr. Sinclair's background may perhaps have helped supply this. The son of a Scottish sea captain, he was educated in England and spent his vacations in the highlands of Scotland. He was apprenticed in 1919 to learn farming, fruit growing, and stock breeding on the farms of the Duke of Buccleuch, Drumlanrig Castle, Dumfriesshire, Scotland. In 1923 he left Scotland for Canada via New Mexico, which was to hold him for the rest of his life. After years of work on the range, he became a research assistant for the Extension Service of the Museum of New Mexico, and in 1940 was appointed curator of the Lincoln County Museum and custodian of the Lincoln State Monument. In this historic old courthouse, from which Billy the Kid made his famous escape, Mr. Sinclair wrote *In Time of Harvest*. Later he served as custodian of the Coronado State Museum near Bernalillo, supervising maintenance of the great ruins of the ancient Kuaua Pueblo. The nearly two hundred short stories and articles he has written attest to his knowledge of New Mexico's history.

*In Time of Harvest* was first published in 1943. It gained immediate wide acceptance. The *Chicago Tribune,* for example, reported, "John L. Sinclair writes like mountain music turned prose and put between bean rows." And perceptive Saul Cohen of Santa Fe lists the novel as one of the ten best about New Mexico.

The Estancia Valley is no longer the Pinto Bean Capital of the World. As Mr. Sinclair has recently written, "It's a land of big ranches, irrigated fields, and long reaches of cactus-spotted land . . . abandoned homes rotting in the sun and rusted farm machinery . . . a graveyard of the prosperous times that were." *In Time of Harvest* stands as a literary monument to this once prosperous homeland of the Pinto Bean.

Frank Waters
Taos, New Mexico

*Chapter One*

WHEN Tod McClung pulled the lines to his mules and brought his
wagon to a stop on the section of land he claimed as a homestead,
way back in 1919, he looked at the sky, then he looked at the land,
then he turned and looked at his family and belongings loaded in the
wagon.

"We've done crossed seven hundred miles of dirt," he said to his
wife, Faybelle, who sat beside him holding the baby. "Seven hundred miles to reach one square mile of it we can call our own."

And so they had; because Tod had whacked those mules on the
butt for seven hundred miles—fifty-five days of mule-whacking and
steady driving from Atoka County, Oklahoma, to Torrance County,
New Mexico. It was a long haul.

Now he said to Faybelle: "I knew this land was ours the minute
the mules set their feet on it; I could smell beans in the dust they
kicked up with their hooves: beans cooked down with side meat;
beans sacked up to sell in Mountainair for good solid cash; beans
to feed and clothe us all."

Faybelle was mighty weary after the long haul, and all she did
was sit and say, "I reckon."

The kids, loaded in the back, jabbered a plenty, and somehow they
wished the trip was not over. They would have liked to keep a-going.
There were five of them—all stout kids even to the youngest, who
slept in Faybelle's arms and still wore didies.

At the tailboard of the wagon sat Faybelle's old daddy, who was
called Piddle, and he said nothing. Piddle seldom said anything. He
looked at the extra mule and saddle pony that were hitched behind,
looked at them like he had done for seven hundred miles. And although Piddle never said much his jaws were always a-moving because he chewed tobacco a plenty. All through the trip he helped
break the monotony by aiming his spit at the star on the pony's forehead and nine times out of ten hitting the mark. So now after that

long haul you couldn't see the white star any more; it was chestnut just like the rest of the pony's hide.

Once when Piddle said something, he said: "Ain't no need for me to talk. There's plenty in this family to make noise! . . . As for exercisin' my jaws, this quid keeps 'em movin'."

Piddle was Faybelle's daddy, and he raised a stout one in that girl. She was now thirty years old, and she married Tod way back when she was eighteen. She made him a good wife because she knew what a man wanted; she knew she would not only have to cook his vittles, but have to do as much work in the fields to raise them as he did, and to slack off only at times when the kids came—and that was steady and often.

There were five of them, those kids—Sudie, ten years old, the only girl so far; Roddy, eight; Tewp, five; Jay Boy, three; and Buster, who still wore didies, was only a year old.

Tod knew something—so did Piddle, so did the kids old enough to savvy: that Faybelle was fixing to have another come October. Because back there in Atoka County, two months before, just before they started out west, Faybelle told them all that Tod had done it again. Sudie said she hoped it would be a sister, Piddle said nothing, and Tod looked at the store of vittles he had put by to tide them over until the first bean harvest, and said: "God damn."

Now they had come to the land; it was April and time to break the soil. The wagon was stopped on the homestead they had travelled so far to reach—there was no time to dally.

But still they just sat there and looked about them.

"Looks like bean country to me," said Tod. "Level and rich—worth comin' out to get and a couple years of starvation to put in shape."

About them rolled the prairie—mile upon mile of it in all directions—flat, and yet tawny from the frost of the past winter. Far to the west they could see the peaks of the Manzano Mountains, north lay the Pedernal Hills, south the long range of the Gallinas, east the endless flat plains over which they had come.

Tod's homestead was a solid square mile of unbroken turf, solid except for one swath that was cut east to west down the middle—

the track of the Santa Fe Railway that stretched plumb from Chicago to California.

"Doggone," said Tod. "I'm glad we've got a railroad near. I like to hear them old rattlers toot and whistle just like the Katy did back in Atoka County."

Sure enough, Tod's wishes were to come true, for right there on that Santa Fe Railway, right there on Tod's homestead, those firemen kept shoveling the coal to the westbound freights and limiteds; and those eagle-eyed engineers kept handling the throttles, fixing to twist their tails over the Abo Pass beyond Willard, and run them down to Belen on the Rio Grande.

So Tod McClung looked up at the sky, and he felt the west wind brush his face; then he looked down on the land and he saw that it was rich, level, and had a slight drainage to the draw. And like in a dream he saw beans sprouting out of the soil; he saw them bush out and bear pods in clusters—long and green—filled with the stuff they pay cash for in Mountainair.

Then he climbed behind on the wagon and unlashed the ropes from the John Deere breaking plow and he pitched it onto the earth. Then he kicked off a set of hickory double-trees. Then he said:

"Me and the mules are fixin' to raise beans, and right here is where we'll grow 'em."

To Piddle, he said:

"Looks like bean country to me. Don't it to you, dad?"

But Piddle said nothing because he was chewing his quid, and what looked all right to Tod McClung looked all right to Piddle.

"Over yonder by the railroad," Tod said to Faybelle, "is where we'll build our house—for I like to watch them old rattlers roll."

The wagon started off toward the tracks while Tod McClung bragged on his land and aimed to raise beans. When he got down by the fence he called the mules to a stop and said: "As good a place as any, I reckon."

He unloaded his junk, and the kids scampered around; then he unhitched the mules and the saddle pony, and he hobbled them to let them graze. He pitched the tent right where the house was going to be.

Tod McClung looked about him in all directions, and he saw houses and the brown fields of nesters just like himself; and the fields were plowed and ready for seed. They were widely scattered and far apart, with stretches of dun-colored prairie between. But that got Tod to studying that if he was going to raise a crop in that year of 1919 he had better get on his high horse.

So the next day he saddled the pony and rode to town to see about the things he had ordered from the John Deere dealer there—things he had written to say he needed and were too heavy to carry all the way from Oklahoma, things to be there by the time he and his folks reached the land.

And sure enough, he found the John Deere dealer with all his farm tools stacked up—a harrow, a middlebuster, a go-devil, a riding cultivator, plenty of hoes for Faybelle and the kids. And then he had also written about material for fencing, so as to close his place in. And he was damned if that John Deere dealer hadn't gotten a Mexican to go out on the mesas and cut cedar posts enough to carry four miles of barbwire fence, enough to close in all of Tod's land. And right there with those farm tools were piled rolls and rolls of barbwire. When Tod saw all this he was plumb tickled to death, for he had saved up enough money to pay for all that stuff.

The John Deere dealer told Tod that he would have the tools and fencing hauled out to the homestead the next day, and that he would tell the Mexican to do the same with the cedar posts. So Tod went home and hitched the mules to the breaking plow—because he was a bean-growing fool and was wasting no time.

Tod yelled to the mules; the plow went forward and the share ripped the earth. It cut a furrow a quarter-mile long from west to east; then he drove another from north to south for a quarter-mile, then from east to west, and back north to the corner from which he started. And when he had done that he had a boundary marked out for a forty-acre field.

He plowed up that prairie turf until the sun set low; then he unhitched the mules from the plow, went back to the tent where were his wife, his kids, and his junk—and he put corn chops in the nose bags so that the mules would be fed and rearing to go when he set to plowing the next day. And by the end of April, Tod McClung had a forty-acre field all plowed up and middlebusted to long, deep furrows that would receive any moisture the elements should offer, all set to be seeded to crop.

What land the nesters had not taken up was open range in Torrance County, New Mexico. There were cattle and horses, even burros, running over the prairie in herds. Tod lost no time in getting together Faybelle, Piddle, and the kids stout enough to work, and they strung up that boundary fence to keep stray stock out of the pasture. They dug the postholes thirty feet apart, and in them set the cedar posts. When they had them all set and tamped they stretched three strands of barbwire stout enough to faze any range bull; and they stapled them securely to the posts. Tod planted the corner and gateposts three feet in the ground and braced them with deadmen and guywires; for he knew what he was doing and he wanted the fence to stay put.

And when the neighbors saw what Tod was doing, they said: "That man from Oklahoma is a workin' fool, and he's out to make a crop; because he gits on his high horse and don't let anything git in his way."

So when Tod got his folks and his junk settled down there by the Santa Fe Railway the neighbors came around to say howdy. The women chewed the rag with Faybelle, the men talked mules and beans with Tod. They came from near by and up by the Salt Lakes country, from the Pedernal Hills and down from Willard.

When they all got together Tod would brag on Faybelle, his kids, and himself; and he would tell them what a rounder Piddle had been in his younger days. And when Piddle heard Tod bragging to the neighbors of his past doings he just shut his mouth and let Tod do all the talking. But Tod always gave Piddle credit for one thing: that he had raised a real honest-to-God woman in Faybelle.

For a fact, Faybelle *was* a real honest-to-God woman. She had stout legs, hard muscles in her arms, wide hips, and enough milk to raise a slew of kids. She could cook heavy food like Tod wanted it, and she could sling a hoe in the field like a man. She was a she-sized woman for a man who worked and got around.

Back in them old Oklahoma days, while Tod left Faybelle at home in Atoka County—to tend the farm and raise the kids—he went off to where the wages were. He went to Muskogee and found him a job of work in the Katy roundhouse; he went to Tulsa, and Drumright, and Konawa, where he made big pay by dressing tools in the oil fields. And one winter he even joined a buddy in the Kiamichi Mountains, where they ran off moonshine whisky and raked in the cash.

When he had all this money earned he came home to his rented farm on the Muddy Boggy—right there in Atoka County—and he found that Faybelle had worked as hard as he had. So with all this money they aimed to come out to New Mexico and take up a homestead.

"A man needs a woman, and a man needs a job of work," Tod told the neighbors; "but he don't want a job that won't pay big wages or a woman he has to support. I've worked and raked in the cash, and I've got a woman who's a hoe-slingin' fool."

The neighbors looked at Faybelle; they saw she had stout legs and arms, wide hips and big breasts—then they saw all the things Tod had bought with the money he earned, and they reckoned he was right.

Now although Tod had six hundred and forty acres he could damn near call his own, and he would get his deed when he had done three years of proving up, there were a few mighty uncomfortable situations that had to be bided by; but these fazed Tod nary a bit— because he was a man who could take it and get around.

There was so much to do in the field—such as plowing it up and seeding it—that he didn't have time to build his house. All eight of them, Tod, Faybelle, Piddle, and the kids, got along in that little ten-by-twelve tent. They slept on pallets: Piddle by himself; Tod, Faybelle, and the baby together; and the four other kids all in one bed. There was no room to cook inside, so Faybelle tended the vittles on a pot rack over a fire in the open. And because Faybelle had a strong man to feed she kept those pots boiling.

Even in summer it got pretty doggone chilly at nights on those open prairies, that rolling grass that just seemed to get higher and higher until it crawled up on the Manzano Mountains; but Tod and his folks kept warm because of all those breathing bodies that were sleeping in that one tent. It was snug, because Tod had the bottom sides of that tent banked with dirt, and every night when they turned in he laced the flap so as that the cool air could not get inside.

One night they had a visitor while they were sleeping that played holy hell with everything and everybody concerned. Faybelle had some covered pots of food around the pot rack outside and somehow a skunk got a whiff of them and came nosing around. He tried to bust open the pots but he found that Faybelle had clamped the lids down solid, and he was a mighty disappointed skunk. Then he got to thinking there might be something in the tent, so he just stuck his head under the flap and crawled in.

Everything went well at first because all were sleeping quietly, and Piddle was only snoring moderate—not enough to scare the skunk. The skunk just nosed about and looked for chuck. Then something woke Buster, the baby, and he started bawling. Faybelle turned and said: "Doggone it, what's ailin' my little hon? I'll bet he's so dog-gone hongry he could eat a skunk!" Then she gave the baby her breast so he could get some dinner.

When the skunk heard that noise he got scared. And what I mean he got *scared*!

He got out from under the flap all right, but before he did he fixed up those pallets and the inside of that tent a plenty. Stink! Lord God!

Then all those folks came out of that tent like bees from a hive. Faybelle yelled: "Lord, Lord!" The kids bawled, and Tod and Piddle cussed like he-men.

They sat up all night by the fire and drank coffee, and the next day Faybelle washed the quilts and aired the tent; but for many weeks after that they could smell skunk about the outfit that they couldn't get shed of.

"Could have been worse," said Tod.

"Praise Jesus it was a skunk that crawled in on us and not a rattle-snake," said Faybelle.

Piddle never said what he thought about it.

After Tod had the beans planted, the west wind turned to the east and the sky clouded over.

"It's gonter rain like a wampus cat," said Tod, while Faybelle gathered up the chuck around the pot rack and packed it into the tent.

And sure enough it did. The rain came down and soaked Tod's field and pasture a plenty; and when the sun shone again the days got hot. The prairie turned green with the new grama grass, and on his field Tod saw the beans sprout in the soil—rows of them a quarter-mile long; and the corn came up, so did the kaffir corn and the sorghum cane.

Tod got ready the go-devil and the middlebuster and fixed to battle the weeds. When the corn crop reached a height of about two feet he ran the middlebuster down the ridges between the rows and banked the soil around the roots, so they could be deep down and feed on the moisture that soaked in from the summer rains. And while he did that Faybelle, Piddle, and the kids got a hoe apiece so they could make hash of the weeds. And the crop came up clean, because they were all working fools and knew what it was all about.

Tod was happy when he ran the go-devil down the rows because he was making a bean crop, too. If he made a crop he would thresh and sack beans come harvest, and they paid cash for sacked beans in Mountainair.

While he worked he sang one of those songs he made up himself; his voice was so loud you could hear it a quarter-mile with the wind blowing.

> *Sweetheart, sweetheart, why're you so doggone mean?*
> *Sweetheart, sweetheart, why're you so doggone mean?*
> *'Cause you don't treat me right,*
> *And now I'm raisin' beans.*

That was Tod's song.

While Tod and his folks worked the field the east wind brought rain and the west wind brought warmth and sunshine. The weeks passed and the months went by; the crop ate the good stuff in the soil and the roots drank up the moisture that came down from the sky. The stalks of the corn and cane got fat and high, and the beans bushed out like bristles on a porcupine. When September came around it looked to Tod like there would be a big harvest to work on, and Tod and his folks were plumb tickled to death.

One time during the summer when the neighbors came over to

chew the rag with Tod, they looked at Tod's kids; and then they got to studying on how young Faybelle was to have so many, and then they thought: "It's a plenty."

"There's a heap of drawbacks we folks out here have to bide," said one of them; "but I figure the worst of all is the lack of schoolin' for the kids. It's a long ways into Willard, and no trottin' distance to any place where there's a schoolteacher. But I reckon we'll get a school in this community in time. Meanwhile, we can all pray to the Lord."

But Tod was content to let things be as they were, for he said: "I'll be a son of a bitch if I want to raise my kids to be jelly beans and educated fools. I can learn 'em all they want to know myself; and if they know how to work that's all the educatin' they need. If they want to read, Faybelle can learn 'em the words in the Bible, and the Lord's word is good enough for anybody."

"The law will make 'em go to school," argued the neighbor.

"Then if the law makes 'em go they can go, and I cain't kick. But I always say enough is enough, and if they git the idea that they want to go beyond the eighth grade I'll whale the hell out of 'em so's they'll git out of the notion."

Then the neighbors looked again at those five poor kids, and then they looked at Faybelle. When they saw Faybelle's waist, which was getting big in the family way, they went home and said among themselves: "Lord God Almighty!"

As early October and the harvest drew near, Faybelle felt like she couldn't do the work as a woman should, for her time was getting mighty close. But although she tired easily she lent her hand as best she could; she chopped the firewood, slung a hoe in the field, and cooked the vittles.

Then the day came when Tod looked at the bean crop and saw that it was ready to pull and gather. The beans rattled in the pods, and when Tod crunched them in his hand he found them to be speckled and dry. Then they all got together and pulled the plants from the rows. They piled them in heaps and left them to dry in the sun.

After a few days Tod went out to the field and kicked into a shock of beans. They were dry and brittle and ready to thresh. He hitched the mules to the wagon, and all the folks took a pitchfork apiece and they drove out to the field to thresh the beans.

"I don't feel good today, Tod," said Faybelle. "I'm tired and plumb heavy all over. I'll do what I can, though."

So Faybelle went out to the field with the folks and they threshed beans. Tod drove the wagon up beside the shocks, Faybelle pitched the forkfuls up over the sideboards while Tod and Piddle whammed hell out of the beans. As fast as Faybelle pitched the stuff up on one side Piddle and Tod threshed it in the wagon and threw the straw and empty pods over the other. When they finished with one shock they moved on to another, leaving the kids to make a neat pile of the straw left behind them. And while they were doing this the beans became thick on the floor of the wagon.

"Pitch 'em up, gal," yelled Tod, for he was busy threshing beans and the forkfuls were not coming fast enough. "We've made a crop and we're harvestin' beans, and we cain't work after the sun goes down."

Then he said, "Damn," because when he looked down beside the wagon he saw that Faybelle was no longer pitching and had fainted to the ground.

Both Tod and Piddle leapt down, and they took Faybelle and laid her in the straw. She was plumb white about the gills. The kids gathered around and tried to figure out what ailed their ma.

"He'p me hist her in the wagon," said Tod to Piddle, "and I'll drive her to the tent quick. . . . Then you run and git the neighbor woman who's got a doctor book, and tell her to come over, for we'll need her he'p."

Faybelle groaned as they lifted her onto the wagon; and Tod said: "Easy, gal, we're with you-all."

Piddle set out at a run for the neighbor's; Tod had told him what to do, and there was no need to talk because he was chewing his quid.

The mules raced over the field and onto the pasture; Faybelle lay on the floor of the wagon, half buried in the beans. Tod jerked the lines and brought the mules to a stop before the tent. Faybelle was no light woman, but Tod took her in those big strong arms of his and carried her into the tent. When Faybelle was laid on the pallet she spoke.

"Doggone it, honey," she said. "It looks like my time has come again, and why it should come in the middle of bean harvest I don't know. But we have no choice in that, I reckon, and it's up to the Lord to decide when. This is one time in a woman's life when she's the weakest and the strongest all mashed up into one."

All Tod said was: "Hush, gal! Easy, hon! We were fixin' to quit anyhow, because the sun was gittin' low and it was time to do up the chores."

He held Faybelle's head in his arms as she lay on the pallet. The kids stood by and Sudie tried to reckon how long it would be before she would have a sister, and figured she would get real mad if it were another brother.

The pain gripped Faybelle.

"Easy, gal—easy, sweetheart," said Tod.

When the pain hit Faybelle she shut her eyes and groaned, but when they were open she looked at Tod.

"Piddle's gone to git the neighbor woman with the doctor book. They'll be here right quick," said the man.

Faybelle held Tod close to her, and her grip around him was strong when the bad spells came. From outside they heard the roar and rattling of a freight train on the railroad. It was going west.

"Listen to that old freight," said Tod, as he kissed Faybelle's forehead and wiped the sweat away. "It's a full mile long, and it's hootin' and tootin' like it had religion; and the red caboose at the end is tryin' hard to keep up."

Faybelle—even in her pain—smiled at Tod, and with her strong arms drew him closer to her. The engineer on the train gave one long blast to the whistle, and the sound rolled over the prairie like the wind.

Then the flap of the tent opened and Piddle and the neighbor woman came in. She had her doctor book.

When the freight train passed Tod's homestead on its way west the engineer pulled the whistle because there was a crossing ahead. It was a fifteen-mile run into Willard and he was giving her the gun because he was behind time. There was no stop this time at Lucy, but he would have to clear the track at Willard for an eastbound limited. The fireman was keeping the steam up, but he was saving his strength for the grade over the Abo Pass—which lay ahead in the Manzanos—and where, he reckoned, he would have to get on his high horse. The engineer was chewing tobacco, and he spat from the cab and nearly hit a lizard that was slithering down from the track.

The train was a solid mile long, and it hauled several empty refrigerator cars heading back to California; it carried boxcars to be switched at Belen—some to go north to Albuquerque, some south to El Paso. About halfway through the train two bums, who had hooked a ride, sat in a gondola swapping big windies of where they had been and where they were going. The conductor had told them that he would kick them off at Willard, but they thought to themselves that they would just crawl back on when the train pulled out again. Back in the caboose the conductor and the brakey talked about the railroad—all they ever talked about was the railroad.

The freight pulled into Willard and it switched some cars. It picked up as many as it dropped, and the brakey kicked the bums off. The eastbound limited came through, and because it was supper-time the dining car was full of people. A couple men stood on the observation platform and waved to some kids as the train pulled out. They stood behind the big glass disc at the end railing that had the blue cross of the Santa Fe on it. They were dudes and wore suits.

When the freight drew out of Willard the conductor found that the two bums had crawled on again and he aimed to kick them off at Mountainair. The fireman got busy and fed coal to the firebox so as to get steam up for the grade over the Abo Pass. The engineer had his hand on the throttle and was twisting her tail.

"In Bakersfield, California," said one bum to the other, "you can get a feed for a dime, and there's a place where you can flop for nothin'—but you'll get the crabs like I did. The Salvation Army gave me a pair of shoes, and I blew town after I was let out of jail."

It was night when they crawled over the Abo Pass; the moon was full and the stars glittered by the thousand. The conductor picked up some cars loaded with beans at Mountainair and kicked the bums off. When the train pulled out again he had the extra cars and the bums too.

From the Abo Pass down to Belen the fireman took it easy, and he wiped the sweat away with his glove. They crossed the river, and one bum said to the other: "I came over the Mississippi at East St. Louis, but it's a bigger river than the Rio Grande."

As the train approached Belen it slowed down to a snail's pace; and just before it reached the yards it stopped. The bums quit the gondola and headed for the jungles beside the track. The dick here would be tough on them, they were told.

The engineer sat in his cab waiting for the signal to flash so he could pull into the Belen yards. The fireman leaned out of his window and yelled something to the brakey who walked up with his lantern. The engineer pulled the whistle and gave three long blasts.

And just as that Santa Fe freight was fixing to pull into the Belen yards—that mile-long train with the red caboose—just as that engineer had his hand on the throttle ready to give her the steam, the very minute he sent those three long blasts from the whistle into the night, back there in the tent in the bean country, way east beyond the Abo Pass, Lyndel, Tod McClung's younger daughter, was born.

## Chapter Two

Now Piddle had been a rambling fool and had got around, and he liked the folks to know about it. So when the summer of 1925 came along he got to studying on how old he was, and he reckoned himself to be sixty-four. He had seen his best days and was now settled down to take it easy. He had horsed around in the big cities back yonder—St. Louis, New Orleans, Memphis, and Little Rock—and in those places he proved himself to be a he-rounder and a studhorse from way back.

Although he was proud to have Tod tell the neighbors about the good old days Piddle would seldom say anything for himself. He just let Tod have full rein and he spoke only when Tod asked him a question—for there was so much rambling and horsing in Piddle's younger years that Tod would forget sometimes, and when Tod asked him about an adventure that he had partly forgotten, but recalled Piddle telling him, the old man spit out his quid and opened up; and when he got done opening up Piddle just put in a fresh quid and started chewing. But when Piddle had the McClung folks together—just them alone—that was different, and he told them a plenty.

"A man cain't set still and be a man," he once told the McClung folks. "He's got to work and git a woman; and a rounder can git a woman easy because he's a he-man, and a he-man is what a woman likes best."

That is how Piddle preached his philosophy.

And when Piddle told of his past doings, while he spoke of way back yonder, Tod would laugh and say, "God damn," Faybelle would blush and say, "I swear, Paw!" and the six kids would look up at him and listen—four of them in admiration, two of them in wonder.

Even at that, the occasions when Piddle opened up were scarce, and he always had to be primed like a dry pump to get him to say something to amuse the folks. Often he would sit alone out on the woodpile, just thinking; and all the time his jaws would be moving, chewing hell out of that old quid. And those who saw him there would know that his thoughts were way back yonder—maybe rambling down the Mississippi, maybe hooking a freight out of Chattanooga, maybe serving out a spell in the jailhouse; but his thoughts were not here, they were way back yonder.

Faybelle often got to thinking if the Lord wouldn't strike her down for allowing Piddle to tell of his wicked doings to the kids.

"I ought to kick like a bay mule," she once said to Tod after Piddle had quit talking and gone to chewing. "Because there's two girls in our bunch and we ought to raise 'em ignorant of such doin's."

When she said that Tod didn't speak, and he looked as though he didn't give a damn. Piddle just put his quid between his back teeth and opened up.

"I cain't git no respect for a woman who don't love a rounder," he said. "Back in St. Louis they ran me down like a pack of hound dogs after a coon; because they talked among themselves of what a studhorse I was, and how I got around and raked in the cash."

In that year of 1925 Tod and Faybelle had a family of six kids —four boys and two girls. Sudie, the oldest of the bunch, was sixteen, and she was showing signs of being a she-woman. She was tall and slim and pretty as a doll. Her hips looked like they were going to be wide, like Faybelle's; her arms and legs were strong and slender, and her breasts made her look like a grown woman. She had dark brown hair and sort of slant eyes; and her lips were thin and red, and folks reckoned she carried them tighter than she should.

Roddy was the oldest boy, and he could work as hard as the grown folks. He was fourteen and already a man-sized kid. He was strong, like Tod, and Piddle taught him to cuss and chew tobacco. He could skin mules from hell to high water, and when they acted decent he got the most worth out of them; but when they balked and got ornery he would whale them with the lines. Sometimes when they sulled * he would get real mad and spit tobacco juice in their eyes. That got them mules on their high horse, because they couldn't buffalo Roddy McClung.

* Sulked.

Tewp and Jay Boy were younger and had not been around the community as Sudie and Roddy had. The two oldest kids had something in common that the others did not have—especially Sudie who was nearly ready enough to get married and have a man of her own.

But the two youngest were Tod's pride and joy. Buster, during that summer of 1925, was seven years old; and Lyndel, the youngest of all, was five and wouldn't turn six until bean harvest. And, just as these two were apart from the others in Tod's heart, so they played together by themselves, away from the other kids. They were as different as two white Holsteins in a herd of black Angus.

Piddle didn't like these two nary a bit, because they were always doing something by themselves and wouldn't give his talk any mind when he went to all that trouble of opening up.

"That Lyndel and that Buster, God damn 'em," Piddle would say, "are like the glibs on a vat of boilin' molasses. When they git older they'll think themselves smarter than the others, but for a fact they'll only be fit to skim off and throw away."

Buster would listen to Piddle but without much show of attention; Lyndel would look at him and sometimes cry, and wonder how her granddaddy could be so mean.

"She's the cryin' kind," said Piddle, plumb disgusted. "She's weak."

Lyndel was different from Sudie in most ways, but she showed she was a daughter of Tod and Faybelle too. Her hair wasn't yellow, it was pure gold. It had a curl to it that Faybelle didn't have to dress up—it was natural, just like the rest of the kid. Her big eyes were bright and kind; and her little lips were full, red, and when she smiled it got Tod all het up with love for the youngster, and he would take his little daughter on his lap and say: "Sweetest lil old young un as ever had a gut."

Tod McClung had improved his homestead right smart since the day he broke the first soil back in 1919. He had attended to all the requirements that the United States of America put on homesteaders, things that had to be done to get the deed, such as living on the place most of the year and building a flood-water tank of banked earth in the draw. Tod and his folks did better than that: they lived on the place all year round because it was their home, and Tod got the mules to working and together they built the tank, because he wanted to catch all the flood water he could and put an end to driving the stock for water to a neighbor's windmill three miles away. For the family's drinking use Roddy would haul water on the wagon, in barrels, from the windmill, and they used a plenty because there were nine of them. After Tod had done the three years of proving up, the United States government gave him his deed.

During those passed years—every fall—Tod harvested and sacked beans, and because the Lord was good to him, he sold them in Mountainair and raked in the cash. With the money he earned he built him a house of rough lumber, and on it he put a tin roof. He got out the Montgomery Ward catalogue and ordered furniture—a cookstove for Faybelle, three rocking chairs for the grownups to sit in, and a guitar and a slew of French harps for the kids. Piddle didn't like his rocking chair and never sat in it. He liked the wood box by the stove and said it was more comfortable and handy to the grate when it came time for him to spit.

The house had one big room—where they all slept and sat around —and a lean-to where Faybelle cooked the vittles. Along the front was a porch. Faybelle pasted newspapers on the inside walls for insulation—three layers thick—and she saved all the picture papers for the outside layer and made sure to get them right side up so the folks could look at them.

With that money Tod bought him an automobile too—a second-hand Cadillac, 1918 model, which cost him seventy-five dollars—and he filled it up with gas and it got them all around. Tod was mighty proud of that Cadillac because he was told that when it was new it cost five thousand dollars and only a rich man could afford to buy one—and Tod reckoned it must be a good car if it cost five thousand dollars. Roddy was a handy mechanic, so he tore off the old body and built on a strip-down bed of rough lumber, big enough to haul the whole family at once. And every time Tod went to Estancia, the county seat, to pay his taxes or attend to big business, he would take all the folks with him, and he would open up the cut-out and give that Cadillac the gun. And when everybody heard the roar of that car and saw the dust climbing up to the sky from off the road, they knew Tod McClung was going to town.

Tod was a man who liked to make money, and he got to thinking of ways of improving his income. He bought ten young Hereford cows all fixing to find a calf. They were high-grade stuff, not scrubs like most of the nesters had—and they all found live calves but two. Tod ran them in his pasture and fed them bean hay. They got fat and sassy in the summer, those cows, but in the winter they got poorly, grass-bellied. Tod shoveled the bean hay to them and brought them through.

While Tod was doing all this the neighbors prayed to the Lord; and, sure enough, in time a little white frame schoolhouse was built in the community and a schoolteacher named Miss Simonson came to educate the nesters' kids.

The neighbors who came over to visit with Tod's folks told him Miss Simonson seemed mighty anxious to have the McClung kids come to school. But Tod answered that he and Faybelle made those kids: it was up to him and her to decide what to do with them, and it was none of Miss Simonson's business.

"There's a law," said the neighbors.

That got Tod rattled.

"I've made moonshine whisky up in the Kiamichi Mountains," he said, "and I've found a heap of fun just laughin' at the law and makin' 'em feel silly. Piddle's rambled and got around, and the law didn't like his doin's; but that didn't faze Piddle a bit, and he's alive and kickin' and as happy as a pig in the slop."

The neighbors listened to Tod, and then they said:

"But times are changin', Tod McClung. You and Piddle are grown, and your best days have been in the past. Them youngsters have yet to work and git around, and the years to come will ask more of the sense in a man or woman's head and won't give much mind to the stoutness of the arms and legs. Ask the kids themselves, Tod. Ask them if they want to go to school!"

But if the kids opened their mouths to speak Tod would tell them to shut up.

Besides, Tod had met Miss Simonson on the road one evening, and he was scared she was going to tell him to send the kids to school. She just kept on coming and passed him without a word except 'How do you do?' and Tod raised his hat like a man should; he saw her, and when he saw her he reckoned he didn't like her.

"She's sickly," Tod said to the neighbors. "She don't git out in the open. Education keeps her indoors away from the sun, and in time it will kill her. She's only a woman from the neck up and nothin' from there down."

"Her skirts are so short you can see her knees," said Faybelle. "I ain't goin' to raise my girls to be nothin' like her."

The neighbors turned to Piddle and asked him what he thought; but Piddle said nothing because he was chewing his quid. He did not need to speak because they all knew for sure what Piddle thought of Miss Simonson and her education.

"There," said Tod, pointing to Piddle, "sits a man who's got around without education. He doesn't know what sickness is—he's only had two sick days in his life that we know of—he's strong and ignorant but knows how to work."

For a fact, as far as anybody knew, Piddle had had only two sick days in his life—once right here on the homestead, and before, long before, when he rambled and gambled around.

The only time Faybelle had seen him sick was on a day in the year they built the house on the homestead—the year Tod got his deed from the United States—the day they all had chicken mulligan and hominy for dinner.

Piddle reckoned he ate too much—that was how come he got sick.

Anyway, after Piddle got up from the table, and had washed his mouth out with a dipper of water, he began to get white around the gills. He sat down by the stove as usual but did not take a chew. Tod looked at Faybelle, and they both looked at Piddle.

"He's sick," said Faybelle.

"I ain't done it," said Piddle, acting kind of mad.

Then he got up and staggered to his bed like he was drunk.

Faybelle knew better than to go near Piddle until he started groaning; but they waited and, sure enough, after a while Piddle groaned.

"I reckon it's a tapeworm," said Faybelle.

"May be," said Tod.

They watched Piddle twist in agony until he spoke.

"Git the hell out of here and let me be!" he cried. "Cain't you-all let a man be sick in peace?"

So Tod and Faybelle let Piddle be and groan.

Now Piddle was Faybelle's daddy, and she was worried about him. She motioned Tod to follow her into the lean-to, where the kids were hunkered down around the stove, and when they got together they talked seriously about Piddle's ailment.

"I reckon he's got a tapeworm, all right," Faybelle said, "because every time it gapes it makes him groan."

Then they got to studying.

Piddle lay on the bed groaning and kicking his bare feet in the air; and every time he made a noise Faybelle got herself into a worry. Then, when she could stand it no longer, she whispered in Tod's ear.

Tod studied a minute.

"I reckon Roddy could saddle up the pony and ride into Willard," he said. "Then we'd know for sure what's ailin' him."

When Piddle heard Tod say that, he got on his high horse. He came off that bed like a mad bull and ran into the lean-to as though nothing bothered him.

"If you send for a doctor," cried Piddle, "I'll tear him up and pitch him into the yard! I'll do that as soon as he sets foot in the house! . . . You know that, daughter, and you-all ain't got no feelin' for your paw when you git such notions. You-all aimin' to murder me?"

The kids ran out in the yard as scared as jack rabbits, but Tod and Faybelle stood their ground and looked at Piddle like he had gone crazy.

"I'll cure myself," said Piddle. "I did it once before, a worser ailment than this, and by God I'll do it agin."

As he said that he took down from the shelf a bottle of black horse medicine—guaranteed to cure any horse ailment from the colic to the bots—and he took a swig of it like he would a dipper of water. And after he did that he picked up his chewing tobacco and went out in his bare feet.

"I'm a sick man," he said as he went out to the yard. "Let me be, and let me have my ailment in peace."

Tod, Faybelle, and all the kids watched Piddle go into the backhouse and close the door.

"That poor human bein' ain't got one lick of sense," said Faybelle sadly.

When suppertime came around, Faybelle said she figured it was about time Piddle should be getting out.

"He's been in there four hours," she said.

They all ate their supper and didn't talk. They were worried. It became dark and the air outside was chilly. Lyndel and Buster went to bed; but the rest of the kids sat up with Tod and Faybelle, and they all talked about people they knew who had gotten sick. Faybelle made a big pot of coffee, and they drank one cup after another until daylight showed itself the next morning. Piddle had not yet come out.

When the sun came up they all went out to the yard and watched where Piddle had gone from a distance. The sunshine made the tin roof glitter, the door was shut tighter than on a jailhouse, and not a sound came from the inside.

Faybelle was not the crying kind—none of Piddle's family had been as soft as that—but now two or three tears were working in her eyes and making them wet.

"Do you reckon he's dead?" she asked Tod.

"It'll take more than a tapeworm and mule medicine to kill Piddle," Tod told her; "but I reckon somebody ought to go over and git him out. He's been in there long enough."

Faybelle could not keep from studying.

"If he's dead we'll have to haul him out and bury him," she said, wiping her eyes with her sleeve; "but if he's alive and we don't let him be we'll only git a cussin'."

Roddy said he was getting sick of fooling around.

"I'm goin' out to git him—dead or alive," said the kid. "There ain't no sense in him keepin' us guessin' which he is!"

Faybelle called as Roddy took off, "Mind out, son, he kicks like a bay mule when he gits mad."

Roddy did not have to go far, for, just as he started out, the door opened, and there they saw Piddle. He spit out his quid, gave the folks a look that said, "Let me be," hooked his toe in the latch, and pulled the door shut again.

"He's alive and kickin'," said Sudie.

Then they all went in to breakfast and let Piddle be.

An hour later Piddle came in stomping like nothing ailed him, chewing tobacco, and said he wanted something to eat.

When Faybelle told the neighbors of Piddle's ailment they said: "We all kind of figured there was a little bit of mule in him."

Piddle heard them say that, and he was mighty proud. But that was the only time Faybelle had seen him sick, seen it with her òwn eyes so she could swear to it on the Bible. The other time, back in his rounder days, she had only heard tell.

It happened in Little Rock, Arkansas, when Piddle had quit his family in Okmulgee County for a spell of horsing around. It was when he was drinking right smart and dressed up like a fancy gent; when he was handy with the cards and dice and followed the Mississippi steamboats as a passenger for a living. He had a pack of marked cards and a set of loaded dice.

In those good old days Piddle wore a suit like a dude, polished his shoes every day, and shaved his face regular. He had a mustache, which he trimmed. He had a fancy tie with a diamond stickpin in it, his starched cuffs came way down over his hands, and his high collar nearly touched the lobes of his ears. On his head was a brown derby. He used perfume, and you could smell him.

One day, on that side-wheel boat the *Seymour Andrews,* Piddle met up with a gambler as handy with the cards and dice as himself. Piddle worked hard at the game, but soon he found himself left with only the fancy clothes on his back and his work clothes bundled up in his traveling bag. Then he got hungry and couldn't do anything about it, because that gambling man had broken him flat.

When he landed in Memphis the whores wouldn't feed him, they who had been so kind to him and fussed over him when he was flush with cash.

"I ought to be whipped over the ear with a dead rabbit!" said Piddle to himself. "I ought to be jailed for lettin' that gamblin' man clean me out!"

He thought about the inhospitable folks of Memphis.

"What is a poor man like me to do?" he said. But no one said anything but his stomach, which growled like a surly dog. Then he got so hungry he thought it best to get him a job of work.

He took out west for Little Rock, changed his fancy suit for his overalls and jumper, and got him a job of work on the Cotton Belt Route. He swung a sledge hammer and hated doing it; and when he got plumb disgusted and had earned some cash, he quit, changed back to his dude's clothes, bought himself a cigar, and headed for the back of town.

"Good eatin' and the love of work has given me an arm to swing a sledge hammer," Piddle told the sporting-house girls. "But the Lord gave me the soul of a man who gits around."

The girls fussed over him because he had earned some cash on the Cotton Belt Route.

While Piddle sat there talking to all those girls he kept his brown derby on his head, because he was feared that if he put it down he would go off and leave it. Then he got hungry, so he said: "Gimme somethin' to eat, gals, for I'm gittin' empty agin. Cook me some ham, and make the meat plenty thick. Fry me a dozen eggs and sprinkle their yeller faces so heavy with black pepper that you cain't tell them from the skillet. I need my oats."

While Piddle was eating his ham and eggs the girls sat around him and bragged on what a rounder he was and how he gave out a heap of big talk. Then the doorbell rang and the landlady yelled: "Company, girls."

Piddle kept on eating ham and eggs, and the girls went out to see who had come. But because Piddle was a he-sized rounder they did not leave him alone for long. He could sit and gas with them the livelong day and make them like it. The bell would ring, now and then, and Piddle didn't give a damn; for, if who had come didn't like the girls, they all came back to Piddle—if who had come *did* like the girls they all came back but one.

When Piddle finished eating he got up and said: "So long." He plunked a silver dollar on the table and stomped out of that kitchen tipping his hat to the girls—because he was a he-rounder who was having a good time.

Piddle went further into the back of town and stopped at a saloon kept by a man named Suggs. He laid his money down on the bar and called for a drink—and he bought all the boys drinks because he had made the cash on the Cotton Belt Railroad. He drank for four hours and a half, and then he drank until the sun went down; then he called for a gallon jug of whisky, so he wouldn't run short, and went into the back room where a poker game was going on.

He sat in a chair by the wall, with his gallon jug of whisky, and did not try to get in the game. He was getting drunk and just wanted to watch those gamblers play their hands.

"Come on, Piddle," said the gamblers. "Git into the game and lay your money down."

But Piddle just sat.

The gamblers were around a big table where the poker chips were stacked high, and the dealer had eyes like a cougar in the brake. There was big talk while the game went on. Piddle watched them until he got sleepy, then he put his billfold and diamond stickpin in one hand and held his gallon jug with the other; he put five chairs together and lay down to sleep, laying his brown derby hat over his face. When he woke up again Suggs brought him a fried-meat sandwich.

For two days Piddle drank and watched the gamblers; when he finished one gallon he bought another, and Suggs thought he was a real man and didn't want to kick him out.

Then Piddle looked in his billfold and saw that he was getting short of cash, so he sat at the table and laid his money down. The dealer dealt him a hand, and Piddle played until he took the jack pot; then he quit playing and bought himself another gallon of whisky. The game went on, and Piddle just sat, watched, and drank.

Now, while he was watching, a funny thing happened to Piddle. He felt as though he was beginning to get drunk. The room somehow changed, and it looked and smelled like a big barn. And in the middle of this barn was a stack of hay, and around the stack were a circle of goats. The goats were eating the hay and making a lot of noise. They stank like goats, but they were not the ordinary kind: they were not white nor were they speckled—they were blue goats.

Among these goats there was one that was different from the others; he had eyes like a panther, and his color would not stay blue—it changed from blue to pink, then from green to pure gold. This goat made more noise than the others, and he kept saying: "Come on, Piddle, git in the game. The pickin's are good, and it ain't all chaff; there's money to be lost and won."

That made Piddle mad.

He figured that the hay was not there for the goats—it was for the mules and no other animal. He decided to do something about it right quick and was wasting no time. So he took his gallon jug and pitched it among them; then he picked up a chair and waded into them without a fear.

The goats scattered.

Then that big goat which changed colors came at Piddle and tried to butt him down, but Piddle let him have it with the chair. Piddle saw goats all around him until everything went black. When he came to he was lying down in a doctor's office and the doctor had put a cool, wet cloth on his head. Piddle felt dizzy in the head and sick all over. There was a bump on his head that didn't look pretty.

"He is coming out of it," said the doctor.

Suggs was there looking at Piddle too.

"Where am I?" asked Piddle.

"You are a sick man, take it easy. . . . Rest, take it easy." That is what the doctor said.

"I ain't never been sick in all my life," said Piddle, "and I ain't goin' to be now. Let me up!"

"Take it easy," said the doctor. "You have had the D.T.'s, and you are a sick man. You saw blue goats when they were not there. Lie down. Take it easy."

"My head's got a bump on it as big as a wagon hub. How come?"

"I laid you out with a baseball bat I keep for fellers such as you." said Suggs.

For a minute Piddle lay still; then he said: "What's wrong with me, if I'm sick?"

"Plenty," said the doctor. "You are an alcoholic."

Now Piddle never took a cussing from any man, and he particularly hated being sassed by doctors. He didn't know the meaning of the doctor's cuss word, but he figured he had better do something about it right quick. He got up and started to wade into the doctor.

"Take him out!" yelled the doctor to Suggs. "Get him out of here and don't bring him back! . . . We haven't got any straitjackets handy, and he isn't safe without one! . . . The river is deep, so take him down there and pitch him in! . . . Take him out, and don't bring him back!"

Suggs took Piddle out on the street and told him to go home.

"Don't come back to my place no more, Piddle," said Suggs. "Because you are too rough with a gallon of whisky and you wrecked my poker room. . . . Go home and cut out the booze, and I tell you this because I'm your friend. Or you can go home and drink and die, and I tell you that because I'm your friend too. . . . But don't die in my poker room!"

"Why did the doctor call me what he did?" asked Piddle of Suggs. "I don't take sass from any man."

"What the doctor told you was the truth and worth ten dollars in cash in any man's pocket. He told you that you are a sick man and had the D.T.'s; that if you don't cut out the booze they'll have to put you in a six-foot coffin without trimmin's and the County will bury you. You are a nuisance to humanity and you wrecked my poker room; you don't play your hand at the game and just sit and git drunk and disorderly. The doctor had to put stitches in the dealer's head where you cold-cocked him with a chair. . . . And above all, you must git out of Little Rock, and don't come back no more!"

When Piddle heard Suggs say that, he got scared, and aimed to cure himself of the booze for all time.

He watched Suggs walk down the street to his saloon; then he looked to the northwest. To the northwest was where his family lived; but he had quit them and didn't aim to go back. Then he looked to the southwest, where Tod and Faybelle lived, and he figured he would go there.

So he polished up his diamond stickpin, and he put his hat straight on his head—over the bump. He went to the freight yards and caught a train going west on the Missouri Pacific Railroad and he rode it plumb to Texarkana. The brakey kicked him off at Arkadelphia and again at Hope, but Piddle was a man who when he was heaved off wouldn't stay put. When that freight pulled into Texarkana the yardmen saw Piddle's brown derby sticking out from the rods, and Piddle was under it telling them howdy.

When he got to the Muddy Boggy, right there in Atoka County, his stickpin was shining but his fancy suit was covered with soot. He said howdy to Tod and Faybelle and asked them for a job of work just for his keep and chewing tobacco.

"Because," said Piddle, "I'm gittin' old and feeble."

When they set him to doing the chores Piddle changed from his fancy suit and diamond stickpin to his overalls and jumper—for his rambling and gambling days were over. And that's how come Piddle cured himself of being a drinking man—and he didn't need a doctor to do it for him.

Now, here in New Mexico, Piddle thought a lot about those good old days and got a heap of fun just telling of them to the kids. Out in the fields, when they were chopping weeds from the rows of corn, beans, and cane, the kids would sling their hoes as fast as they could just to keep up with Piddle and listen to the talk of his past doings. Lyndel and Buster would fall behind, but they were little and not interested nohow.

"Ain't worth their salt," said Piddle, looking back at the two youngest kids, and he was plumb disgusted. "Two worthless, no-account young uns!"

During those summer months Tod would watch the oldest go down the rows slinging their hoes. He would see Lyndel and Buster, far behind by themselves, stop to talk now and then of things that did not interest Piddle or the rest of the kids.

"Funny critters, those two," said their daddy.

Tod rode the John Deere riding cultivator behind the mules. The rows were a quarter-mile long and those hard-tails kept pulling him along at a steady pace, ripping out the weeds and churning up the earth. Tod guided the swinging sweeps of the cultivator with his feet and left the crop in the rows—but he plowed out the careless weed, the purple verbena, and the tumbleweeds, and left them to wilt in the sun.

As he cultivated down the rows, one after another, Piddle and the kids would do the same on foot with their hoes. When Tod reached the end of one row he swung his mules around and tackled another. Sometimes he stopped the team to leave them rest while he walked over to the wagon, reached down under where the keg of water lay in the shade, and took a long swig to wet his whistle.

At times, when he was still driving down the rows, he would see Piddle and the kids go to the wagon to sit down and rest, to drink the water and sharpen the blades of their hoes with the files. And Tod knew that while they were there, resting and filing, Piddle was spitting long windies of his past doings.

As the mules plodded on Tod sang a song:

> *"Old man Piddle was a ramblin' fool,*
> *Sweet stuff!*
> *Old man Piddle was a ramblin' fool,*
> *Hon-ee!*
> *Old man Piddle was a ramblin' fool,*
> *Drunk and gambled and never went to school.*
> *Please, child, gimme some water,*
> *'Cause my mouth is really dry!"*

That was what Tod sang; but when he got to the end of the row he left the mules to stand while he went to the wagon for a swig of water.

He found Piddle telling about big times in De Queen, Arkansas. Sudie listened to every word and thought how easy those rounder girls made their living; Roddy thought of hooking freights and getting over the country; Tewp pictured himself sitting at the gambling table and raking in the cash; Jay Boy got ambitious to make the law take a lot of sass and like it.

Tod looked about, but he could not see Lyndel or Buster anywhere. He asked Piddle where they were, but the old man said he was damned if he knew. But when Tod reached under the wagon to get a keg of water he found them both in the shade. They were fast asleep.

## Chapter Three

MARY SIMONSON lived in a little white frame house beside the school —about a mile and a half from the McClung homestead. She lived alone, cooked her own vittles, and kept the place tidy. And because she had a brand-new Chevrolet car she took off every Saturday morning for Albuquerque, where her kinfolks lived, and she didn't come back until Sunday night.

Folks in the community didn't mind her going off on those week-end trips so long as she stayed by her duties from Monday morning to Friday night, but they figured she used up a lot of gasoline for her own pleasure and kept them guessing as to what she did while she was away. Still they all figured that that was her business, and that was all there was to it.

Mrs. Smeet, one of the neighbors, said she had heard that Mary Simonson had a young man in Albuquerque; and Mrs. Mudgett, another neighbor, wondered if it were true that the teacher had kinfolks there or was she just going off to see the young man. And it took Mrs. Smeet over three weeks to get Mary Simonson primed so she would open up and tell her that her father and mother lived in Albuquerque, and that she was engaged to marry the young man, who kept a cleaning and pressing shop there. He had given Mary a diamond ring, and Mary showed it to Mrs. Smeet.

Mrs. Smeet used up a heap of gasoline in her Oakland car, after she had told Mrs. Mudgett what she had heard of Mary Simonson's young man, by going around visiting the neighbors, all except the McClungs, before Mrs. Mudgett could get to them first—but she figured the neighbors ought to know.

When she told them everything she knew, Mrs. Smeet reckoned that Mary Simonson was a good schoolteacher and wasn't transgressing against the Lord on week ends off; and every woman in the community, other than the McClungs, seemed right proud to have her teach their kids education.

29

As Mrs. Smeet drove home she got to thinking about the Bible, the prophets, and the sinful ways of most people.

" 'And I will bring distress upon men,' " she quoted, " 'that they shall walk like blind men, because they have sinned against the Lord: and their blood shall be poured out as dust, and their flesh as the dung.' "

She remembered that it was the prophet Zephaniah who said those noble words, for she had read her Bible through six times and was three-quarter way through it again, and if Zephaniah said them it was O.K. with her, because he had always been her favorite prophet.

Mrs. Smeet had a daughter, Earlene, who got her education from Mary Simonson. Earlene was sixteen years old and was the smartest pupil, and folks reckoned she should be in Willard where she could go to high school. She could figure arithmetic and spell jawbreaking words.

"If I thought for a minute that Earlene wanted to be a stenographer or a schoolteacher," Mrs. Smeet told the neighbors, "I'd ship her off to high school right quick so's she could git smarter. But when the Lord shined his countenance on me and gave her to me, I figured she was born to be the wife of an honest-to-goodness dirt farmer who needed no extra learnin'."

Marvin Smeet, father of Earlene, had homesteaded his three-quarter section of land in 1917, when they were having all that war across the water, two years before Tod McClung and his folks came to the country. Earlene, the only child, was born back in Texas—in Throckmorton County.

"I swan before Jonah," Mrs. Smeet told Mrs. Mudgett. "I think the sweetest thing that ever happened to me was when the dear Lord steered Marvin in my direction and inspired his soul to ask me to marry him. Marvin's not only an honest-to-goodness dirt farmer but he's a Christian from way down the line. He's got more righteousness in him than a dozen Methodist preachers and a Hard-Shell Baptist all together at a camp meetin'."

About Earlene, Mary Simonson had told Mrs. Smeet: "Earlene is the brightest pupil I have." And that made Mrs. Smeet mighty proud.

On the following week end Mary said the same thing to her young man in Albuquerque: "Earlene is the brightest pupil I have." But she added: "And she has reason to be, for she is sixteen years old and should be in high school where she could find some competition. She knows simple arithmetic and reads very well, and that is really all I can say for her."

That's how Mary came to tell her young man about Earlene. She told him how the girl was bright in her own way but wasn't no genius for a fact. How the next in brightness were two Mexicans, younger than Earlene, who when they reached sixteen would make the Smeet girl seem like a primary grader compared with them. And after the young man heard Mary's talk he knew all about Earlene.

Mary told him of the kid's daddy and mammy, too, and after he had sat and listened for a spell he got the notion that Marvin and Virgie Smeet were hypocrites from down the line, and that poor Earlene wasn't so much to blame for lacking the horse sense she did.

Now among Mary Simonson's eighteen pupils at the community school only a few of the youngest Anglo children were born New Mexicans. Earlene was a native Texan, like most of the kids. Others came from Oklahoma, Arkansas, and Mississippi.

"My two Mexicans," said Mary, "are the only pupils I have who are likely to reach the Willard High School. When the others finish such 'book learning' as I can give them they will go back to the land —the boys to the barnyard, and each girl to the bed and kitchen of a dirt farmer. The Mexicans will go to the University awhile, I suppose, and then take some political job in Santa Fe. How they love politics!"

It was indeed a fact that the two Mexican kids were the smartest in the school; Earlene had the advantage over them only of being older. The other kids wouldn't pay the Mexicans much mind out in the schoolyard because back in Texas they had been taught to keep clear of any kind of Mexican.

"Their language ain't American, and their religion ain't the same," their mammies and daddies told them.

Now Marvin Smeet was known in the community to be somewhat of the east end of a horse going west. He had his faults like any other man; and although he tried to hide them, those pesky faults would keep coming out to slap the neighbors smack on the jaw. But he claimed to be a righteous man who loved his neighbor as himself —all but the McClungs—and did unto others as he aimed them to do by him. He was a full-blood Baptist, as was his wife, and he was a Christian from way back.

That's what he claimed, but the folks knew different. Marvin Smeet couldn't fool a whole community of people. They knew him to be pure evil in a heap of his ways, try as he might to conceal them. But again, he was like anybody else—most of him was good.

Virgie spent a powerful amount of time reading the Bible, but she made more of a show about it when someone was around to watch her doing it. Like, for instance, she'd be doing up an important chore in the kitchen and be quite happy about it until she heard the gate go smack. Then she knew somebody was on his or her way in and it was time to quit the chore and make a show of religion.

Lord! Would Virgie rush for the Bible and start in to finger the pages!

She'd meet the caller with the good book in hand and look so dog-gone pious that any folks who didn't know her would be feared to get close lest they contaminate her.

Sham!

That was all.

They had Earlene trained, like a pet filly colt, to do tricks for them; to spread the word at school and around the community how plumb Christian her mammy and daddy were, and how they were raising her to be the same; to lie like it were the gospel truth.

Big talk can't deceive a whole settlement of people, though, and in spite of Marvin and Virgie's sanctimonious doings the folks reckoned them to be scribes or Pharisees or some suchlike critters.

Marvin and Virgie got scared at times and wondered if the Lord wouldn't send a bolt of fire to strike them down. The lightning struck in summer around the Smeet homestead but never got within hitting distance of Marvin and Virgie.

"The time will come," said one of the good folks round about, "when the Lord will make the Smeets atone for the high-up religion they're tryin' to fool us with. That punishment won't happen in heaven or hell, nor will it come ridin' down on a lightnin' streak and make hash of 'em for all time. . . . It will be somethin' plumb natural on earth—on their own spread of land—and that alone will make honest Christians of Marvin and Virgie Smeet: a grief that'll do more good to the hearts of 'em than all the baptizin' the preacher can give 'em, more than if he soaked 'em in the horse-trough for a week."

"The time will come," said those who listened to that neighbor.

"Somethin' natural—right here on earth," said the folks who talked sound sense.

Mr. Flowers, the local preacher, was a full-blooded Baptist like Mr. and Mrs. Smeet, and like a lot of other folks in the community, but the Baptist Church didn't recognize him as an ordained preacher. The regular church and the Baptist ministers figured that Mr. Flowers was ignorant and not fit to preach God's word. They said it took training to conduct a church service; and Mr. Flowers had no training except what he gave himself by reading the Bible. They said he should get out and farm; but Mr. Flowers didn't like to farm, so he reckoned he could be a service to the community by preaching to the people and passing around his hat for pay. It was a good and godly way of making a living, he thought. He was absolutely on his own hook with nobody to boss him around but the Lord. He and Marvin Smeet had a heap in common.

It was quite a piece of a ways into Willard, so the folks of the community gathered in Mr. Flowers' house on Sunday mornings to worship and glorify and listen to Mr. Flowers preach. Everybody went to these gatherings whether they were Baptists, Methodists, or Holiness—all but the McClungs and Mary Simonson. The folks forgave Mary Simonson because she went to Albuquerque on week ends, but they reckoned the McClungs to be downright heathen.

"There's a den of serpents in our midst, Brethren and Sistern," preached Mr. Flowers one Sunday morning. "Two twistin' snakes, and one daddy of 'em all, with a litter of young uns growin' steady to be mean with orneriness. They eat of the Lord's Tree of Life and then coil up and rattle when his countenance is shined on 'em. But the Lord is out to git even, I'll tell you-all for sure! . . . Believe you me, he'll burn 'em up like somebody pitched the Devil's own lit-up cigarette in a barrel of gasoline!"

Then Mr. Flowers spoke more reverend words by telling the congregation about the wrath of God.

The next morning at school, Earlene told the teacher what Mr. Flowers had said about the Lord.

"Mr. Flowers told us yesterday at preachin' that the Lord is so big he can take the world in his mouth and grind it up to nothin' with his teeth—just like a stick of candy. . . . Mr. Flowers said the Lord had one eye for every sinner on earth and a hand for each so he could smite him down. . . . And he said the Lord was gittin' sick and tired of all the transgressin' most of the folks he made was doin'."

"Heavens, what a monster!" said Mary Simonson. "But I'm glad he gets sick and tired of things like anybody else."

"But he's sweet and kind to them that love him and don't git him filled with wrath. That's what Mr. Flowers said."

"He sounds almost human," said the teacher.

"Who, Mr. Flowers?"

"No. Not Mr. Flowers," said Mary. "The Lord."

One day Marvin Smeet went out of his way to talk to Mr. Flowers and asked him if something could be done about Tod McClung and his family.

"They're sealin' their own fate," said the preacher. "They don't come to meetin' and don't contribute to the collection hat for the furtherance of the Lord's word. . . . But that ain't no skin off my arm, and the Lord will stand so much and then He'll git 'em. He'll fix 'em up so's they'll only be fit to haul off in a sack. . . . I repeat, Brother Smeet, they're only sealin' their own fate."

"But Tod McClung brazenly spreads his wickedness among the righteous!" yelled Marvin Smeet, all hot and bothered.

"How come?" Mr. Flowers wanted to know.

Then Marvin told the preacher how Tod McClung sent his transgressions right up to the front door of the house of the righteous.

It all happened because Marvin had a fine Hereford bull named Silas Domino. He had gone to Amarillo two years before and bought the bull at a sale of registered Herefords. He gave a hundred dollars for him and had him shipped out to his farm in New Mexico. Silas Domino was one of the finest-looking bulls that ever grazed a pasture: he was white-faced, was all beef, was like a big loaf of bread set on four short legs, and had a pedigree from way back like all the Dominos have. But there was a heap of a lot wrong with him as far as bulls go. He couldn't, for the life of him, make a cow find a calf.

Of course Marvin didn't know the bull's failing when he bought him, else he wouldn't have paid a hundred dollars for him; and the fellow who sold Silas to Marvin didn't know what kind of an animal it was going to be—it being just a calf—so Silas Domino showed every sign of making a Hereford of the finest kind.

After Marvin kept him a year in the pasture with his cows Silas showed himself up to be no kind of daddy to the calf crop. So Marvin got himself another bull and just let Silas be—to eat and drink and lay around chewing his cud, and to keep all those cows worrying over him and wondering what kind of a bull he was anyway.

But every time Marvin saw a hundred dollars and the cost of shipment from Amarillo laying around doing nothing he got rattled.

"Virgie," he said one day—Mrs. Smeet's given name was Virgie—"I feel like butcherin' that worthless male animal come the first day it gits cold enough. I wonder if we couldn't peddle the meat out and git part of our money back."

Mrs. Smeet thought different. She reckoned that Silas Domino, if killed and cut up, would only bring thirty dollars at the most.

"Mrs. Mudgett told me," she said, "that Tod McClung hasn't got a male animal for his herd, and he wants one right smart. Maybe we can sell Silas to him."

Marvin Smeet frowned, because he was a righteous man.

"But this male animal is only fit for meat," he said. "He ain't never performed the duty I intended him to do. It ain't right, to sell such an animal—even to Tod McClung."

Virgie aimed to get some return from Silas, nevertheless.

"I hope the Lord won't strike us down," she said, "but I think you ought to see Tod McClung about buyin' the male animal. This is a business matter—even the prophets had to go among sinners on business matters."

"But it ain't just right to—"

Mrs. Smeet looked him straight in the eye.

"Marvin Smeet," she said. "You are my lawfully wedded husband, and I'm here to tell you what ought to be done. I'll tell you just like Zachariah or any righteous prophet would tell you if he was livin'. It ain't right to have aught to do with Tod McClung, because he's Satan's own handiwork; but here we have a chance to show the Lord we can outwit the Devil. If Tod is such a rattlin'-good farmer as the neighbors say he is, maybe he can tell beforehand that Silas ain't the kind of male animal we bought him for. It ain't wicked—it's business."

So Marvin went out to the barn where he could be alone and meditate, where no pesky woman could bother him. He got down on his knees and asked the Lord to forgive his wife her wicked intentions, and to enlighten him as to how much Silas Domino was worth. He asked God if he thought a hundred and twenty dollars would be too much for a registered Hereford male animal with papers to prove his pedigree and two years' pasturage with no return. He reminded the Lord that the price of cattle had gone up that season. He requested that a sign be given him if this business deal was wicked in the sight of Heaven. He asked the Lord to strike him down with a bolt of fire if it were.

Marvin prayed and crouched his shoulders, ready for the bolt to smack him; but the only sound that interrupted his meditation was the cackling of hens; and Marvin was glad to hear the hens cackle because it was a sign that they were laying eggs.

He got up and brushed the chaff from his knees, and went to the house so Virgie could get word down the line by way of Mrs. Mudgett, to Mr. Mudgett, who would pass it on to a neighbor friendly with the McClungs, that Silas Domino was up for sale.

When Tod McClung heard that there was a registered bull for sale in the community, one that didn't have to be shipped in, he was plumb tickled to death. He figured his breeding problem was long gone. He wasted no time and told Roddy to ride over to Marvin Smeet's on horseback, while he himself drove over in his Cadillac car. Roddy could drive the bull back after Tod bought it.

So Roddy saddled up the pony and hunted down his brother Tewp. He found Tewp behind the barn reading *Ranch Romances*.

Tewp's ambition in life was to be cowpuncher and get around the country by riding bronc's and making them like it. He wanted to be a bronc' snapper from way back and have nothing to do with beans and cultivators. He wanted to follow the rodeos and shoot craps and play poker between contests. He aimed to be a cowpuncher like they have in *Ranch Romances,* and nobody was going to stop him.

Tod and Faybelle wouldn't let the kids read anything but the Bible. It was through the words in that book that Faybelle taught the whole bunch to read—even to Lyndel, the littlest of them all. If Tod or Faybelle caught any of those kids reading anything but the Bible, that one who was doing the reading would get his or her hide smacked until he or she hollered "Calf rope." That was how Tod and Faybelle felt about book reading.

So, because of his fear of Tod and Faybelle, Tewp kept his *Ranch Romances* and his *Lariat* story magazines hid out back of the barn. Sudie kept her love story magazines hid there too, because she liked reading right smart. And that's where Roddy found Tewp—right at the part of a story where a pretty girl was kissing a cowpuncher named Tex.

"Loan me your spurs, boots, and chaps," said Roddy to Tewp. "For the old man's done told me to git the bull and twist his tail over here. Loan me them, or I'll tell Maw you're out here readin'."

Now Tewp figured that the things Roddy asked for were his and Roddy could go to hell and stay there; but he feared too that if he didn't let his brother have his way Tod would get to know that he was reading love stories.

So he stretched out his legs and let Roddy pull the boots from him, and then he told where the spurs and chaps were. Tewp told his brother to get going, and when Roddy got going Tewp went back to the pretty girl kissing Tex.

Roddy McClung thought himself some punkins when he rode off to Marvin Smeet's all dressed up in Tewp's cowboy outfit. He kept the pony at a running walk, and the motion made the spurs jingle and the chaps flap like a buzzard's wings. He sang the song he had heard on a phonograph record:

> *"Some like Chicago,*
> *Some like Memphis, Tennessee.*

*But gimme good ol' Dallas, Texas,*
*Where the women are all crazy over me."*

On the way he turned down a lane and passed the schoolhouse. It was afternoon recess, and the kids were all playing and chasing about the yard. Among them was the teacher, Mary Simonson.

"She's a pretty bitch," said Roddy to himself.

It wasn't far over to Marvin Smeet's—only two miles and a half —and Roddy made the stretch in no time. He loped into the yard like an honest-to-God cowpuncher; he dismounted and hitched the pony to the fence.

Tod had not yet arrived in his Cadillac car, so Roddy just rolled himself a smoke and waited.

But Marvin and his old lady had seen Roddy ride up. They saw him from the window of the house. So Mrs. Smeet pushed Marvin out of the door and told him to go sell Silas Domino.

"Remember," warned Virgie. "All through this transaction you will be in Satan's presence. When you are tempted, don't git violent. Be calm and brave!"

Marvin walked out to where Roddy sat hunkered down and smoking.

"I'll be proud," said Marvin, "if you don't smoke cigarettes on my property."

Roddy puffed away at his cigarette. "I'll be careful," he said. "There ain't no hay aroun'."

"It ain't that," said Marvin. "This here is a Christian household, and I don't permit smokin'."

Roddy threw his cigarette to the ground and stamped on it.

"God bless you," said Marvin.

Marvin was fixing to question Roddy, just to find out if the boy hadn't just one mite of Christianity about him, when Tod drove up in the car.

"I hear you've got a bull for sale," said Tod.

"I have," replied Marvin. "Are you in the market for a male animal?"

"That's what I came over here for," Tod said. "Strictly business, Mr. Smeet, strictly business. No pleasure call between me and you."

"I'll show him to you."

Marvin led Tod and Roddy over to the corral where Silas Domino lay in the sun chewing his cud. But Virgie was standing all this while watching from the window of the house, and she figured that as there were two devils to one Christian in this deal she had better get out and make sides even.

"Good evenin', Mr. McClung," she said—all sweetening up. "And Roddy! . . . My, what a big boy you have grown up to be! I'm right proud, as I'm sure Mr. Smeet is, that you two good neighbors have paid us a friendly call."

"We've come to look at the bull," said Tod, tipping his hat.

Virgie blushed red, and Marvin's face twitched with wrath.

"I'll be proud, Mr. McClung," Marvin said, "if you'll speak of this creature as a male animal in the presence of my wife."

Tod didn't pay any mind to Marvin's words but gave the bull a thorough looking over. He kicked Silas in the rump and made him get up on his feet. Silas stretched and walked over to the hay rack.

"He's a good-lookin' bull," said Tod to Roddy.

But Tod wanted more proof as to Silas' worth, so he asked: "How long have you-all had him?"

"Silas is three years old, and I've had him for two years."

"All right," said Tod. "Let's see some of the calves you've got from him in that time."

Neither Marvin or Virgie was prepared for this question, and they didn't know how to answer Tod without telling a lie. They had no calves of Silas' to show Tod. They figured that this demand to see the calf increase was a trick of the Devil's to tempt them into sin. Both of them shuddered, because they felt Satan near.

Marvin was fixing to say that there were no calves of Silas' around when Virgie saw Tod's checkbook sticking out from his pocket. She handled the situation right quick.

"There's two calves here," she said, leading Tod to a pen where two yearlings were standing. "They are sired by Silas Domino, and they are fine Herefords. Of course their mammies were grade cows and they ain't registered—but they've got the Domino blood. There's a lot more like 'em in the pasture."

These calves were the get of the other bull—the registered Hereford Marvin had bought when he found Silas to be no account for a daddy. Virgie told a downright lie, thought Marvin, and they would both have to atone for it before the Lord, but he knew better than to horn in while Virgie held the pulpit.

The transaction got under way and Marvin said he wanted a hundred and twenty dollars for Silas.

Tod said it was too much.

Marvin said Silas was a fine male animal.

Roddy said he was damned if he would pay a hundred and twenty dollars for any man's bull.

Marvin lowered the price to a hundred and ten, so Tod got out his checkbook and said O.K.

As soon as Virgie saw that the deal was done she took off to the house. She heard Tod crank up his car; and from the window she saw Roddy chouse Silas out of the yard gate and haze him down the road toward the McClung farm. She was pleased that they had outwitted the Devil, but she was forced to hold her hands over her ears because Roddy was shouting cusswords at Silas.

"I'll speak to Mr. Flowers about that," Marvin said when he came into the house. "It don't seem right that we cain't make a business deal without them bringin' their evil ways right up to our front door."

Virgie hung her head in shame.

"Let us pray," she said.

They got down on their knees, and Virgie led off:

"Lord, we thank thee for the hundred and ten dollars that thou saw fittest to come to the household of thy servants. . . . We thank thee for thy grace in takin' that worthless male animal off our pasture and puttin' him on the hay of sinners. Amen."

Then Marvin spoke up.

"And if we sinned in thy sight during the previous business deal, we ask thy forgiveness. Amen."

They both knelt in silence.

"Let us meditate," said Marvin.

Then he raised his eyes to heaven, and under his breath he conversed only with his God.

"And for the sinner's sake, O Lord; and for thy servant's sake— please make Silas Domino fertile. Amen."

While Marvin and Virgie were doing all this praying Roddy was raking the pony with the spurs and hazing Silas down the road like a cowpuncher from way back. He was cussing the bull and walloping him on the rump with his lariat rope.

Silas trotted his big bulk along, all the time mumbling and grumbling. When Roddy let up on him for a spell Silas got his snout down to the grass and would go to grazing, or he would paw the dirt and bellow.

After Roddy had ridden a ways he saw a slew of kids from the school on their way home. It was four in the evening, and they had all called their education quits for the day. One of them, a girl, was walking along the road in Roddy's direction. She was Earlene Smeet.

"Don't be scared of him," Roddy called, as the bull met the girl. "He's gentle."

Earlene stopped, holding her books under her arm.

"That's Silas!" she said. "No, I ain't scared of him. When he was a yearlin' I used to ride him around the corral. He's gentle as a Shetland pony."

She stood looking at Roddy, while he reined the pony still so he could chew the rag with her.

"Where you goin' with Silas?" Earlene inquired.

"My paw's done bought him," said Roddy. "We ain't gittin' no calves without a bull among the cows."

Earlene knew of Silas' failing, but she kept her mouth shut.

"I hate to see him go," she said. "I used to feed him sugar."

She gazed at Roddy. He looked handsome in his chaps and with the spurs on his boots. He looked just like a cowboy she had seen in *True Story Magazine,* except that the cowboy in the magazine was better-looking than Roddy and didn't have freckles. Roddy looked like he stayed in the open air more than the magazine cowboy. She liked Roddy's looks and figured he was a nice boy in spite of what her folks said about him.

Roddy thought Earlene was nice-looking too. She was sixteen years old and had yellow hair. Her dress came way down below her knees because her folks thought it only decent; and Roddy thought she acted right clever and friendly. But she was a woman, and she was built right, and that suited Roddy to a T.

"I once read about a cowboy like you in a magazine," Earlene said. "He rode a horse called Pal, and the cowboy's name was Sidewinder Lee. He saved a girl from a terrible fate, but I don't know if he married her or not."

"How come?"

"I didn't git to the end of the story. Maw caught me readin' the magazine and burnt it up."

"My folks do the same if they catch us readin' magazines," said Roddy, " 'cept they give us a lickin' too. But only my brother Tewp and my sister Sudie read magazines, and they keep 'em hid out back of the barn."

"That's where I keep my *True Story Magazine* hid," said Earlene.

"Lyndel—that's my youngest sister—she don't go for magazines much, but she picks up old tin cans layin' around and reads the labels on 'em. She's locoed. . . . Whenever a freight passes our place on the railroad, Lyndel gits out and reads the letters and numbers on the boxcars. She wants to go to school, but the folks won't let her."

"Why not?"

"Because Paw says if she goes to school she'll git education and she won't want to live on the farm no more. He's feared she'll go off and marry a jelly bean. He says it will make her uppity."

"I go to school, and I ain't uppity."

"I know," said Roddy. "I think you're right friendly."

Earlene liked the looks of Roddy McClung.

"It ain't much of a walk from school to my house," she said, "but it sure's a lonesome one. I git out every evenin' but Saturday and Sunday at four o'clock. I pass here about ten minutes after."

"Maybe I'll git to see you sometimes," said Roddy.

Earlene smiled. She was just a little country girl who liked Roddy because he was so doggone good-looking.

"I've got to git goin' now," she said. "I won't tell my folks I talked to you; I always say that what they don't know don't hurt 'em."

"That's what I say too," Roddy agreed. He set himself straight in the saddle ready to give the pony the spurs and haze Silas home. "Well," he added, "I reckon I ain't doin' nothing' special tomorrow, so I might be 'round here about the same time in the evenin'."

That suited Earlene fine.

Roddy hazed Silas down the road, whooping and hollering like an honest-to-God cowpuncher, and Earlene walked on home as happy as any country girl who had met a good-looking boy. She aimed to see him again.

"She'll be as easy as fallin' off a log," said Roddy to himself as he rode along.

As Earlene walked home she thought about the handsome cowboy in *True Story Magazine*. She thought about the girl who maybe married him and lived happily ever after. She remembered the beautiful picture of the two of them alone—the cowpuncher and the girl—kissing in the moonlight. And in back of them was a log cabin with pine trees all around it. And what a romantic caption the picture had! And she thought how mean it was of her mother to burn the magazine up.

"This ain't fittin' for no girl like you to read," Mrs. Smeet had said.

"But they're only love stories," sobbed Earlene.

"They're stories of man's love, which is sinful," said the old lady, het up because of Earlene's shameful reading. "The Bible will tell you about the Lord's love, which is pure."

And now, as Earlene walked along, she thought of the love stories in the Bible. She thought of Ruth and Boaz and the rest of those long-gone folks.

" 'Whither thou goest, I will go,' " Earlene quoted.

So it was because of that bull trade with Tod McClung that Marvin Smeet had to go to Mr. Flowers and tell him about Tod bringing his cusswords right up to the door of the righteous.

"They're sealin' their own fate," said Mr. Flowers.

Mr. Flowers was a man of God who was out to make a living whether the Baptist Church liked it or not.

"And I aim to save 'em before they got done sealin' it," he said. "I will go unto the wilderness and call on them poor lost sheep and try to git 'em penned up in the fold."

He said that because he knew Tod McClung to be an honest-to-God dirt farmer who sold his crops and calves and raked in the cash; and Mr. Flowers would like to see some of that money fall into his hat.

## Chapter Four

WHEN the late September of 1928 came along the folks up and down the Estancia Valley—from Cedarvale clean up to Galisteo, around about Moriarty and Estancia, way east to Encino and high up at Mountainair—felt the wind blow cool, and they said, "Fall is here." And they looked to the yellowing crops and said, "Time to cut 'em down and haul 'em in."

It was then that Tod McClung drove into Willard in his Cadillac car to buy bean sacks so as to pack off the main crop; and for the corn and cane harvest he got new parts to replace those worn out on the row binder, and spools a plenty of binder twine.

"Because," he said, "the summer's done over and it's time to git on our high horse and gather the crop in; for before we know it frost will come and old winter will be on us as sudden as a hawk swoopin' down on a pullet."

And, because Tod was a man who spoke what he thought, all the McClungs got ready to haul in the bean harvest before frost.

October came. The bean crop in; corn and cane cut and stocked.

Big things were happening in the Estancia valley during that fall of 1928. In fact all the United States were het up with politics— they were fixing to elect a new President, and New Mexico was aiming to set up a new governor in the capitol in Santa Fe. And the Estancia valley was astir a plenty, for the governor at that time, Dick Dillon of Encino, a Torrance County man, was nominated to run a second term on the Republican ticket.

"I never split a ballot before," said those solid Democrats from Texas, "but I aim to, this election—in favor of old Dick Dillon, that Torrance County man."

"He's give us roads, and we need roads; if we keep him up there where he belongs he'll lay them down like only old Dick Dillon can. . . . He's a Torrance County man who knows his highways," said those folks who drove automobiles.

"I've heard tell he's an honest-to-goodness Christian," said the Baptist ladies.

"He's a dirt farmer's friend, and Lord knows we need a friend! . . . He'll do a heap for Torrance County," said those who raised beans.

"One good term deserves another. . . . Torrance County's proud of old Governor Dick Dillon," said those who used their thinkers.

"He's a Republican who's agin booze," said the prohibes.

All in all, the folks of Torrance County thought Dick Dillon was a governor of New Mexico from way back yonder.

"Dillon is bound to be reelected," said the people, "but who, in this wide weary world, is goin' to be the next President of the United States?"

And that was what the whole country was wanting to know. That was what all those high-up politicians were making speeches about—that was what most of the noise on the radio was concerned with: Which one, Al Smith or Herbert Hoover, would be the next President of the United States of America?

"Al Smith," said the wets and those hard old Democrats.

"Hoover," said the prohibes and Republicans.

"The Lord will provide," said the Baptist ladies.

It was that sort of political ranting—that which came in over the radio from the high moguls over the country—that Mary Simonson was trying to shut off so she could get some music. It was on a cool October night, and she sat alone in her white frame house by the school, reading books and just acting lazy.

Mary Simonson's room was the most comfortable in the community. She had a wood heater for warmth and a gasoline lamp for light. She had curtains on the windows and pictures on the walls; she had rugs on the floor and an easy-chair to sit in. Her battery radio set made music when the politicians shut up, and she had a lot of storybooks laying around.

Most folks would think, if they saw Mary's room, that she was uppity, but those who knew her said she was right clever and ordinary.

She kept her Chevrolet car in a garage outside.

Mary smoked cigarettes, which Mrs. Smeet didn't like, but the teacher never took a whiff in the presence of the kids, for which the ladies of the community were thankful. Mrs. Smeet had gone to the trouble of praying to the Lord for Mary Simonson. She asked God to forgive the poor girl this one sin—the teacher's only sin that Virgie Smeet knew of, try as hard as she might to find others—and petitioned the Almighty to strike Mary down with a bolt of fire if he didn't approve. Mrs. Smeet always asked for some sign from heaven as an answer to her prayers, and if no sign came she figured it was O.K. with the Lord; and what was O.K. with the Lord was O.K. with Virgie Smeet. The sign never came.

"To think that that dear, sweet soul should be tainted with tobacco fumes!" Mrs. Smeet said to the preacher one day.

"She's sealin' her own fate," said Mr. Flowers.

Here alone in her room, Mary was dressed comfortably in a bathrobe colored light blue. She had soft bedroom slippers on her feet and a cigarette in her mouth. She kept turning the dial of the radio and saying: "Damn."

"Hullo, World, doggone it," came a voice from a Louisiana station. "You-all are now in the asbestos-lined studio, so don't go 'way. You have just heard 'The Sidewalks of New York' played for our next President, Alfred E. Smith. I wonder how 'Lord Hoover'—"

"Damn," said Mary as she shut off the voice.

She switched the dial and caught the tail end of "By the Waters of Minnetonka."

"That's better."

Mary found the book she had been reading, sat down in the easy-chair, crossed her legs, and tried to relax; but she couldn't relax, for she had been to visit the McClungs that day and she had a worry on her mind.

That poor kid! she thought. That uncombed golden hair, that sweet face, those beautiful teeth that have never known Colgate's, the little head so eager to learn!

An organ solo now came from the radio.

She's like a—what? asked Mary to herself.

She tried to think: I would say a nice clean piece of imported Roquefort cheese melting down to nothing in a greasy pot of mulligan stew. That was how Mary figured up Lyndel McClung.

She remembered how, a short while before, she had driven to Albuquerque and on the way passed through the Salt Lakes country east of Willard. Somehow she got curious when she saw a cowboy on the flat beside the road pulling a heifer from a bog hole. She stopped her car so she could watch him.

The heifer was lying down in the mud, stuck like a fly in flypaper; the poor critter couldn't move. So when the cowboy rode up he aimed to pull her out, and he built a loop in his catch rope and tied the end to his saddle horn. Then with one neat swing over his head he sent the noose over the bog hole to catch the heifer around the neck.

The horse took up the slack, and, easily and steadily, he dragged the heifer to dry earth. Before the heifer gained her feet the cowboy was off his horse, had the rope free, and was again mounted. The heifer was plenty mad, but she took off across the flats without trying to molest the cowboy.

"You know," said the cowboy, after he had reined his horse over to where Mary sat in the car, because he saw she was a pretty girl, "those darn critters are the most ungrateful cusses in the world. . . . They git stuck in the mud—held as tight as a coyote in a trap—and all they can do is wait for us humans to come along and pull 'em out. . . . Then, when we *do* assist 'em to gittin' to dry land, they don't waste no time in lettin' us know how insulted they are, and they try to hook us down. As though we are to blame for them stickin' there! . . . They always git to proddin' when we git off'n our horse to let the rope loose; when they find us afoot, by golly! . . . A bog-hole rider who knows his business, and don't aim to find a scrap on his hands, will git back in the saddle before the critter can git onto her feet."

"That's interesting to know," Mary said; "but I suppose it is worth the risk of a goring when you consider what a heifer will bring you at the Kansas City stockyards at shipping time."

"You bet," said the cowboy. "And the critter you see there high-tailin' it across the flat is worth it—even if she's only a scrub. She's young yet, and if she's bred to a registered Hereford bull she'll maybe find some high-grade calves. If she don't git to be a mammy she'll make good beef if she's handled right. I always say, and I've told the boss the same, that even the sorriest scrub is worth pullin' out of the bog hole—specially the young ones."

Now, weeks after, as Mary sat alone in her room listening to the radio and trying to read her book, she thought of that chat with the cowboy in the Salt Lakes country.

"Poor little Lyndel McClung," she thought. "Poor little mud-crusted heifer in the bog hole! She's waiting for someone with a strong rope to come along and fish her out. She's worth it—any scrub heifer is worth it, if you catch 'em young; she might be mammy to some high-grade young uns; she might even— Oh, for God's sake!"

Mary Simonson opened her book and tried to put her mind into reading. But she couldn't because she was plumb heckled about Lyndel—she couldn't read, she couldn't relax.

Mary Simonson had never been over to say howdy to the Mc-Clungs before that day. She figured it would be of no use talking education with Tod because he was so hell-fired against it—*it* in any form from simple reading plumb up to long division. He didn't like Mary because she was a schoolteacher and, worst of all, because she was a schoolteacher close at hand.

"I don't like rattlesnakes," Tod said to the folks once when his mind got onto schools, "but I ain't got half as much a hate for a six-foot diamond-back down in south Texas as I have for a two-foot twister which crawls into my own back yard."

That was the way Tod felt about Mary; he felt that she was close by, and he didn't like her because she was near enough to do him some harm. But as much as he hated rattlesnakes he was afeared of them; and he was scared of that slim little teacher, too—fright-ened gutless that she wanted to educate his kids. He was feared of book learning as he was of snake-bite; more so, because a human can always kill a rattlesnake and, if he is bitten, most times can get the poison out of his system; but once he gets struck by book learning he can't get shed of it, try as he might.

Because Tod McClung was scared he said:

"I ain't afeared of the kick in the pants I got two years ago be-cause I don't feel it no more, but I've got me a scare for the one I might git in the next five minutes."

He said that because he expected any moment, without a hint of warning, the little teacher to pounce on his kids and educate them.

In spite of all his big talk, when Tod met Mary on the road one day—she coming along in her Chevrolet car—he said, but not loud enough for the teacher to hear: "I wish I had that nice shiny car you're drivin' and you had to walk for a change." But when Mary passed him, all smiling and nodding her head, Tod raised his hat and said "Howdy."

Now Mary Simonson had right smart of an itch to talk with the McClungs—to get a close-up look at the kids and see them at home. All she needed was an excuse for a visit, and on that October evening the excuse came. It was this way:

On account of it being harvest time, beans hauled in and the corn crop cut and shocked, and so near to election day, the folks of the community fixed to give an old-fashioned square dance at the schoolhouse one night late in the month. All the women would doll up in old-timy dresses with long skirts. They would wear sunbonnets, too. The men would come just in their work clothes. Big things were planned, a real old hoedown, and there would be eats out in the yard with chuck for all—meat, goodies, and lemonade. They would have a fiddler and guitar player to make music—but who? Who, by God?

They wanted to get the best fiddler in all Torrance County, and somebody who could tickle that old guitar down to making those folks stomp like they didn't know what; and they heard that the man who could make a fiddle speak music was right in the community. That man was Tod McClung.

"Somebody," said the old dirt farmer who was to be master of ceremonies, "has got to go see that fiddlin' man and give him an invite to the dance. I reckon he'll be right proud to come. But somebody has to go git him. I'm here to tell you-all I won't do it myself."

Nobody seemed anxious to go see Tod but Mary.

Mrs. Smeet said she would be right proud to help with the dance provided there would be no hug dancing or modern stuff, and she got the master of ceremonies to promise there would be nothing that wasn't old-fashioned and decent.

"It will be a joy to the eyes to see women all decked up in old-timy ginghams, with only their faces and hands bare as the Lord intended," said Mrs. Smeet to Mrs. Mudgett. "I'm havin' such fun makin' all the doodads. Pink! Effie Lee, do you think pink matches my complexion?"

"Gray would be most becomin', I think, Virgie. Gray and black are such old-timy and Christian colors!"

"But gray don't match my complexion," protested Virgie Smeet. Effie Lee didn't say anything.

"When I was a girl," said Mrs. Smeet, "I wore pink to dances— that was until I got saved and quit 'em. . . . And don't take me wrong, Effie Lee, and git the notion I'm sinnin' jes' 'cause I'm goin' to this one! Lord, Lord, Mr. Flowers is to be there so's he can watch out for no hug dancin', and I aim to he'p him. He'll ask a blessin' before the eats, and I'm sure the dear Lord will have his countenance shined on us all."

"Tod McClung will be there and fiddlin'," said Mrs. Mudgett grimly.

Mrs. Smeet winced.

"Effie Lee," she said sternly, "as a true Christian you should know there were serpents in Eden."

Mrs. Smeet didn't know at that time how close to her and hers the wicked were really getting. She didn't know that on certain evenings, on more than a few, Roddy McClung saddled up the pony and rode over to a deep wash on the prairie—the Juan Largo, people called it—a wash halfway between the school and the Smeet home. She didn't know that the boy let the pony graze among the brush deep down in the draw, while he himself sat and waited for four o'clock to come around, when the school kids were let out.

Mary Simonson thought it strange when she saw Earlene, on those same evenings, set off in the direction of the Juan Largo instead of taking the road straight for home.

"Why do you go home that way?" Mary asked Earlene.

"It's shorter," said the girl.

"But it isn't. . . . The road is direct; you are going out of your way."

"I like to go home by way of Juan Largo," said Earlene, who had all kinds of excuses ready for home and school, "because there's nature there. I like to be close to nature."

Smart kid, thought Mary. Or is she?

So when Mrs. Smeet and Mrs. Mudgett got to talking about serpents in Eden they shuddered—not because of the snakes so much, but the thought of being close up with McClung wickedness at a country dance gave them the all-overs.

"And that shameless daddy of Mrs. McClung's will be there," said Mrs. Mudgett.

"And that profane, freckle-faced boy," added Mrs. Smeet.

They meant Piddle and Roddy, of course, but they just didn't know about the meanness Piddle had cooked Roddy up to doing when the dance should finally get under way and every man would start swinging the women around the floor. They didn't have a hint of the fun that shameless old man and that freckle-faced boy would have at their expense.

Because Piddle told Roddy of a dance he attended years before at Tushka, Oklahoma—a dance such as the folks aimed to put on at Mary Simonson's school. He told of the devilment he made at that long-gone hoedown, and Roddy thought it the best joke he had ever heard tell of.

"It'll make them old gals scratch like they had the seven-year itch," promised Piddle.

Roddy thought it would be no dance at all without Piddle's devilment, and they both looked forward to the night when they would split their sides laughing at all those women scratching and getting tickled.

So both those ladies, Mrs. Smeet and Mrs. Mudgett, ignorant of Piddle's devilment, screwed their faces and clicked their tongues when they thought of that profane McClung tribe.

"They'll come to no good," said Mrs. Smeet to Mrs. Mudgett; "but with the Lord's help we'll abide 'em, and that's all there is to it."

Mary Simonson was just waiting for an excuse to visit with the McClungs, so she was plumb rearing to go when the master of ceremonies called for a volunteer to ask Tod to play the fiddle.

When Mary dismissed the school kids at four o'clock on that October day she got in her Chevrolet car and drove over to the McClungs. Tod saw her pull up in the yard and he said, "Hell!" and when he saw that she had Lyndel and Buster sitting there in the front seat with her he got rattling-mad.

"How'd she git hold of them two kids?" Faybelle asked Tod as she watched the car from the window of the house.

"I don't know, but I'm damned if I'm goin' to stand here and do nothin' while she handles 'em as she pleases. I kind of reckoned she'd git around here sooner or later. Kids are her meat."

As Tod made for the door he turned to Faybelle.

"You-all stay here—'cause I'm goin' to give her some mind she's never had before."

When Tod went outside and met Mary he raised his hat like a gentleman and said: "Howdy."

While Tod was outside Faybelle gathered up Piddle, Sudie, Tewp, and Jay Boy and had them stay in the house. Roddy had saddled up the pony and ridden over to the Juan Largo—and Tod was getting plumb sick of all this riding off he was doing lately while there was work to be done on the farm, now that it was past bean harvest and the corn was ready to haul in. But Roddy was a boy set in his ways, and there was no holding him back.

They all watched the teacher's car from the window.

"I ain't never seen her this close before," said Faybelle. "Look at them short skirts, will you! And them silk stockin's!"

Now this was how come Mary had Lyndel and Buster in the car. She had picked them up down the road where the kids had been off by themselves horsing around the railroad tracks. She met them just as she was getting out to open the gate into the McClung land, about a half-mile from the house. But Buster beat her to it, and it was he who let the fence gap loose so she could pass through; and when he had set it back again both kids piled into the car with Mary.

"I'm ten past," said Buster.

"And I was nine yesterday," said Lyndel.

Mary just sat in the car and didn't aim to start it up.

"You know," she said, "this is the first chance I've had to know you children. I hope you will like me as much as I am sure I will like you."

Buster thought the teacher talked funny—Lyndel liked her and didn't feel bashful.

"I'd like to have you two at school," said Mary, not wasting any time.

"When?" asked Lyndel.

"Now. . . . Tomorrow."

"You-all better not let Paw know what you're thinkin'. . . . He'd git mad."

"He sure gits rambunctious when he gits mad," added Buster. "He's worser'n Piddle."

"Who's Piddle?" asked Mary, although she knew because she had heard everyone tell.

"He's our grandpaw, and he's sure got around a lot. He's horsed—"

"Horsed?"

"Got around—went from one place to 'nother. He got drunk in Arkansas and nearly died. He—"

"He don't talk much," said Lyndel, "but he likes to tell us kids of his doin's and his horsin' around."

"But we don't pay him much mind," said Buster.

"But Sudie and our brothers do," put in Lyndel. "They think Piddle's big punkins 'cause he's rambled around."

Mary said: "They must know a lot about the world, then. Do you know any of the children in the community?"

"Some," said Lyndel, "but they think us kids are a bunch of bastards."

Mary expected this, so she didn't show surprise. All she could do was sit there and listen and think.

Nine years of it, she thought. And the boy has her beaten by perhaps a year and a half.

High on the embankment that carried the railroad track, Mary saw the arm of a block signal descend from its upright position to the halfway drop; at the same time a freight train whistled down the line.

Lyndel raised her eyes to Mary Simonson.

"Where you aimin' to go?" she asked.

Mary turned the key in the dashboard, ready to give the car the gun.

"No. Wait!" cried Lyndel, holding Mary's hand back. "After the train goes by." Then: "If you're goin' to see Paw about gittin' us kids to school you'd better turn 'round and go home. It won't do you no good."

"Is he home?"

"Yes. He's fixin' the binder after cutting the corn crop down. It won't do you no good to see him about us kids."

"We don't want to see you git a cussin' out," said Buster.

The arm of the block signal dropped to a horizontal position—the train whistled closer.

"No, it isn't that I want you at school if he would rather have you at home," said Mary, "but— He plays the fiddle, doesn't he?"

"Boy, howdy!" said Buster. "I'll say he does!"

"That's what I want to see him about."

"He'll be right glad to talk to you about fiddlin'," said Lyndel.

A crew of Mexican section hands, who were working on the track, stepped down the embankment as the train drew near. It was a long freight—nearly a mile from engine to caboose. As it was westbound it had a grade to pull, the smoke from the stack came black and thick—the cars hauled merchandise, oil, livestock, and coal—a thousand wheels bore the weight of the load and clattered along the track. The fireman was shoveling and sweating: and the engineer was driving her toward Willard.

Lyndel pointed to one of the boxcars.

"That car says 'Chesapeake and Ohio,' " she said. "Chesapeake is a big bay in the ocean near where the President lives, and Ohio is a state way back yonder."

"Good Lord!" Mary said in surprise. "Where did you learn that?"

"We got a school, just me and Buster, in—"

"In that culvert under the tracks," said Buster. "We got—"

"We got a map there," Lyndel let Mary know.

Mary's eyes were fixed on the dark tunnel under the tracks—Lyndel and Buster's school.

"We tore it out of the Montgomery Ward catalogue," Buster added.

"We ain't got no reg'lar geography book 'cause Paw would give us a whippin'. He don't know about the school nohow. . . . You won't tell him we got books, will you?"

"What other books have you at your school?" Mary asked.

"We got another map, of the whole United States, in a little book somebody pitched off'n the train and—"

"We got some pitchers and writin' we tore off'n old tin cans," added Buster.

"And we learn a heap by watchin' the letters and numbers on the freight cars as they go by. . . . Paw would give us a whippin' if he knew what we was doin'."

Mary sat watching these two. Except for the two Mexicans at the school she didn't know of a kid in the community who was as eager to learn.

The train passed on to the west; the Mexican section crew climbed back on the track and took up their picks and shovels. Mary stepped on the starter and got the car into motion.

I want to get a good close look at this Tod McClung, she thought.

The kids jabbered a plenty as they drove toward the house.

"You won't talk to Paw about us kids?" asked Lyndel, anxious-like.

"No," said Mary.

That was how Mary had Lyndel and Buster in the car with her when she drove into the McClung yard; and that was why Tod went out to meet her, aiming to give her hell. But he walked up to her and said "Howdy" and tipped his hat like a gentleman should.

Tod was mighty shaky when he fixed himself to talk to Mary. He knew there was a law about folks sending their kids to school —the neighbors had told him so, and he reckoned they were right —and he was afraid of the law.

Besides, he was getting sick of all these people coming around to tell him how he should bring up his kids. Only the week before, Mr. Flowers had collared Tod out in the field and started in on him about Roddy and said he had heard that the boy used profane language in the presence of the neighbors.

"Looky here," said Tod, all het up. "If that's the way my boy talks it's his way of makin' himself understood. I ain't got no respect for a man without guts enough to tell his neighbor to go to hell. My boy—"

Mr. Flowers was pious but stern.

"Mr. McClung," he said, "your boy is only sealin' his own fate, but I'll be proud to remind you that you're talkin' to a man of God. It's profanity that's brought me here to see you, and—"

"By God," yelled Tod, "it's profanity you're goin' to git."

Tod fixed himself ready to whip Mr. Flowers if the preacher gave him any more sass—but before he knew it he was alone again and yelling to the mules to get on their high horse. Mr. Flowers was long gone.

Mr. Flowers, after promising Marvin Smeet that he would do so, had put off this interview with Tod as long as he could, because he didn't like to get out among sinners and was satisfied with those good neighbors who came to his Sunday meetings and who understood, without being told, the reason for his wearing a hat. The preacher would have liked to see a dime or two of Tod McClung's go into his hat, because he had to make a living like anyone else, but now he figured that the dimes would only be the shekels of scribes and Pharisees, and he didn't want any truck with folks such as that. After he had suffered the cussing Tod gave him in the field the preacher figured that his pious thought of Tod's folks putting dimes in his hat was long gone and that Satan could have them for all he cared.

"Curse them!" prayed Mr. Flowers to his God that night. "Land, beans, kids and all!"

So when Tod went out to meet Mary he thought, God damn it to hell. He reckoned that this schoolteacher had come to devil him and tell him how he should run his business. He didn't need anyone to tell him how to make a living for his family. The soil gave them food and shelter, clothing and health; and if they stuck by the soil they would live right and like it. Tod hadn't had a crop failure since the time he first put his plow into the dirt of Torrance County.

Short crops, yes—but nothing to gripe about; heavy crops, plenty —when the rains fell and the frosts stayed off. And Tod was thankful to the Lord for the goodness bestowed upon him by Heaven, and there wasn't a man or woman on earth who could put themselves between Tod McClung and the Lord.

But this hussy! This schoolteacher! She was aiming to wean Tod's kids away from the soil; to educate and make jelly beans of them, to take the man out of the boys and the she out of the girls—and Tod was damned if he was going to let her get away with it.

He tipped his hat and said "Howdy," but all the time he was thinking up fighting words.

"Git out," said Tod to the kids. "You-all git in the house and stay by your maw, or I'll lick the hell out of you."

Both Lyndel and Buster looked at Mary and went. Tod said nothing but waited for Mary to speak.

"I wonder, Mr. McClung, if you can guess what I have come to see you about."

"I reckon," said Tod, "it's somethin' to do with schoolin' my kids. I can use my head *that* much."

"But why should you think that? . . . Because I am a teacher? . . . No, it's because of music."

"I can learn my kids music myself."

"I am sure you can, and you would be a very able teacher. They tell me you are the best fiddler in Torrance County."

"What's that got to do with schoolin' my kids?"

"Nothing. . . . But are you anxious to have them go to school?"

"Not by a damned sight, and let's git that straight right now."

Mary leaned on the steering wheel and made herself comfortable.

"I've come to ask you if you would play for the dance at the schoolhouse," she said. "We need a fiddler. . . . And by the way, Mr. Flowers and Mr. Smeet are not asking you. . . . I am. . . . Will you do it?"

Talking education with Tod was one thing and fiddling was another. He was the best fiddler that ever came out of eastern Oklahoma, and he knew it. He was a fiddling fool from way back, and he would like the folks of the community to hear him make music.

"I reckon myself pretty good," he said, "but what's that got to do with kids and school?"

"Absolutely nothing. I am not going to talk to you about kids and school. . . . You can keep your kids at home. . . . I'm asking you to fiddle for the dance."

Then Tod changed. He changed to a right clever man. He opened the car door so Mary could get out.

"Won't you-all come in?" he said. "I'd be right proud to have you meet my old lady."

"Thanks," said Mary, stepping out, silk stockings and all.

All this time Faybelle was watching from the window.

"Lord save us!" she said to Piddle and the kids. "She's comin' in. I swear to God if Tod ain't bringin' her in!"

So Piddle spat out his quid and took a fresh one so he wouldn't be expected to talk.

"Git in the lean-to, you-all kids," Faybelle yelled at Sudie and Jay Boy and Tewp, and at the two youngest who had just come in. "It ain't fittin' for young uns to be in the presence of such as her."

Faybelle thought of Jezebel and wondered if they wore silk in them long-gone days.

When Tod and Mary came in, only Faybelle and Piddle were in the room. The teacher had a feeling that someone was watching her from behind the gunny-sack curtain which hung over the door of the lean-to. She heard whispers and saw the curtain move. She thought she saw eyes peeping through the crack.

"This is my wife," said Tod to Mary. "And this man here is her daddy." . . . Then to the folks: "This is the teacher. She's come to say howdy."

Faybelle acted cold.

"Proud to meet you," she said.

Piddle didn't say anything.

Faybelle looked Mary over from the feet up. She noticed the high-heeled shoes, the shameless stockings, the short-skirted blue dress with the lace collar, the coat that should have been buttoned in October, and the dressed-up hair without a hat.

Why don't she wear a hat with all that uppity riggin'? thought Faybelle.

Piddle gave some attention to Mary too. He figured she had the

build and looks of a girl he had met, long ago, on the street in
Nashville. He had picked the girl up and saw she had a pretty face,
but he couldn't tell about the rest of her, because of all the stuffing
and petticoats, until he had her locked up with him in the hotel room.
It took the girl ten minutes of stripping to get down to what Mary
had on right here before decent folks.

"Miss Simonson has come over to talk to us about fiddlin'," Tod
said.

"Fiddlin'!" said Faybelle, surprised.

"Sure. Fiddlin'. She wants me to play for the hoedown they're
puttin' on at the school."

"I reckon it's O.K."

"I'll be proud to do it."

"But what about the kids? . . . I thought—"

"Shut up about the kids!" cried Tod. "Do you want to start
somethin' unpleasant!"

Mary thought the place smelled of cold fried potatoes. All these
people seemed to have an odor about them that reeked of grease.
Marvin Smeet's house had the whiff of cold fried onions and vinegar
about it. Here, too, was the barnyard stink; Mary wondered if
there couldn't be living pork and poultry around the house somewhere—maybe under the four double beds that took up most of the
room.

"We've often aimed to pay you a visit," said Faybelle.

"And ask you over for dinner some time," added Tod.

Piddle chewed his quid and looked at Mary's legs.

Tod figured there was something missing in the room. "Where-
all's them kids?" he asked of Faybelle.

"They ran to the lean-to when they saw the teacher comin'. I
reckon they got scared when they saw her."

Mary wished they had a mirror somewhere—she wondered if she
possibly could look that bad.

Tod drew the gunny-sack curtain aside and called to the kids.
The smell of cold fried potatoes became stronger.

"Git in here and meet the teacher. What you-all scared about?
. . . I'll whale the hell out of you if you don't act clever. . . .
Git in here!"

The brown-haired Sudie with the thin lips was the first to come out from the lean-to. She was tall, slim, and slightly knock-kneed; she blushed because Tod had cussed her out before the teacher. She didn't speak.

"This is my oldest girl," said Tod. "The oldest of the bunch. Her name's Sudie, and she's nineteen."

By the time Tod finished saying that, the rest of the kids were in the room.

"This here is Tewp—he aims to be a cowpuncher. Roddy, my oldest boy, has done rid off somewheres."

"And the son of a bitch took my boots with him," cussed Tewp.

"Talk different, son, before the teacher. Or I'll knock your teeth down your throat." That is what Tod said to Tewp, and he meant it.

Faybelle cut in before any more arguments could get mixed up between Tod and Tewp. "And this here is Jay Boy. He's twelve and plays the guitar," she said. "And right well, too."

Now Piddle was right smart of a wag, and he had to have his say-so, as much as he hated talking to strangers. He spat in the stove, put his quid between his back teeth, and opened up.

"And I'm sixty-seven and I need educatin'. I want to go to school with the rest of the kids. I want to learn 'rithmetic."

Tod and Faybelle laughed at Piddle because they thought he was one hell of a cut-up, but Mary thought he should wipe the tobacco juice from his chin.

"From what I have heard about you, Mr.—" Mary tried to say.

"Call me Piddle. As old as I am I like pretty gals to git familiar," invited Faybelle's daddy.

"From what I have heard about you, you don't seem to need educating. I think—"

"Tell her about the time in Fort Smith," urged Tod.

Piddle cackled like he was having a lot of fun.

Faybelle turned on Tod. "Now, Tod McClung, you hush your big mouth," she said, blushing all over. "I swan!"

Lyndel moved over to Mary, and the teacher reached down and held her by the hand.

"About the schoolmarm," continued Tod, all full of devilment, "who said she'd learn you what she couldn't tell the kids 'cause you was done growed up and they wasn't. And you said—"

Faybelle got rambunctious and slapped Tod over the mouth all in fun. Then she said to Mary: "I'd be right proud if you-all'd stay for supper. It's doggone nigh time."

Mary accepted the invitation; she would like to learn more about Lyndel.

"May I help?" she asked Faybelle.

"No, ma'am," Faybelle told her. "You-all set and make yourself comfy. Me and Sudie will stir up the vittles." And then to Tewp and Jay Boy: "You-all git out and do up the chores."

Tod asked Mary if she would like to hear some music.

"Paw, make them boys git out and do up the chores," Faybelle yelled to Tod from the lean-to.

"Me and Jay Boy's fixin' to make some music for the teacher," Tod called back, "but Tewp ain't doin' nothin'—he can fix 'em up."

Tewp asked Piddle for a chew of tobacco.

"Git out and do 'em up, son," said Tod, stern-like. "You-all will have to be gittin' over to your business come dark."

Tewp bit off a piece of Piddle's plug and got himself outside.

Lyndel stood close to Mary all this time but kept silent. Now and then she would ask the teacher a question, about her clothes or how she had fixed her hair so pretty, but every time she spoke Tod would tell her to shut up and let the grownups do the talking.

Tod and Jay Boy tuned up their instruments and fixed to give the teacher some music. For Tod and Jay Boy were musicians from way back and they were out to make some noise.

In the lean-to Faybelle and Sudie busied themselves about getting supper. "You-all make the piecrust, Sudie, and I'll fix the fillin'," Faybelle was saying.

Tod got that old fiddle under his chin and asked Jay Boy what it would be.

" 'Green Corn,' " said Jay Boy, all set with his guitar.

So Tod sawed the fiddle and Jay Boy tickled the guitar, and, both together, they mowed that music down.

Piddle sat by the stove making hash of his quid and tapped his foot to the tune. Lyndel stood by Mary, unable to take her eyes away. Buster listened to that old mountain country song and thought his brother and daddy were big stuff. In the lean-to Faybelle and Sudie fussed about the supper. Mary smelled fried onions.

While everybody was paying mind to the music Lyndel leaned over and whispered in Mary's ear. "I wish you was kinfolks," she said. Mary smiled and reached for Lyndel's hand.

The way Tod was stamping his foot as he sawed on that fiddle indicated that the tune would soon be coming to an end and that the last note would stop sudden with a loud bang. It came, and Jay Boy figured that "Short'nin' Bread" would be a good number to pull down. Mary heard something frying in the lean-to, and then Tod said: "Let's go." Again the fiddle whined and the guitar strummed.

The next to be offered to Mary was a song, which Jay Boy would render with his own loud voice, because Jay Boy was a singing fool, so the folks reckoned. The selection he chose was "The Death of Floyd Collins," which was slow and mournful. Mary wondered how Jay Boy could possibly sing with a chew of tobacco in his mouth. She figured that that was the reason the words were so nasal—no room in the mouth for a song and a chew at the same time.

"It's about a man gittin' suffocated in a cave," Lyndel whispered to Mary.

"How long does he take to die?" the teacher whispered back.

The song went on, verse after verse. Tod kept time to Jay Boy's voice and guitar strumming with a slow swing on the fiddle strings. By the time it came to an end Tewp had passed through the room and into the lean-to with a bucket of milk.

"Let's have that old Jimmy Rodgers song from the record," said Tod. "The ladies like that love stuff. You know, the one we like, 'My Carolina Sunshine Girl.' "

Again Jay Boy broke into singing—this time all set to talk love to that old Carolina sunshine girl.

> *"My Carolina sunshine girl,*
> *You've turned my heart to stone—"*

They were going to have coffee for supper—that cheap kind. Mary could smell it boiling in the lean-to.

*"My Carolina sunshine girl,*
*You've left me all alone—"*

The fried onions still made themselves smelt all over the house. Mary sniffed at her handkerchief which she had luckily perfumed up before setting out on this visit.

*"But you're the sweetest angel in this world,*
*And I love—love—love you.*
*My Carolina sunshine girl."*

When Jay Boy got done singing that Jimmy Rodgers song, after Tod had made a long sweep of the bow and gave the last tap with his foot, Faybelle came out from the lean-to and said: "You-all git washed, 'cause supper's done ready."

They all washed but Mary; she didn't like the look of the towel, and Faybelle thought, Maybe she *is* uppity.

Mary looked over the assortment of food on the table and was right glad she had a box of bicarbonate of soda in her own kitchen at home. Then they all sat down to eat.

Tod said: "You-all care for some soup?"

So Mary poured some soup in her plate and wondered how she should eat it. She waited until she saw Piddle fixing to break some corn bread and mix it all up in the soup; she figured she should do likewise but couldn't get herself into the notion. The mess on Piddle's plate looked muddy.

"This is bean soup—it's the soup from the beans. It's got meat grease in it," said Faybelle.

There was noise a plenty as everyone got down to eating supper. There was the clattering of dishes and the scrape of folks scooping out food, and Piddle plumb bubbling at the mouth while he ate his soup.

"I'll thank you for the beans," said Tod.

"You-all pass the meat," demanded Jay Boy.

"I want some coffee," said Sudie, aiming to get the pot from the stove.

When Mary finished her soup she hoped she would not be offered any more supper, but Faybelle handed her a bowl of beans. "These here are the beans from the soup—this year's crop. They're mixed up with fried onions and grease. We eat a heap of beans in this house."

The corn bread was crumbly and hard to handle, the meat was sowbelly and plenty salty, the coffee was black and cheap. Mary burped and said, "Pardon."

"You ready for pie?" Faybelle asked the teacher. "It's bean pie."

"Bean pie!"

"It's beans from the soup," Faybelle told her.

"Beans from the soup!" said Mary, like as though she had never heard of bean pie.

Faybelle scooped her off a piece.

"It's easy made and good eatin'." Faybelle knew because she had mixed it up herself. "All you do is mash up the beans and add sugar and cinnamon. You can put in vanilla, too, if you want."

"And meat grease to make it stick together," said Sudie.

"Yes, and plenty meat grease. . . . Then you bake it in a crust like apple pie. It's good eatin'."

Mary tried the pie. Good Lord, she thought, how they make the most of a bean crop!

And just as she finished eating her pie and burped and said "Pardon," just as all were fixing to go wash their mouths out with a dipper of water, Roddy McClung came into the room. His spurs jingled as he walked, and he said he was hungry. He paid no mind to Mary but went over to the stove and scooped him out some beans on a plate. Then Tewp cussed him out.

"God damn it," Tewp said. "Why-all cain't you go bitchin' around the Juan Largo without takin' my boots with you? Why-all cain't you lay the girl in your own shoes?"

"Shut up, son," scolded Tod. "We got company."

"Take 'em off," yelled Tewp.

"No. . . . His feet stink," protested Sudie. "Wait till the teacher goes home before you take the boots off, Roddy."

Roddy said nothing but just went on mashing up beans and scooping them into his mouth.

"Let's leave him be," said Tod, leading everybody but Roddy into the big room. "Maybe the teacher would like to hear some more music." Then to Tewp: "Son, it's dark, you-all better be gittin' about your business."

"As soon as that bastard gives me my boots."

"Shut up your God-damned coarse language," said Tod, plumb disgusted with Tewp's cussing.

Mary put on her coat.

"I'd like to stay, Mr. McClung," she said, "and just listen to your playing all night, but I have a lot of school work to do before bedtime. . . . Thank you so much for a pleasant evening, and ever so much for your offer to play at the dance." Then to Jay Boy she said: "I hope you can help out with the guitar, Jay Boy. We will need you too."

"Me and Paw always play together."

"That's settled, then."

"He'd be right proud."

"You-all come back," invited Faybelle.

"You bet," said Sudie.

Lyndel said nothing, but she looked at the teacher as though she was God Almighty.

Mary had been afraid to say what she wanted to, but now, with all these friendly folks around her she came out with it and nothing was holding her back.

"Mr. McClung," she said. "I have been thinking of this girl here." She had her hand resting on Lyndel's shoulder. "I would like to have her meet the children at the school—"

A frown came to Tod's forehead.

"No. . . . Don't misunderstand me," she went on to say. "I just want to see her again. Take her on rides in the car. . . . I would even like to take her to Albuquerque with me some week end."

Tod did not reply but opened the door and led the way out for Mary.

"You-all come back," called everybody from the house.

Tod opened the car door for Mary. He said nothing for a moment, until Mary had herself settled comfortable in her Chevrolet. Then he opened up.

"Miss Simonson," he said. "I know what you-all think of me. . . . I know it without hearin' you speak your mind. Without you tellin' me how low-lifed I am."

Mary figured she had better keep silent.

"Funny feller, that's me. But Lord knows I ain't like most folks. . . . I'm tryin' to do right by my kids. . . . And the farm."

Tod raised his hand, pointing to the darkness.

"You cain't see it now, but you've looked at it a plenty in the daytime: the country, the fields with the growin' crops of summer and the bare stubble of winter; the brown soil that feeds and keeps us folks who ain't like you. . . . We's so different, us and you, that it ain't pitiful. You're one kind—like a sleek race horse runnin' over ground that's smooth and green, and we're like mules that bust clods and sweat and know we ain't good for nothin' but just that. You're of the soft breed—the best kind; we're hard and tough and down in the dirt where we belong. . . . Don't try to lift us out of the soil, for it's our meat and livin'."

Mary just sat.

"Switch your lights on," said Tod.

The headlights flashed onto the barn, and the rough-lumber shed came before the eyes of the two human beings alone in the yard.

"That shed there holds the bean crop; it's all harvested and sacked up. In a day or two the trucks will come and haul it off to Mountainair. The buyers will look it over and weigh it and pay me cash for my summer's work. The sweat of me and my kids raised that crop. We ain't altogether ignorant 'cause we's bright in our own way. . . . We know the soil. We don't need to know anything else; we don't want to—we know the dirt and how to eat from the dirt. . . . We know the taste and feel of it—what's good about it, and what's bad.

"Leave us few folks on the soil, and we won't molest nobody. Somehow I feel . . ."

Tod paused in his talk as a breeze came up from the west. It was cold; it smelled of frost, of yellow pumpkins, of dry fodder, of everything that made up the harvest. He sniffed at the air, and Mary felt through the darkness, without touching him, the man's body quiver with pleasure.

"Smell it," said Tod. "God Almighty! Smell that air comin' over the cornfield. . . . It's comin' over them shocks all standin' ready to be shucked and shelled. . . . Me and my kids made them all. We made them come out of the ground. We worked them even to the littlest—"

"Lyndel?" asked Mary.

"Yes. She's my favorite young un."

Tod pointed in the direction of the field—it was all black out there. "You know, Miss Simonson, my kids are so close to the soil that that young un—that Lyndel—was darn near born in a shock of beans. Nine years ago yesterday it was. By God, I'd plumb forgot! . . . I got Faybelle to the tent before it happened. . . . Been pitchin' beans up to me in the wagon, was Faybelle. She's a strong woman. It was our first bean harvest."

"And you've raised a bean crop every year since," said Mary, thinking hard.

"Ain't had a single failure—even in dry years and short seasons."

Now came Mary's say-so.

"But you've failed in your kid harvest, Tod McClung," she said. "Failures that will drain on the field crop money you've turned into the bank. The six youngsters you have seeded and reaped have all turned out failures but two; and if you don't come out of the rut these two, your only salvation, will go to ruin with the rest. . . . But give them a chance and they will pay out. They will bring up your balance and give you back what you will lose on the others. It is all the same kind of farming. They will—"

But Tod McClung was a man set in his ways, and he wasn't going to let any schoolteacher tell him different—even this one, whom he had learned to like in a couple brief hours.

He opened his mouth to speak.

"Wait, Tod," Mary said, for she was not done with her say-so. "These two will come up out of the dirt of their own accord, try as hard as you may to hold them down."

Tod couldn't say anything; he got to scratching around the dirt with his foot: he was trying to think.

"What is your children's destiny, as you see it?" Mary asked him.

"Destiny?"

"What you aim for them to do," explained Mary in Tod's own language.

Then Tod opened up.

"Raise 'em to love the soil," he said, "this here six hundred and forty acres of it, like nothin' else in the world. Make 'em see no other way of livin' but from what comes out of the field. To let 'em have a spell of ramblin' around and then git it out of their systems. To have my girls marry up with dirt farmers like me—their own kind. To make 'em feel so damned foolish anywhere else but on the farm so's they just cain't eat and breathe away from it."

"They will all go away, and only two will come back," prophesied Mary.

"The youngest?"

"Lyndel and Buster."

"So I reckon," said Tod, and there was a worry on his mind. "But you cain't say I didn't try to hold 'em. . . . Maybe they've got a stubborn head like me. . . . I won't blame them if they go away, only the one who takes 'em."

Tod held out his hand to Mary. "There's a heap of difference in the feel of our skin, Miss Simonson. . . . Mine's hard, and yours soft. . . . Lyndel's hand feels more like yours, what I've felt of it, but maybe it's 'cause she's so young. . . . We grow up to be hard, us folks, and I reckon the oldest of our bunch are past softenin' down. But them youngest—"

Mary turned the switch and stepped on the starter.

Then Tod said, hastily, as though he was afraid Mary would get away before he had his say-so: "But I'd be right proud if you want to take Lyndel to Albuquerque with you some Saturday. . . . She'd maybe like to see a pitcher show. She ain't never yet."

The teacher put her car into low gear and released the clutch.

"See you at the dance, Tod," she called as she drove off.

"Me and Jay Boy will make them folks stomp like they don't know what," Tod yelled after her, loud so he could be heard.

In the house Tod found Faybelle and Sudie looking at the Montgomery Ward catalogue just to see how much silk stockings cost, and Tewp was fixing to go out on his business.

"Hurry up, son," said Tod to Tewp. "Old man Buck Smiles will be waitin' for you in the dugout and cussin' you to high water."

Old man Buck Smiles was a neighbor friendly with the McClungs. He had been a moonshiner when he lived way back in Georgia.

He had a boy called T. J. who was right smart fond of Sudie.

"I want my boots," said Tewp, mad. "Make Roddy gimme my boots."

The room stank of sweaty feet while Roddy took off the boots.

"How's the beer workin'?" asked Tod of Tewp.

"Fine. . . . It was bubblin' and rarin' to be worked today. We'll run it off tonight and we'll have altogether eight gallons. . . . Eight gallons of good corn whisky! . . . Old man Buck Smiles says we can git sixteen dollars a gallon for it at the dance."

"There'll be a good market for it," agreed Tod.

"You're darn tootin'," said Tewp.

The boy started out for the still in old man Buck's dugout— to make that bubbling corn beer into good hard, white whisky.

"Watch out for the prohibes, son," warned Tod, as Tewp took off.

Piddle and Roddy were in the lean-to planning devilment.

"What color is the floor of the schoolhouse?" asked Piddle.

"God damned if I know," said Roddy. "Brown, I reckon. It's wood."

"Then we'll need to git the tail of a brown horse."

"Old man Mudgett's got a chestnut mare with a brown tail," Roddy said.

"Hell," Piddle cackled, like he was having fun. "You-all git out and dock the tail off'n old man Mudgett's mare. . . . Just what we need, by Jesus!"

So with Tod and Jay Boy to make music, Tewp to sell bootleg whisky on the quiet, and Roddy and Piddle to get their devilment going, the dance at the schoolhouse promised to be a grand affair.

As Mary Simonson drove home she did a heap of thinking.

"So Roddy rode off to the Juan Largo wearing Tewp's boots," she said to herself. "And Earlene goes home that way because she likes to be close to nature. . . . Oh, Earlene! And after all the nice things St. Paul said about virginity!"

Mary thought of Earlene, but she gave most of her heart to Lyndel.

And that was how Mary Simonson had a worry on her mind that night—and why she couldn't relax while she read her storybook.

## Chapter Five

VIRGIE SMEET and Effie Lee Mudgett were all aflutter the evening before the night of the dance.

Were they aflutter!

It being a Saturday, there was no school, and Mary Simonson sat in her room fixing the doodads on the long dress she aimed to wear at the dance. She just sat and thought and hummed and sewed, and then she got herself pestered by Virgie and Effie Lee.

"I'll swan before Jonah!" said Virgie, as she and Mrs. Mudgett walked in on Mary. "There's more chores to gittin' this dance a-goin' than a month of Sundays on a black-land farm in Texas. It wears a Christian soul down for sure."

Effie Lee had to have her say-so, too: "The folks'll be gittin' here come eight o'clock," she said, "and it's four-twenty-five right now. We've yet to hang the floomagadunjets in the schoolroom."

The floomagadunjets were the bright cloth decorations and streamers the womenfolks had ripped up.

"Marvin will be over when he gits the chores done up, and Earlene will he'p him," Virgie said. "Lord, Lord, it's sweet to have such a lovin' husband with all the trimmin's of an honest-to-goodness Christian. It's a shame Mr. Mudgett don't come over and lend a hand, Effie Lee."

But Effie Lee was in a stew over Mr. Mudgett's trouble.

"He's done got himself into such a heat," she said, "I don't reckon he'll even come to the dance. . . . Such a low, sneakin' trick to play on a good Christian and a poor dumb brute! . . . I don't know what the world's comin' to, as I've often told Mr. Mudgett, and I don't know what's what, and that's all there is to it."

Both Mary and Virgie had heard of Mr. Mudgett's trouble earlier in the day. He made a discovery when he went to grain the horses at sunup that morning. He found his fine chestnut mare with half her tail gone. Cut off with scissors, by God!

Mary sewed and hummed, not giving the ladies much mind.

"I cain't imagine who," sighed Effie Lee.

"I can," said Virgie.

"Who-all?"

Then Virgie Smeet opened up.

"That Mexican sheepherder who works for Dan Blakey, that's who. They say he's always plaitin' somethin' while he's herdin' them sheep: quirts, hatbands, and ropes. . . . Cain't keep his hands still, that greaser. He ran out of horsehair and he took it out on old Tulip, I'll tell you for sure, Effie Lee."

Tulip was the name of Mr. Mudgett's chestnut mare.

Both the ladies clicked their tongues.

Mary sewed and listened while the visiting ladies rattled off, cackled away like a pair of Minorca hens laying eggs, plumb heckled over Tulip's half-docked tail. Nobody could blame Effie Lee for being so doggone mad, because who done it maybe aimed to use the horsehair for some useful purpose—such as plaiting quirts and ropes like a Mexican sheepherder will—or likely it was done for plain ornery meanness and nothing else but.

She didn't know that Roddy McClung had climbed quietly into the corral during the night, while the folks were sleeping soundly, and said, "Whoa, nice horsey," to the mare, and patted her on the flanks and got to work on the tail. And all the while Tulip thought he was just ridding her of cockleburrs and didn't know different until that mean McClung boy took out for home with half her tail stowed away in a sack. So when Virgie Smeet said she reckoned it was Dan Blakey's sheepherder who did the cutting both ladies clicked their tongues, and Mary just said nothing because it was none of her business. She couldn't guess who did it, anyway.

Then the teacher reckoned she had better say something, because the ladies had come to pay her a visit.

"I suppose the dance will bring folks from all around," said Mary. "From the Salt Lakes and up by Pedernal. . . . Tod McClung is known far and wide as a fiddler, and that will be an attraction."

"There'll be a heap of a crowd there," said Virgie, sourly. "But to my way of thinkin' Tod McClung or any of his tribe ain't much of an attraction. . . . They're plumb infidel."

"Down to the littlest," said Effie Lee.

"Lyndel?" asked Mary.

"All of 'em," said the Mudgett woman. "They're all kin by blood and marriage to that wicked old granddaddy. Piddle's a good name for him 'cause he just piddles around and don't do nothin' useful to better Christianity. He's a Pharisee or I don't know one. I'll swan they're all tainted the same."

Tares in the wheat, thought Mary; ugly McClung weeds among useful Smeet, Mudgett, and Flowers grain.

"I think the youngest is a cute kid," she said aloud, "and smart. If she could be taken away from the family for a while and have a chance to learn something—just attend school—she would make a fine woman some day. She's—"

"A McClung," snapped Virgie, like that was enough to damn any girl.

"And hopeless," abetted Effie Lee.

Mary sighed.

"That youngest boy, Buster, seems a smart kid too. If he had schooling he'd turn out to be a first-class farmer. I wish Tod would let me teach him—both of them."

"If a McClung 'tends the school," said Virgie, "I'll take Earlene out and keep her home. . . . My girl ain't goin' to be tainted by none of them. And that's how much use I've got for that tribe, teacher."

Effie Lee thought Virgie talked sound preaching.

"And what gits me plumb riled," said Effie Lee, "is that the Lord lets Tod go on havin' so much luck with his farm. He's been here since 1919 and ain't had a crop failure in all that time. Us folks have had our beans nipped by the frost and ruined more times than one, but that infidel goes on harvestin' and takin' in good money and the Lord don't seem to mind how prosperous he gits. . . . It gits my dander up for sure, but I'm Christian enough to let be if the Lord ordains it."

Virgie got a hanker to speak.

"Wait, Effie Lee," she cried. "You-all just wait till the time comes for Tod to go back on his luck. Give him a chance to build up his place and git head over heels in debt with the bank. Let him prosper and enjoy it till he don't know nothin' else but and cain't do without it. Then the Lord will ruin his crop with an early frost and bring misery to him—even put blackleg among his cattle—and raise havoc with all he's built up from nothin'. . . . As a full-blood Christian you-all should know that's the way the Lord sends his vengeance to infidels. When his wrath will be felt most."

And because Virgie spoke honest-to-goodness Christianity such as that, Effie Lee Mudgett thought her to be a sister in God from way down the line.

Mary thought to herself while she sewed doodads to her long pink dance dress. She glanced up now and then to take a squint at the visiting ladies, who sat up straight in their chairs like a pair of Minorca hens. But the teacher kept quiet, for she figured that whatever she should say in favor of the McClungs would have as much effect as though she'd talk to a pair of genuine feathered Minorcas sitting on a perch in the chicken house.

Then somebody called "Howdy" from the yard. It was Marvin and Earlene come to fix the floomagadunjets.

Virgie and Effie Lee rose, said a polite "Good day" and left like the house was on fire. Left quick as though they needed fresh air; away from a body who talked like she was a McClung lover.

Mary was damned glad of it.

A dance such as was to take place was something special for the community folks to enjoy. So everybody lent a hand to make it a grand affair. It was up to Mr. Flowers to ask a blessing before the eats and to watch out for sinful hug dancing when the folks got going on the floor. Tod and Jay Boy McClung were to make music; and unbeknownst to the Christians gathered, Tewp would peddle bootleg whisky on the Q.T. Old man Buck Smiles, who helped Tewp make the likker, was to call the dance while the fiddle whined and the guitar strummed and the dancers were sweating and blowing and having a good time. The Widow Burge, who lived out close to the tracks like the McClungs and who had two grown sons, would cook the vittles at home and pack it all to the school yard where it would be served on tables set in a circle around a blazing fire of cedar and piñon. Virgie Smeet would help dish out the food to the folks, and Marvin would patrol the school yard to watch out for any sparking among the young people in the dark.

The Widow Burge had two sons; one was bright and lazy, and the other half-witted but worth his salt because he chopped wood for the neighbors and raked in the cash and kept the weeds down in the bean patch. The folks in the community called the half-wit "Craze Rufe," because his given name was Rufe and there was no doubt about him being off his noggin.

The other son's name was Tennis—Tennis Burge, that was the name he was born with. And the neighbors did a heap of thinking and wondering as to just what Tennis was born for. He was a good boy and never got into any meanness. He wouldn't move far enough from the front porch to get into any kind of devilment. He ate a lot and slept a plenty, which didn't hurt the neighbors, and the Widow didn't kick ary a bit. He was right friendly and clever, so the folks reckoned; and a *good* boy—but just what Tennis was *good for* nobody could figure out.

So the Widow Burge fixed the vittles for the dance, and Craze Rufe helped her, and Tennis just sat and watched. She roasted two whole hindquarters of beef and boiled six big pots of beans cooked down with sowbelly. She had corn bread and biscuits stacked up like a bean shock and would have made gallons of coffee, too, if Mr. Flowers had let her; but the preacher would stand for no coffee drinking at the dance, and he wanted it known to all. So the Widow made lemonade instead. The neighbor women packed all the stuff to make the vittles over to the Widow, and all she had to do was simply cook it.

But oh, Lord!

That pesky old Satan always keeps sticking his head and horns in where he isn't wanted.

Just outside the fence of the school yard was an acre or so where the sacaton grass grew rank and high; and it was there that Tewp cached his bootleg whisky and where he aimed to sell it to anybody who wanted to get lit higher than a kite. The night before that of the dance he and old man Buck Smiles put the likker in a ten-gallon keg—they had eight gallons altogether—and hid it deep in the sacaton. They made sure it would be in the shade when the sun shone the next day, because the stuff was *that* powerful they were feared it would get hot and blow the stopper out of the keg.

At this moment, while Mr. Flowers was thinking up a blessing for the folks, while the Widow Burge was making nice soft lemonade, while Virgie Smeet was rehearsing a good scolding with lots of Bible sayings she would give to anyone she caught hug dancing, and while Marvin and Earlene were fixing the floomagadunjets, out there in the sacaton rested a keg of the Devil's own brew, just waiting to make mischief a plenty.

While the women were fixing their dresses with doodads, and everybody was fixing to have fun that night, Piddle and Roddy were busy too. They were sitting out on the McClung woodpile and Roddy was holding a paper sack open while Piddle used scissors to cut the tail of old man Mudgett's chestnut mare up into shreds of not more than a quarter-inch long. The sack was getting full.

"How long you aim to let 'em dance?" asked Roddy.

"Till midnight," said Piddle. "They'll want to go on stompin' till two o'clock in the mornin', but I figure I don't want 'em to, and when I aim for 'em to quit they'll quit, by golly."

"You and me both."

"Anyway," said Piddle, "Preacher Flowers ought to be in bed by midnight, 'cause late hours ain't good for his complexion. It's too late for him and kids."

"You're damned whistlin'. . . . They'll dance for four hours, then, and by that time Tewp will have the bulk of the menfolks stinkin'-drunk."

"You bet, and then we'll be ready to work on the women with the horsehair," said Piddle, giggling like a schoolboy.

So Satan would be there in person. He would be there with Piddle and Roddy making the girls itch and scratch with what was left of Tulip's tail. He would make Tewp's likker get the menfolks drunk and stinking. And right now he was putting a bug in the ear of T. J., old man Buck Smiles' rounder boy, and giving him a hanker to get to Sudie McClung's britches.

T. J. was a young man of twenty-five who had got around. He had worked as a roustabout in the oil fields, east of Artesia, he had followed the wheat harvest from the Texas Panhandle clean up to Montana, he had been to the Salt River Valley in Arizona where he picked cotton and hired himself out in the citrus groves, and he had been to the west coast and had even seen the ocean. In Tod McClung's eyes T. J. was big punkins.

So when T. J. got himself sweet on Sudie, Tod said to Faybelle: "The right man for our oldest girl, 'cause he works and gits around."

T. J. was a man who had love for Sudie in his heart and a ramble on his mind. He spoke loving words to her one night when they sat together in the cab of his Reo truck, and he told Sudie what he aimed to do.

"I need a woman to love, but I want one who's got a ramblin' soul and a body that's healthy and don't crave medicine," he said. " 'Cause she's got to travel with me and keep a-goin' without proppin' up, and she's got to take all I give her on the chin, 'cause I don't give the dust time to settle on my tracks."

And what T. J. said pleased Sudie right smart.

"I got an itch on my heel that I cain't git shed of," said the girl in answer to his words of love. "And I aim to be a hasher in a restaurant while my man works too. This world is too big for a body to stay put all the time. I've got to make a livin', and what else can a poor girl do! When she's got a job and a man, she's set, and that's all there is to it."

After the talk in the Reo truck, when Sudie told Tod that she and T. J. might get married up and travel around, Tod said to Faybelle: "They'll ramble and work till they git their fill, then they'll come back to the farm like a prairie dog huntin' his hole."

So when T. J. talked sweet loving to Sudie the girl asked: "How much does it cost to git married?"

"It takes two dollars for a license," said T. J., "and five for a preacher. It's a lot of dough and would buy a heap of gas for this old Reo to git around."

"Sounds crazy to me, spendin' all that money." That is what Sudie said.

"I reckon so too," agreed T. J.

"And what folks don't know don't hurt 'em, and I've told a heap of lies before."

"Well," said T. J., seeing right there that Sudie would take him for her loving husband, "will you-all marry me without spendin' any money?"

"Sure thing," said Sudie.

So T. J. took his loving wife and kissed her smack on the face like a husband should, and they didn't aim to give Mr. Flowers five dollars to make it legal.

"We cain't live together till we git to ramblin'," T. J. told her. "We'll tell the folks we'll git married in Artesia, and they'll all be happy. . . . We'll live in a hotel, and you-all can hash in a restaurant while I git me a job of work in the oil fields. I aim to gamble some, 'cause I like to lay my money down."

That is how T. J. and Sudie fixed to get married up without a license—for they were young folks starting out on life, and it was none of the old folks's business. And that was the reason, too, on this night of the dance, that T. J. figured Sudie's britches were his and there was nothing holding him back.

When eight o'clock came on that October night it was well after dark. The school was lit up with gasoline lanterns, and the gay streamers and doodads made it look like the folks were out to have a good time. In the yard the Widow Burge was fixing up the tables around the fire and was setting out the vittles.

Eats! Lord God!

You never saw such heaps of brown roasted meat. Or such stacks of mashed potatoes. And cake. Or so many buckets of lemonade. There was enough to feed the United States Army hunting Pancho Villa, and a plenty left for Pancho Villa when they found him. And the folks looked at all that food and said, "Golly," and smacked their lips and wished it was time to eat—all except Tennis, who had grabbed himself a hunk of beef and was chewing it to hash. Craze Rufe was helping his mama.

The McClungs arrived in their strip-down Cadillac, and Tod and Jay Boy were all dressed up in clean overalls ready to make music. Tewp had on his boots, and Sudie wore the dress she bought after looking at page 90 of the Montgomery Ward catalogue. Piddle and Roddy didn't dress up because they both said, "To hell with it," but Lyndel, of all the McClung womenfolks, looked prettiest and cleanest.

The Smeets arrived in their Oakland car, and they had driven by Preacher Flowers' house and picked him up. Mr. Flowers had on clean overalls and looked even more reverend than he did at preaching. He saw the food and said, "Hallelujah."

Although Mr. Mudgett would have liked to get his claws into the man who ran off with Tulip's tail, he came to the dance anyway. Effie Lee was all dressed up in gray gingham and wore a sunbonnet with dangling strings.

Mr. Flowers walked about and shook hands with everybody but the McClungs and said, "God bless you." Then he reckoned he had better say something funny, so he called:

"Now don't any you-all Baptist feet step on them Methodist feet while you're dancin'."

So everybody but the McClungs laughed and thought Preacher Flowers was a right witty man when he aimed to be.

"He's such a cut-up," said Virgie Smeet, who was admiring Mrs. Mudgett's old-timy dress and Mrs. Mudgett was admiring hers. "He's a catch for some widder-woman if I ever knew one. . . . He's goin' to be the life of this here dance, or I don't know what's what, Effie Lee."

Mary Simonson looked anxiously at the door and left the rest of the folks to have a good time by themselves, although all the women had made a point of saying something to the teacher. She didn't wear a sunbonnet but her dark brown hair was fixed up right pretty. Her face was powdered, and her lips were red with lipstick, and her eyes had a sparkle to them that the other women didn't have, except maybe, little Lyndel. Her dress wasn't so old-timy like the rest of the womenfolks', and yet it was old-timy too. It was long and pink and made of pure silk. Around her waist was a sash tied with a big bow at the back and on the front of it, at the middle, was a bunch of flowers.

A beautiful woman!

Lord, Lord!

But every time Virgie and Effie Lee looked at Mary they blushed, and when the teacher turned her back on them they turned too—for Mary's dress was cut shamelessly low behind. Every man thought Mary was built like a brick outhouse and all said so except Marvin Smeet and Mr. Flowers.

Now while the women were jabbering, the men talking and laughing, Mr. Flowers shaking hands, and some kids giggling and others bawling—a strange young man in a gray jelly-bean suit came in. Mary spied him and went over to say howdy.

"You look like Mary Garden," said the young man, taking Mary's hand and holding on to it.

Virgie Smeet, sitting there on a bench by the wall, cupped her hand over her mouth and whispered to Effie Lee: "Who-all, do you reckon?"

All Effie Lee could say was: "Well!"

"Looks like a high mogul to me," said Virgie, "in that fine gray suit and all."

The way Mary looked at the young man showed she thought a heap of him for sure, and the two ladies noticed it.

"Lord save us, Effie Lee," said Virgie Smeet. "May the dear Lord strike me down with fire for bein' so dumb! . . . That's the teacher's young man from Albuquerque. I'll swan before Jonah, it is!"

"So I reckon," Mrs. Mudgett agreed.

Now Mr. Flowers quit shaking hands when the stranger came in, because he had to look him over. He saw the fine gray suit, the polished shoes, the necktie, and even an overcoat—and he figured that the man inside all that dude apparel didn't farm or work for wages, and it scared the preacher nigh out of his shoes. He thought the young man might be a regular ordained Baptist minister and Preacher Flowers was just scared sick of real ministers, because they reckoned he was an impostor and was not fit to teach the Lord's word on earth.

An impostor! That is what the high-ups reckoned Luke Flowers to be. He a Reverend as much as they were, who had received the call from God himself, and who got religious spasms nigh every day and half a dozen on Sundays! Mr. Flowers didn't like ordained ministers because they thought themselves so doggone smart. But more than the hating of them he was scared of them. If this young man *was* a real preacher, an honest-to-goodness ordained one, Mr. Flowers would be plumb ashamed to pass around his hat after he had asked a blessing.

If that's a man of God, thought Mr. Flowers, I *do* hope he's a

Methodist or Assembly of God, or even a Holiness; but if he's a Baptist the Devil's brought him here, and that's all there is to it.

Was Mr. Flowers worried!

Mary said to the young man: "Bob, they are wondering who you are, and I don't like the thought of making you known to every individual here. I'll introduce you to Mrs. Smeet and let human nature take its course."

Mary did just that, and Virgie was right pleased to meet the teacher's young man from Albuquerque, and before five minutes had passed everybody there gathered knew that the stranger had come to see Miss Simonson, and that it was all right because they aimed to get legally married, and that Mrs. Smeet reckoned he was too good for the likes of the teacher.

When Virgie told Mr. Flowers about the young man the preacher seemed right pleased and started in shaking hands again and patted the men on the shoulder and kids on the head as a reverend man should.

"Look, Bob," said Mary, holding on to his arm as shameless as Potiphar's wife ready to take his garment from him if he aimed to run like Joseph did in those long-gone Bible days. "The little girl in the blue dress. She's the kid I've been telling you about. . . . We must do something about her."

Bob nodded.

By this time old man Buck Smiles was sprinkling corn meal on the floor so that the dancing feet would slide easily and get around, and Tod and Jay Boy were tuning up their instruments fixing to make music.

Then that old dirt farmer, who was manager of this community dance, called out:

"Ladies and gentlemen of the vicinity here gathered:

"The hour has come when we all see fit to make merry and have a good time. With the Lord's permission we're out to put on a real old-timy hoedown like our paws and grandpappies talk about and the likes of which some of you-all folks who're past fryin' size can remember. . . . And now I say if you've got any hates for anybody here tonight, I say forgit it, and have a good time.

"Because Reveren' Flowers is here to guard us agin wickedness, the Devil will be afeared to stick his ugly old face in at this here dance, I'll tell you-all for sure. Mr. Flowers will chase him out till he's long gone.

"Lord, Lord, what a blessin'!

"For this grand occasion, and on the part of you-all folks, I give thanks to the Reveren' Luke Z. Flowers for his offered services agin the Devil; also to Brother and Mistress Marvin Smeet, who you-all know to be good Christians; and to the good-lookin' ladies of the community for providin' the eats and lemonade. To the mentioned lady, gentleman, and reveren' I give them you-all folks's thanks."

The people clapped their hands, and that old dirt farmer felt himself mighty important.

"The son of a bitch!" said Tod to Jay Boy. "He ain't a-thankin' us none for givin' music."

The Widow Burge was rattled, too. "After all the cookin' I've done, and not a solitary word!" she said to Craze Rufe.

"And the way I'm a-goin' to yell my throat raw callin' this dance! . . . Not a God-damned thank you!" said old man Buck Smiles to T. J. and Sudie who were standing close by him.

"I'd like to get up and give a word of thanks to Tod McClung and old lady Burge," said Mary to her young man, "and to let everyone know what little effort Brother Flowers and his disciple Smeet gave to the making of this party, but I'd feel as conspicuous as if I were a vocalist in a hog-calling contest."

Bob nodded his head, indicating Piddle.

"Hold your horses," he said. "The night's young yet. In spite of Brother Flowers I'll bet the Devil crashes this party and will be the life of it. I think I see horns on that old reprobate over there."

Piddle was chewing his quid. Mary had given him an empty coffee can in which he could spit.

Then Mr. Flowers took the floor.

"On with the dance, if the Lord is willin'!" he called.

He gave the signal to the master of ceremonies because he didn't want to converse with a McClung, and that old dirt farmer called, "Let's go!" to Tod, and that McClung band handled their instruments and mowed that music down.

What a dance!

Now Tod McClung was a man who could grow beans; he could raise a family, too—and he could make that good old mountain-country music come from way back yonder. My, oh, my, how Tod could cause that fiddle to whine, and how Jay Boy could make that guitar speak language!

"Line up, ladies and gents!" called old man Buck Smiles. "Line up and git your feet primed for this old-timy hoedown. . . . 'Cause I'm goin' to call this dance and make you-all puff and blow like freights on the Santa Fe Railway. . . . Line up, you gents and ladies! . . . We'll dance awhile, and then we'll eat them goodies. . . . Come out, you bashful boy, and git in the middle, while I call 'Chase That Rabbit,' and make you-all go round and round!"

Oh, did Tod saw that fiddle and Jay Boy tickle that guitar! The music turned somersaults in the air, and everybody was on their high horse rearing to get in on the dance.

Virgie Smeet lifted her skirt above her ankle and tapped her foot to the tune. She whispered to Effie Lee: "I feel so naughty, I swan before Jonah I do."

Then old man Buck called—and what I mean he *called!*

> *"Swing your pardner round and round,*
> *Pocket full of rocks to hold you down,*
> *Ducks in the river goin' to the ford,*
> *Coffee in the pot, sugar in the gourd."*

That's how old man Buck called the dance.

All the people not in the set tapped their feet to the swing of the music. There in the ring, Lord how they danced!

> *"Ladies to the center, how do you do?*
> *Right hand cross and how are you?"*

Along the wall everybody clapped hands to the time; the dancers promenaded and reversed, they joined hands and let go, they swung and crossed.

> *"Chicken in the bread pan kickin' up dough,*
> *Gran'maw, will your dog bite?*
> *No, by Joe!"*

Old man Buck had a voice like a barker at the county fair. How the folks did all he aimed for them to do!

> *"Swing corners all,*
> *Now your pardners,*
> *Promenade the hall.*
> *You swing me and I'll swing you,*
> *All go to heaven in the same old shoe."*

Virgie Smeet sweat with excitement, although she only tapped her foot and watched out for huggers.

> *"Everybody dance as fast as you can,*
> *Catch your pardner by the hand.*
> *Two little pretty gals form a ring,*
> *And when they've done it everybody swing!"*

The McClungs made music better than any phonograph record the folks ever heard tell of, and old man Buck's voice came high and nasal.

Everybody got hot.

> *"Meet your pardner, pat her on the head,*
> *If she don't like biscuits*
> *Give her corn bread."*

Music!

Shuffling and stomping!

Clapping of hands, tapping of feet!

Shouts from the men, yells from the kids!

Old man Buck called that dance high, wide, and handsome!

Lord, Lord!

> *"Gal after boy!*
> *Chase that rabbit, chase that coon,*
> *Chase that cowboy round the room.*
> *Reverse!"*

And boy, howdy, did they chase that rabbit!

> *"Chase that rabbit, chase that squirrel,*
> *Chase that pretty gal round the world.*
> *Promenade!"*

Old man Buck was getting plumb wound up. Now for a circle, and everybody pranced like a studhorse.

> *"All hands up and circle round,*
> *Don't let the pretty gals git out of town.*
> *Dance!*
> *Everybody dance!*
> *Swing your pardners, swing 'em all,*
> *Swing them pretty gals round the hall."*

The dance was coming to an end and Tod gave the sign by the way he swung the bow.

> *"Ladies domineck, gents shanghai,*
> *You'll all git to heaven*
> *In the sweet by-and-by."*

The music stopped, and the dancers took to the benches along the wall. They told each other how well they could swing and promenade. Virgie Smeet eyed a young man who was holding the hand of a girl. Piddle spat in his can.

Now all this while Tewp got himself outside and built a fire in the sacaton patch. He squatted down beside it on his hunkers and waited for T. J. to do his stuff. Inside, T. J. was doing his stuff, and that old dirt farmer called:

"Folks. . . . We'll dance another round and then go out and load up on the chuck which the ladies were so kind to provide. Reveren' Flowers will give us his benediction, and then I'll advise you-all to eat fast and stay at it a long time."

T. J. walked about the room and whispered to the men—all except Mr. Flowers, Marvin Smeet, Mudgett, and that old dirt farmer—and told them there was a keg of corn whisky of the finest kind out in the sacaton, and that Tewp was selling it at two bits a shot. He spoke to Piddle, too; but Piddle said he wanted no more to do with likker; for he had done cured himself of drinking in Little Rock, Arkansas, and didn't aim to start in again.

"Because," said Piddle, "when I take a dip of corn likker I see phantoms which ain't no such thing. I git violent and make devilment for which I'm 'shamed."

T. J. just went around and put the bug in the ear of the more prospective customers. There was wickedness a-brewing.

The Widow Burge was outside attending the eats and goodies, and Virgie Smeet came out to help her. Mr. Flowers, looking so doggoned reverend, joined them ready to give the folks his blessing. Inside, the music whined and the dancers went around and around.

Craze Rufe was helping his mama.

Mr. Flowers stared at the sacaton patch; the fire that the Widow Burge was nursing up to a bright blaze cast a light on his face. He looked worried.

"Mrs. Smeet," he asked Virgie. "Do you see the fire of hell in our midst—out there in the tall grass?"

Virgie did for sure.

"Tewp McClung," she said.

"Satan himself—the Lord's enemy in the flesh—fire and brimstone—blackness!"

"Lord save us," muttered Virgie.

The Widow Burge didn't give the evil any mind. She watched the firelight play on the faces of Virgie and the preacher. They both looked hungry, she thought; perhaps they wouldn't be so scared of Tewp McClung when they had something to eat. She told Craze Rufe to dish out the pickles.

"We must first ask God's blessin'—then we must *fight!*" said Preacher Flowers solemnly.

But the Widow Burge thought to herself: The only fightin' you two will do will be makin' hash of the meat and potatoes. . . . The Lord asks a body to follow His teachin', but He don't aim for him to make a fool of hisself.

That is what the Widow Burge thought, but no one paid her any mind because she didn't speak aloud.

Just then the music stopped in the schoolroom, and that old dirt farmer's voice came out loud and let the Widow and Virgie know they had better get busy with the eats. The folks were hungry, and he was calling them to chuck.

"Citizens of the community," that old dirt farmer was heard to say, "our good neighbor, Mistress Smeet, is outside ready to serve you food. And good eatin', I'll tell you-all for sure. And . . ."

There was loud jabbering and shuffling around indoors.

Then the Widow Burge said something that made Virgie and Preacher Flowers look on her with scorn.

"And now that her flunky, the Widow Burge," she said, "has done the dirty work, Mistress Smeet will smile sweetly at all who says, 'Thank you.' "

Mr. Flowers was fixing to admonish the Widow as he would a sinner, but just then the door flew open and that old dirt farmer called: "Chuck! . . . Come and git it!"

The folks left the school like bats out of hell and milled around the tables as a thirsty herd of cattle at a water hole.

But Preacher Flowers thought about the Lord and told the folks to take it easy. He looked toward the sacaton patch. Tewp still sat by his fire and didn't aim to move—chuck or no chuck.

All gathered formed a circle around Mr. Flowers and fixed to lend their ears to his preaching. Their eyes were on the food and everybody hoped the preacher's blessing would be short. Mr. Flowers took off his hat and set it on the ground before him—crown down, brim side up, ready to receive the nickels and dimes he hoped to get for his divine services.

The folks shut up—they told the kids to shut up—then they waited for the preacher to do his stuff.

"Brethren and sistern here gathered," began Mr. Flowers. "The dear Lord has seen fit to let this here dance take place; he's right glad you-all 're here to have a good time and be old-fashioned and Christianlike. . . . We are tryin' our doggonedest to keep the Devil out of your midst so's you-all will go home pure of heart and ready to come to meetin' at my house tomorrer mornin'.

"But I smell serpents in Eden. They stinketh to heaven and maketh the angels holdeth their noses. . . . The sinners are here among us at this old-timy hoedown, but they're only a few of the thousands of wicked people in Torrance County, New Mexico."

Virgie got het up with religion and aimed for the folks to know about it.

"Oh, the wickedness!" she yelled. "Oh, the wickedness of Torrance County, New Mexico!"

"Amen," hollered Mr. Flowers.

"Praise the Lord," Virgie called back.

"God bless you, sister," replied Mr. Flowers. "You're an honest-to-goodness Christian—the best that ever came out of Throck-morton County, Texas, and that's all there is to it."

"Amen," screamed Virgie.

"Amen!" yelled Mr. Flowers, and the way he said it was enough to tell Virgie to shut up.

Bob was standing by Mary, and he said: "I wouldn't miss this even if it costs me a hundred pressed suits at ninety cents apiece." He eyed the hat on the ground. "When this blessing is over I'm going to do something wicked."

But Preacher Flowers hadn't done with his say-so.

"Friends in righteousness," he began again, now that Virgie had shut up. "I'm here to ask you-all a serious question. I'm goin' to quiz you like the Lord would if he talked to you-all from the top of Pedernal Mountain. This is what I'm goin' to ask you-all: Have you ever been tempted? Has Satan ever sat down by a fire in the sacaton and made devils out of you-all? given you tails and horns and made you think of huggin' and lovin' each other and got you-all het up to drink his alcoholic beverages? . . . No, by golly, say you-all! No, say you sinners who-all think Satan is way down close to Chiny and cain't git to Torrance County 'cause he ain't got the carfare. . . . But you-all are wrong, brethren and sistern, 'cause Satan has trans-portation charges paid by the government of hell to all communities in the world—from Greenland's icy mountains to India's coral strand. He travels around askin' folks to homestead in his colony way down yonder, where he says everything is hunky-dory; but when the sinners git there they find it hotter'n south Texas, the soil is pure brimstone and won't raise beans. . . . He ain't afeared to travel in Pullman cars with the high moguls, and I tell you-all folks for sure it's them that he gits most of. . . . He ain't scared of gittin' seasick, and he goes plumb to Halifax. . . . Oh, the wickedness of Satan! Oh, the wickedness of that there heathen!"

Mr. Flowers paused.

Bob told Mary what he was about to do, and the Widow Burge

wished the preacher would hurry up and get done blessing because the food was getting cold.

"Satan is now in your midst!" called Mr. Flowers with a loud voice. "The fires of hell are in the sacaton. . . . Lord save us!"

Everybody looked toward Tewp's fire, but none got scared except the Smeets and Mudgetts and that old dirt farmer.

That ain't Satan, thought those who were not so righteous. It's only Tewp.

Then they fixed to eat the goodies.

"Stand back!" called Mr. Flowers, mad-like. "Will you please, sir! The Lord ain't done with you yit. I ain't given you my blessin', doggone it!"

So everybody stood still and thought how proud they would be if the preacher would hurry up. Mr. Flowers squirmed about until he looked his most reverendest. He let one arm hang down to his hip and the other he raised in blessing. He set his eyes on the Lord, who he knew to be way up yonder. Then he spoke.

"Lord, scatter thy blessin' on these folks here gathered. Cast thy light on those who are righteous, and give them health to come to thy meetin'house tomorrer. . . . He'p them digest this grand feed they're goin' to eat. . . . Make them appreciate and be generous to thy servants who preach thy word. . . . But, O Lord . . ."

He raised both arms toward heaven; he clutched at the air as though he needed a fiery sword and had to feel around to get hold of it.

"But, O Lord, send thy fire of vengeance on those among this multitude who rebuke Thy servant's preachin'. . . . Roast them in brimstone and send them to eternal damnation. . . . In Thy holy name."

Mr. Flowers let his arms drop; his eyes fell to the upturned hat on the ground; he hoped Marvin Smeet would put fifty cents in it.

"Amen," said the preacher.

He had made his blessing and was now rearing to eat. He would leave his hat where all could see it.

"Chuck!" called that old dirt farmer. "It's all yours, folkses."

The people stampeded for the tables and gave no mind to the preacher's hat. A hungry lady kicked it over and a man following her stepped in the middle of it. Lord, Lord, it was a wild rush!

Mr. Flowers got rattled and aimed to go pick up his hat, but before he could reach it Bob had it in his hands and was brushing off the dust.

"I'm going to take up a collection," Bob told the preacher.

Mr. Flowers smiled and let him have his hat.

"Lord bless you, brother," he said.

So Bob went around with the preacher's hat. In a low voice he asked every man to contribute and told them all how the money would be spent.

"I'd be right proud to give," said a lean man in overalls, forking out four bits.

"Somebody ought to have thought of this before," said a fat woman with a blue-spotted sunbonnet.

Bob didn't say anything to Marvin Smeet but just held out the hat. Marvin was right willing to give a contribution to Preacher Flowers. He dropped in a whole fifty-cent piece.

Oh, was Mr. Flowers happy, and pleased with Mary's young man! He walked among those generous Christians, smiling, saying, "God bless you," and eating from a plate heaped with meat and potatoes. Virgie Smeet followed him around, dishing him pickles and beans and buttering biscuits for him. He saw Mary Simonson drop a dollar bill into his hat, and he walked over to where she stood, and said: "May the Lord forgive you all your sins, sister." He figured heaven would be something like this.

When Bob had collected from all the folks he put a dollar bill in the hat himself, and then handed it to old man Buck Smiles and told him to count the money.

"You know what to do with it," he told old man Buck. "Fifty-fifty."

So old man Buck Smiles counted the money, and Mr. Flowers beamed with satisfaction as he ate good food and saw all those silver coins come out of his hat.

"Thirty-two dollars and fifty cents," said old man Buck, and Mr. Flowers thought it was a fair price for admonishing sinners.

"Thirty-two dollars and fifty cents," old man Buck called out to the folks; and all stopped eating so they could listen to what he had to say. "And I'm sure the good folks who are the high-ups at this grand occasion, includin' the Reveren' Preacher Flowers, thank you-all for bein' so generous—"

"Lord bless you all," cried Mr. Flowers.

"—and," continued old man Buck Smiles, "we thank the Almighty for puttin' the bug in the heart of this young man from Albuquerque —to collect money for a worthy cause. . . . As a result of your generosity, sixteen dollars and twenty-five cents will be given to the best fiddler and guitar player in Torrance County—Tod and Jay Boy McClung—who volunteered their services for nothin'. . . . And the other half of the money collected will go to Mistress Burge, who cooked without pay all the good vittles you-all are eatin' now; and when you git done digestin' it you'll figure she's the best cocinero in Torrance County and points west of the Pecos."

The people cheered; then they went on eating.

The food in the preacher's plate suddenly became tasteless; the beef turned to mud, the mashed potatoes to dry wool, and the lemonade to pure ditch water. He laid his plate on the table, walked over to Mary's young man, picked up his hat, and put it on his head.

"Judas Iscariot!" he snapped between closed teeth.

Then he strutted over to the schoolroom, where he could be alone to meditate, where he could rehearse tomorrow's sermon—seasoned with hell and damnation for jelly beans in gray suits—while everybody outside ate, laughed, and bragged on the Widow Burge for being such a doggoned good cook. They were all having fun but the Smeets, the Mudgetts, and that old dirt farmer.

"That was the Lord's money," sniffed Virgie, eating roast beef. "Marvin gave fifty cents."

"A sneakin' trick to persecute a good Christian," grumbled Effie Lee, eating mashed potatoes. "Mr. Mudgett gave two bits to a McClung! . . . Lord forgive us!"

When everybody had filled up on the chuck they went into the school for a spell of dancing.

Now all this while Tewp McClung squatted by his fire. He gave no mind to anybody in the yard but just kept throwing sticks and bits of stray brush on the blaze. Close by him, hidden in a clump of sacaton, was his keg of whisky.

T. J. brought him out some meat and biscuits, and Tewp asked about the customers.

"They'll be comin' out now," T. J. told him. "They'll tank up and git drunk, and then you'd better ditch what's left of the booze 'cause that old son of a bitch Flowers is a prohibe from way back."

The first to come out was Dan Blakey's cowpuncher, who the folks called Scatterwhiskers because he always needed a shave. He asked Tewp if he had anything to drink, and Tewp poured him out some whisky in a cup.

"This rotgut ought to cook that beef a little more doner," said Scatterwhiskers, " 'cause I've seen better roasted meat runnin' on the range."

Tewp laughed and said, "God damn."

The cowpuncher bought a second drink and was soon joined by five farmers all rearing to get lit higher than a kite.

Virgie, while out in the yard scouting for huggers, watched the men take off for Tewp's fire; but she figured there was no harm a-brewing if women didn't join them. She didn't know there was a keg of rotgut there.

"Women are the root of all evil," she said to herself as she saw the firelight play on the sacaton. She wished the Lord had used good judgment and had not given women any anatomy—she wished men had no anatomy either. "Only in the flesh are we vile," she mourned.

Virgie had never seen Marvin entirely in the flesh—he wore a long nightshirt, and she was thankful. She made the nightshirt herself. She had not shared her bed with Marvin for sixteen long, weary years—she was thankful for that, too.

Out in the sacaton Scatterwhiskers was getting drunk. He was getting nasty and craving a fight, and he wanted it known.

"I'm a hootin', shootin' son of a bitch," he was ranting, "and I don't let no man look down on the crown of my hat. . . . I'm a poor lonesome cowboy, and ornery and dirty; I'm mean, and I'm crooked; and I'm a bastard, 'cause I didn't have no daddy that I know of—but I'm a real man 'cause I can hold my likker and don't let nobody look down on the crown of my hat."

And because Scatterwhiskers was Dan Blakey's cowpuncher Tewp thought he was big punkins. He gave him a drink on the house.

Back in the schoolroom Tod and Jay Boy made the music come fast and furious; the dancers promenaded and reversed, and old man Buck Smiles was right there calling high, wide, and handsome. Even Virgie took time off from watching out for huggers and got in the set. Oh, how she stepped daintily over the floor! Her long old-timy skirt churned up the cornmeal that old man Buck had scattered about. She crossed and joined hands, but wouldn't hold on to a man for long because it wasn't the right thing to do.

Faybelle sat with Lyndel and Buster on the bench along the wall. Sudie was with T. J., both standing near the musicians; Roddy was hunkered down in a corner and kept wondering as to what ailed Earlene, who seemed weighed down with the blues and had red circles around her eyes. She had been crying, by golly!

Marvin and Virgie had caught Earlene crying that day, and the girl bust out bawling again when she was helping with the flooma-gadunjets, and when she was asked what ailed her she said she had a toothache. Marvin said he would drive her to Vaughn and get the tooth fixed by a dentist, but Earlene said to let it be and it would get well by itself. Marvin figured it was Earlene's tooth that was troubling, not his, and that she ought to know whether it needed doctoring or not. He told her to quit her bawling, anyway.

While the folks were dancing that old dirt farmer kept piling the wood into the stove and getting the room entirely too hot for the folks to abide. For a fact the room was overcrowded, and the sweating bodies helped nary a bit to cool the atmosphere. Roddy wanted air, he was going outside, and nobody was holding him back.

So he went.

Outside, the air was cool and pleasant, warm for late October. A patchwork of stars glittered above in the sky; and right here on earth Tewp's fire sent cedar sparks upward. Roddy saw Tewp attending to his customers, and he felt like a good stiff drink.

What-all's ailin' that Smeet gal? Roddy asked himself.

And, inside, Earlene saw Roddy take out for the yard. She made to follow but Marvin spied her and called her back.

"Where-all you goin', daughter?" he said.

"I gotta go to the ladies'," Earlene told him.

"Wait for your mama, she'll run along with you."

"Maw's dancin'," said Earlene, sort of restless-like. "I cain't wait."

But Marvin saw that she acted kind of restless, and he figured she had better go. He was no kind of a man to argue about such matters, even if Earlene was his own flesh and blood, so he told her she had better hurry.

The girl caught Roddy just as he aimed to walk over to the sacaton patch and ask Tewp for a free drink because he was his brother and knew all about his reading *Ranch Romances* behind the barn.

Earlene brushed him as she walked by, and said: "Oh, Roddy, please meet me tomorrer evenin' at the Juan Largo. . . . I must talk to you. . . . I cain't talk to nobody else."

"What the hell?" asked Roddy.

But Earlene had to go to the ladies' because she had told Marvin she would.

"I'll tell you-all tomorrer. . . . Will you come? . . . Please, Roddy!"

And because Roddy hadn't seen Earlene down in the brush of the Juan Largo for nigh onto three weeks he was getting lonesome, like a feller will, and he said: "Sure thing. The same time."

Roddy took out to the sacaton to bum a drink from Tewp; and Earlene went to the ladies', where she figured everyone would let her be, and there she bawled her eyes out.

The menfolks went trailing back and forth from the school to the sacaton patch; those going out were rearing to get lit, those coming back had the stink of secondhand rotgut on their breath and were talking loud and hollering. When Roddy reached the fire there were a dozen standing about.

Scatterwhiskers talked and aimed for everybody to hear him.

"So old Dan Blakey gave me a string of six horses for summer ridin'," he was saying—hunkered down, smoking his cigarette, and all standing by looking down on the crown of his hat. "Six of the prettiest bronc's you ever set your peepers on. . . . And old Dan says, 'Scatterwhiskers, you rusty son of a bitch, here's a string of bronc's with personality, and I'm givin' 'em to you 'cause you're a man with personality.' . . . That's what old Dan said, by God.

"And I rode that blaze-face sorrel with the flax mane and tail, and he was an old crowbait with no mean tricks. . . . A work horse, by golly! . . . I couldn't git him to bust in two and buck. He didn't savvy. He didn't have no personality, and I told old Dan he was a God-damned liar for sayin' he had.

"But that little pecker-necked bay! . . . Christ, boys, there was a horse with personality! . . . So I said, 'Dan, here's a horse with personality.' And I said that 'cause that little bastard pitched me off and bust my collarbone.

"And after I'd done rid them six horses down, I said to Dan, 'You're a God-damned liar, Dan.' That's what I said to Dan. ' 'Cause in this whole string of bronc's there's just one with personality. The others are just no-account, chisel-headed crowbaits with no personality.' . . . And I said that to Dan 'cause I don't let no man look down on the crown of my hat."

Roddy asked Tewp for a drink, and Tewp let him have it because he wanted to save a fuss.

"When we goin' to eat again, big shorty?" Scatterwhiskers asked Roddy.

"Midnight, I reckon," said Roddy. "The Widow Burge is fixin' sandwiches."

"Cain't she git that beef a little doner!" growled Scatterwhiskers. "I sure don't love raw meat."

The men looking down on Scatterwhiskers laughed, and one of them said: "But you sure love raw whisky, by God. You cain't git stuff any rawer than this."

And for a fact, it was mighty green booze Tewp was selling the boys around the fire.

Back at the tables the Widow Burge had done fixed the sandwiches and squeezed another batch of lemonade. All that was left to be done with them now was for the folks to come out and gulp them down. That wouldn't be until midnight, and there was an hour's dancing ahead before that time.

The Widow told Tennis to watch the food and not eat too many sandwiches while he was doing it. She went inside to see how the dance was coming along. Craze Rufe, now that he couldn't do any-

thing to help his mama, just wandered about the schoolroom and
yard and didn't get in anybody's way.

Mary and her young man were not keeping the folks company,
for they had gone over to the house to make coffee and they had
taken Lyndel and Buster with them. Faybelle said it was O.K., and
she reckoned it was all right with Tod. Tod thought a heap of Mary
Simonson, and right this night he had gotten a kick out of the fun
the young man played with the preacher's hat. And both Tod and
Faybelle liked the way these two city folks had taken a shine to
their youngest young un.

Mr. Flowers sat on the bench feeling gloomy. He didn't have a
hate for the people gathered; he was sorry for them because they
had been tricked and persecuted as he had—good Christians, most
of them. They had donated their hard-earned cash, thinking it was
going to the Lord, but Satan came up from hell all dressed up in a
gray suit and gave the proceeds of the collection to Tod McClung
and the Widow Burge.

Oh, the iniquity of Torrance County!

He was heartsick for sure, was Preacher Flowers; a man of God
in the proximity of sinners. Virgie and Mrs. Mudgett came to where
he sat and offered their sympathy, but it didn't do any good. He had
lost the collection money, and the bulk of the people didn't seem to
get het up about their money going to hell instead of heaven. So
to get some clean air, away from folks who would get a hot
sermon the next morning, he walked out to the yard.

He found Cletus Woods in the yard.

Cletus was drunk.

The big farmer threw his arms around Mr. Flowers' neck and
his weight was heavy. His calloused hands gripped the preacher and
held him like a vise. The stink of stale whisky hit the greatest
prohibe in Torrance County smack in the face.

"Where'd you git that stuff?" cried Mr. Flowers, his voice carrying all the wrath of a temperate man.

Cletus lovingly rested his head on the preacher's shoulder.

"You want a drink?" he drawled, sleepy-like. "Good ol' Luke
Flowers! . . . Come on, and we'll git a drink. . . . A drink, by

Jesus. . . . A drink with the preacher, the good ol' son of a bitch."

The farmer's dirty hand fell from the back of Mr. Flowers' neck and gripped his nice clean shirt.

"Come on," said Cletus.

The preacher stared at Tewp's fire. He saw the drunken gathering standing, squatting, and sitting in the light of the flames. His eyes were fixed on a figure, standing behind the sparks and smoke that brazenly rose to heaven; a short, bowlegged man who waved his arms about and whose voice was loud, blasphemous, and drunken. It was Scatterwhiskers telling the boys of the bronc's he had ridden and how he didn't let any man look down on the crown of his hat.

A cold sweat came over Preacher Flowers. He could not speak, he was powerless to admonish Cletus for his iniquity; he wished the Lord would give him courage to attack the group in the sacaton, hurl the whisky in the Devil's own fire, and preach to those assembled until they cowered under his wrath. But Mr. Flowers was a man of peace—he was not brave enough to do that.

But praise the Lord!

He now saw before his very eyes the hell he had read about, and of which he had preached to his congregation every Sunday since he received the call. He saw the flames and the black demons, he watched Satan himself squat by the fire to pour the damnable brew from a keg into a cup.

"Come on," drawled Cletus. "Good ol' Luke! . . . Me and him's goin'—"

With a whimper and the sound of ripping cloth Mr. Flowers tore himself from the grip of Cletus and ran as fast as his legs would carry him into the darkness, down the road and to the safety of his rough-pine house. Cletus staggered over to the sacaton patch carrying the back of the preacher's shirt in his hand.

From the schoolroom came the whining and strumming music and the voice of old man Buck Smiles as he called the dance.

> "You swing me and I'll swing you,
> All git to Heaven in the same ol' shoe.
> Same ol' boys sittin' on a rail,
> Same ol' possum runnin' down the trail."

When midnight came around, the folks stampeded for the tables, and all told the Widow Burge that she was the best sandwich maker in the community. The boys came from the sacaton patch, all except Tewp who had to watch his likker, and Scatterwhiskers who was too drunk to move. They all came out of the schoolroom but Piddle, because he didn't like sandwiches nohow.

When the room was cleared Piddle was joined by Roddy who carried a paper sack and was all set for devilment.

"I see you've got the makin's," said Piddle.

Roddy nodded.

"Scatter it over the floor," Piddle told him. "Mostly over the spot where them long skirts will swoop it up like drawin' a coke out of a glass with a straw. . . . Right where it will riz up to the place where it tickles. . . . Git goin', son, before any of the folks come in and git an idee what's up."

So Roddy took handfuls of the cut horsehair, that which was once old Tulip's tail, and sprinkled the floor with it. The brown, clipped horsehair just matched the color of the stained floor.

Piddle and Roddy went out to the yard and aimed to get a glass of lemonade each, just so the folks wouldn't suspicion they were up to any meanness, them alone in the schoolroom.

Piddle giggled like a schoolboy who had just lit a firecracker and was waiting for it to go off.

"It made me plumb itch to touch it," said Roddy.

Outside, the people were laughing, talking, and telling how they were all set to go on dancing until two o'clock. So they went on talking and laughing until Tennis grabbed the last sandwich—then they all went back to dance.

Both Virgie and Mrs. Mudgett, now that the eats had begun again and were over, wondered where Mr. Flowers had got himself to. They had not seen him for over an hour, and at first figured he must have gone to the gents'—they thought that but didn't suggest it to one another. But now, they reckoned, he should be around somewhere.

"Where-all?" asked Virgie, puzzled.

"I cain't think of no place but his house," said Effie Lee. "I reckon he was so weighed down with remorse over the dirty doin's of sinners that he's took off home to pray and meditate. . . . This ain't no place for a Christian, Virgie, and we guessed wrong when we thought it would be—even with the preacher around. . . . The sooner we git home and to our beds, the more decent I'll feel."

So they both envied Mr. Flowers, who they reckoned had gone home.

"No more eats, folkses," called that old dirt farmer, " 'cause we're goin' to dance till two o'clock, and then the 'Home Waltz' will tell you-all that this grand occasion is long gone. . . . Strike up the band, musicians, 'cause we're rarin' to go!"

Again Tod and Jay Boy fingered their instruments and mowed that music down.

Lyndel and Buster had returned from the teacher's house and were sitting with Faybelle. Virgie saw them there and—

Oh, Lord!

She wondered if it could possibly be that Mary and her young man were alone together in the bedroom.

"Could it possibly be?" asked Virgie of herself.

Well, it could!

Any man who'll steal the Lord's money, she thought, will be sorry enough to do anything else—anything sinful and scarlet.

She went out to the yard to see if maybe there would be a light in the teacher's bedroom window, and she hoped the blind would be up just a mite at the bottom. She rounded the corner of the school and—

Oh, Lord!

There she saw Bob and Mary standing in the dark. Their arms were clasped around each other's neck in the most sinful fashion—their lips were together just like Potiphar's wife and Joseph's would have been if Joseph hadn't been an honest-to-goodness Christian, and how Virgie reckoned David and Uriah's wife actually did.

Lord, Lord! They were kissing, and Bob's hand was stroking Mary's hair.

Virgie shrieked and ran for the schoolroom door. On the way she collided with Cletus Woods, who was staggering about and had part of Mr. Flowers' shirt stuck in his belt. Cletus took the torn cloth and waved it over his head.

"Whoop-ee!" hollered Cletus. "I'm an Apache buck. . . . I got me a scalp."

Virgie didn't recognize the preacher's shirt but shrieked again; she ran in among all those folks in the schoolroom plumb pale and shaking.

All were too interested in the dance to pay any mind to Virgie— all but Mrs. Mudgett, who could see Virgie had something to tell her; even Marvin and Earlene didn't notice her.

"Oh, Lord!" said Effie Lee, after Virgie had told her of all she had seen around the corner of the school. "Don't tell a livin' soul till you see the preacher in the mornin', Virgie. . . . Tell him at the meetin', and we'll expose this wicked Jezebel from earth to heaven. We'll—"

"We'll have a new teacher in this here school within a month," said Virgie. "I'll swan before Jonah we will!"

But Effie Lee just bit her lip and said nothing, lest she get rambunctious, and thought about the iniquity of Babylon long gone, and the wickedness of Torrance County, New Mexico, at this day and time.

While these two ladies were chatting inside, Bob and Mary were walking arm in arm around the yard. The night was warm for the fall of the year, and even at midnight the two were coatless.

"I think it would be best if I tell them to go to hell on election day," Mary said. "That will be next Tuesday—but after hearing Virgie Smeet scream and scram as she did maybe I will be fired tonight, before Tod thumps down on the 'Home Waltz.'"

They started for the schoolroom.

"Let's dance," said Bob.

But Roddy McClung was standing by, and he heard Bob say, "Let's dance." He met the teacher and her young man just as they were going inside.

"Don't dance any time from now on, Miss Simonson," he said, low, so nobody else could hear, " 'cause if you do you'll git the seven-year itch."

Mary laughed.

"Perhaps you are right, Roddy," she said, "but we'll chance it anyway." Then to Bob: "Come on, this will be the last chance we'll have to get in a set with Virgie Smeet."

Roddy watched them go inside.

There were only two hours left for dancing, and the folks were making the best of it. Virgie Smeet, to get her mind off sin, pranced in the circle to show everyone what a hand she was at a hoedown. Old man Buck called promenade and reverse, and Virgie did just what he aimed for her to do. Effie Lee got herself into the set, too, nimble for a woman of fifty-three, and was right cuttish-uppish.

Bob and Mary joined the next dance and Virgie and Effie Lee returned to their bench to chat. To them, now that secret transgressions had come to light, the teacher and her young man were two rattlesnakes crawled out of a den. The ladies didn't want any truck with the likes of them. But when these two city folks quit and sat down, then Virgie got up to dance; and when Virgie was on the floor strutting her stuff she was one big hallelujah straight out of the Bible.

Piddle and Roddy sat and waited. The old man chewed his tobacco and spat in his can; the boy hunkered down on his hockers and waited for the first woman to start scratching.

"It takes a short time for them horsehairs to git tangled up in the women's underpinnin's," said Piddle, thinking back on the good old days in Oklahoma.

Bob and Mary went outside for some fresh air. The room was entirely too stuffy and hot. They walked about arm in arm for the night was pleasant and they were happy—happy until the teacher felt an itch around the tops of her stockings.

"Oh Lord, Bob!" she said, scratching.

"What, honey?"

"Do you remember what that McClung boy said just as we were going in to dance? . . . Something about the seven-year itch?"

Bob laughed. "Have you got it?" he said, jokingly. "The hillbillies say you must bathe in kerosene daily or you will scratch for seven years. . . . Listen, I'm not marrying any woman with the seven-year itch."

They saw Roddy standing at the door of the school and decided they would get to the root of this ticklish business right there and then. Bob called Roddy, and the boy slouched over.

"Look here, Roddy," said Bob. "What about this itch epidemic that seems to be in the air? You gave us the warning signal when we went in to dance. . . . We believe there is really something to it because the symptoms have been felt. . . . Come out with it, like a good pal."

"It's only horsehair," Roddy told them. "I figured I'd warn Miss Simonson so's the clippin's wouldn't bother her. . . . We all like her at our house. . . . If you-all want to see some fun wait till that ol' Smeet woman gits tangled up with 'em."

Then Roddy told them how this particular kind of devilment worked.

"You've seen one of them vacuum cleaners?" he asked.

"Sure," said Bob. "Millions of them."

"Well," Roddy told them, "when them long old-timy skirts git swirlin' around the floor they act like a vacuum cleaner on the horsehairs and draw 'em up to the underpinnin's. . . . It was Piddle's idee, not mine."

"Nothing more serious than eating crackers in bed, kid," Bob said to Mary, "but while Roddy and I go inside and watch Virgie Smeet suffer, you had better go to the house and unload the horsehairs."

As Bob and Roddy entered the building they passed Marvin Smeet coming out. Marvin chewed peanuts and kept spitting the inedible parts on the ground; his teeth munched the nuts, his eyes watched out for huggers—the same eyes that caught Mary going around the corner of the building.

He followed.

Now around this corner of the school there were no lighted windows shining onto the yard; it was dark, other than faint moonlight, and everybody seemed to be inside enjoying themselves or were grouped about in conversation near the sacaton patch far to the other end. So Mary could think of no good reason why she should go to the house just to get rid of a few pesky horsehairs in her stocking-tops. She figured that a deserted yard would be as good as any place.

Marvin, quietly and vigilantly, crept to the corner and peeped around.

Oh, Lord!

Preacher Flowers' right-hand man didn't scream as his wife had. He even held his breath lest the sound disturb the girl before his eyes. His heart pounded ready to burst, still he held the air deep down in his lungs. The sight held Marvin to the spot; try as he might to break away, run back to the lighted room and ask the Lord to forgive him and blot the vision of those white limbs from his mind. His eyes were glued to the scene—he was truly a weak man in the grip of Satan. Only when Mary adjusted her clothes could the man tear himself away. He made a bolt for the outer yard and commenced chewing his peanuts. He tipped his hat to Mary as he passed her on her way to the schoolroom.

But the mischief was done; the teacher had unconsciously aroused the man in the mind of this frigid symbol of all that's good and holy. He asked God to forgive him, and in the same breath thanked the Almighty for his wife, Virgie. He spat peanut shells while he planned a way to attract, after many years of righteous distance, his lawful wife to his bed. After more than sixteen years of continence this suggestion he had in mind would be difficult, but the worst he could expect from his mate would be a cry of shame and perhaps a sharp smack on the face.

He remembered that occasion, a year before the birth of Earlene, when Virgie and he had seriously talked over the problem they would have to face in order to have a child. . . . They wanted a child, and figured they would have to give themselves up to the Lord's price of payment. It would be hard to do, they decided with many blushes, but it was what the Lord ordained and there was no way of getting around it—that is, if they wanted a baby.

Oh, those unholy nights! The warmth of Virgie's bed after Marvin had left his own for a brief half-hour; the prayers that were muttered to overcome their shame as they lay in each other's arms; the relief the man enjoyed when he returned to his room; the greater joy when Virgie got herself pregnant and the shame need no longer be suffered. It was like leading a bull to the cow yard and putting him back in his own pen when the service was done.

And now, after those many years!

Lord, Lord!

Mary found Bob with Roddy and Piddle. The dancers circled and swung, and the musicians weighed down like a ton of bricks on that old fiddle and guitar.

Virgie was in the set, and she scratched.

Effie Lee Mudgett pranced, but her hands kept busy fumbling around the folds of her long, old-timy skirt.

The Widow Burge, who had been doing right smart of dancing now that the eats were over, had gone somewhere outside for a minute. She itched.

All the other dancing ladies kept wondering as to what it was made them tickle around the legs.

Lord, Piddle's devilment had got plumb into action.

"I was young once," said Piddle, when Mary congratulated him on his genius.

Now all this while trouble was brewing at Tewp's fire in the sacaton. Scatterwhiskers was drunk, and mean, and rearing for a fight. He wanted to scrap with Cletus, but Cletus cried like a baby at the thought of blows with Scatterwhiskers—the best friend and bosom pal he ever had. Scatterwhiskers argued with Tewp, but was told to shut up or he wouldn't get any more whisky. Then he saw Bob walking with Mary in the yard, and he said: "Who-all's that jelly-bean son of a bitch in the ice-cream pants?"

Tewp told him to shut up or that jelly bean would come over and mop up on him.

"Him!" yelled Scatterwhiskers. "When I'm rarin' to fight, a dude like that is my meat. . . . All he's got to do is look down on the crown of my hat and he'll git the worst whippin' he's got in his long, weary life."

Tewp gave Scatterwhiskers another drink to shut him up; but the more the cowboy drank, the meaner he got. He reckoned he was a *muy bravo hombre* who didn't take sass from nobody.

"He ain't too damned big," Tewp said to Scatterwhiskers, "but he might know how to handle his mitts. . . . Them city fellers will fool you."

That started Scatterwhiskers off on his ranting again.

"He cain't whip me," said Dan Blakey's cowpuncher, " 'cause it takes two men the size of him to carry a dude off in a stretcher after I git done layin' him out. . . . It takes more of a man . . ."

Scatterwhiskers stopped his self palaver because a newcomer had walked into the firelight and was looking down on the cowboy.

"Who the hell are you?" said Scatterwhiskers, mean-like.

"It's only me," the newcomer told him. "I ain't aimin' to git in nobody's way. . . . I don't want to devil nobody. . . . I want to mind my mama, and they're goin' to make me President of the whole United States."

Craze Rufe had joined the boys at the fire and all got set to have some fun with the half-wit. They all laughed, and Cletus slapped Rufe on the back and told Tewp to give him a drink.

"I ain't goin' to give Rufe no drink," said Tewp. "He's crazy enough as he is. I'm scared of a drunk crazy man, by God."

Rufe looked down on the group of men hunkered around the fire. His eyes were beady, and the way he puckered his lips they figured he would talk and that they were in for some devilment.

"What you-all been dealin' at today, Rufe?" began Cletus, winking at the other men so as to let them know he was starting Rufe off on his crazy talk. "What-all big business you been doin'?"

Scatterwhiskers scowled, and Tewp said: "Leave him alone, Cletus. . . . For Christ's sake don't start him off around here." Then to Rufe: "Go help your mama, Rufe."

But Rufe was rearing to talk big doings, and Tewp or any of them couldn't hold him back when he got his crazy mind onto important business.

"Today," said Rufe, drooling out of his puckered lips and with a wild look in his eyes, "I bought that ol' Santa Fe Railroad. I got me an engine, and I'm goin' to run it myse'f, and I'm goin' to haul beans, and I ain't goin' to let nobody ride on it, by crikey. I got me a Mexican to he'p me. I give thirty cents for that ol' Santa Fe Railroad. . . . You won't tell Mama I bought that engine and that Mexican? She'll git mad. You won't tell Mama, by crikey?"

Rufe's eyes got brighter, and he sat down because he was talking business.

"Shut up, Rufe, and go to your mama," said Tewp.

"What about your bank?" prompted Cletus. "What about that fancy bank you got, Rufe?"

Craze Rufe puckered his lips a minute before he spoke. "I got me a bank in Willard. It ain't got no doors and windows, and nobody can git in and steal my money, by crikey. I got thirty cents in it."

Cletus laughed. They all laughed but Tewp who raked at the fire, and Scatterwhiskers who sat there looking his meanest.

"How much did it cost you-all to build that bank, Rufe?" asked Cletus, and he could hardly hold himself together for laughing, for Rufe was such a doggone fool.

"Thirty cents," said the half-wit, all puckered up.

Lord, Lord, the boys nearly split their sides!

Tewp looked up and saw that two more people had joined them; they stood off from the firelight and were not noticed by the others who were too occupied with Rufe.

Bob and Mary stood watching the circle. Tewp told the boys to let Rufe be. Scatterwhiskers glared at the half-wit.

A brisk wind came up from the west and the sparks from the fire blew upward by its fanning.

"They tell me you got a post office too, Rufe," said one of the drunks. "I want to mail me a letter to the folks back in Texas. How much does it cost to mail a letter in your post office, Rufe?"

"Thirty cents," drooled Rufe.

They all laughed but Tewp, Scatterwhiskers, Bob, and Mary.

The wind blew strong.

Scatterwhiskers rose to his feet and clenched his fists.

"You're a God-damned liar," he cried, walking up to Rufe. "You're a crazy bastard who ain't got no sense."

Tewp rose, too, and faced Scatterwhiskers. "Leave him alone, I tell you," he warned the cowboy. "Before I cold-cock you with this here cedar post. . . . Stand back before I lay it on!"

But Scatterwhiskers was all set to wade into Rufe.

Mary took Bob's hand and they both stepped forward; the teacher's pink dress shone bright in the firelight.

"You had better go home before you get into trouble," Mary said to Scatterwhiskers. Then she turned to Rufe. "Go and help your mama, Rufe. Maybe she needs you."

"I don't want to devil nobody," said Rufe. "I mind my mama and don't git in nobody's way. . . . I don't want no fight, by crikey."

"Go to the school, Rufe," Mary said. "These men are trying to make a fool of you, and they are just proving themselves the biggest fools of all."

Bob gave Rufe a push in the direction of the school, and the half-wit went his way.

Scatterwhiskers staggered up to Bob.

"I reckon you must think you're big stuff in them ice-cream pants and with your pretty jelly-bean face," he said, sneering, drunk and mean. "Who-all the hell are you, anyway?"

The cowpuncher came forward and had his dirty whiskered face close to Bob's; he thought he was a tough hombre for sure.

"In just about thirty seconds," Bob told him, "I'm going to introduce myself to you in a way that suits bums of your kind. One more crack out of you, and I'll let you have it."

Scatterwhiskers snickered.

"And that God-damned pink slut that's hangin' on to you-all—"

"All right, Bob," said Mary, calm and with a heap of confidence. "Give it to him. The landing place will be tough and shaggy, so let him have it hard."

"When I get more of an invitation," said Bob, because he wanted Scatterwhiskers to hit first.

The invitation came with a clumsy, drunken punch from Scatterwhiskers; the reply was dealt with a sharp right hook from Bob. The cowpuncher fell like a ton of bricks.

The rest of the group, all but Tewp and Cletus, stampeded for the yard. Cletus was so doggoned full of likker he got plumb wild.

"Whoopee!" he hollered. "I'm an Apache buck!" And taking a burning stick from the fire he flung it out in the dry sacaton.

The wind was blowing from the west—it was a strong, dry wind.

Now the trouble was that nobody saw Cletus throw the stick. Bob, Mary, and Tewp were too bent on looking at Scatterwhiskers, all laid out, to pay Cletus any mind.

"He'll come out of it," said Bob. "His kind always do—unfortunately."

Scatterwhiskers was breathing, very much alive, but a mighty help-less cowpuncher.

The coarse sacaton grass was tall, dry, and brittle. All through the night Tewp had been mighty careful not to let sparks hit the clumps near by, for it would be plumb explosive, like touching a match to kerosene, and nobody had a hankering to fight a prairie fire. But right now, where Cletus' stick hit the ground fifty feet to the west, the waving blades were turning to a fiery blaze.

"He'll wake up with a terrible hangover," commented Bob, "as well as a nasty soreness under the whiskers."

Cletus looked fondly at his pal. He wept because he reckoned that this was how Scatterwhiskers would look when dead and only fit for the graveyard. It was a sad thought. Cletus figured Dan Blakey's cowpuncher wasn't good company all knocked out cold, and he missed his big talk for sure. He wiped his eyes with the fragment of Preacher Flowers' shirt.

They all studied Scatterwhiskers lying there flat and quiet.

Then Tewp looked up.

"Hell!" he cried. "The God-damned prairie's afire! . . . Look! To the west!"

Sure enough, tongues of flame were dancing over the sacaton. The brittle grass crackled and roared under the sweep of the strong, dry wind. Every second the blaze caught on to a neighboring clump and the fiery swath moved east.

No one who knows the Southwest would dare to say a prairie fire would happen in late October or early November. January, maybe; March, surely, if a sizable spark lights on the flat sea of grass winter has turned from juicy green to dry brown. But nobody with a lick of judgment would predict a grass fire at this time of year.

But New Mexico is tricky. The folks here say only a newcomer can reckon what the weather is going to do—and after a while he gets to know better. Men who have looked at the sky there for years know that, soon or late something violent and unexpected will hap-pen. If the wind blows from the west it may be a baby hurricane; when it comes out of the east direction it will bring rain—and Lord, what a rain!

June heat will fry eggs on the bare rocks; winter frost can shoot the thermometer plumb down to sea level. The elements don't dribble in this country. Maybe it's because of the altitude—over six thousand feet of it below the foothills of the mountains—that the elements think the earth is too close to their range right here and give the prairie folks enough of their curses and blessings to make them holler, "Calf rope."

No, the sky and air down here don't dribble: drouth or moisture, heat or cold,—they do business only in wholesale lots.

But two weeks before the dance, right in mid-October, a frost came down on the land, the first frost of the winter season. It held the prairie in its grip two nights and then let up to noondays of dry heat. It took the life out of the passed summer's grass; the roots stayed alive, but the feathery tops dropped their seed and the stems turned yellow and sick.

"Damn good thing we got the beans harvested in time," Tod McClung said during that frost. "Lord! This is the best country in the world for a bean farmer if he can only beat old man Winter to the draw; but I'd sure hate to be a brass monkey out on these prairies."

And because of that frost the sacaton patch was brittle and dry.

The wind blew, and the fire roared.

Bob grabbed Scatterwhiskers by the shirt collar and dragged him out of the sacaton and onto the schoolyard. Only Cletus wanted to hold back as they all stampeded.

"The whisky!" yelled Cletus; for Tewp still had a gallon left in the keg.

"To hell with the whisky!" cried Tewp. "Git your shirt off and help fight that fire before it hits the school."

Those hanging around the yard gave the alarm inside. The folks swarmed out, hollering and yelling. The women and kids watched, the men ran to put that prairie fire out.

Cletus took off his bib overalls, which he used as a beater, and worked in his shirt and long-handles. Lord, he was a sight!

Some men used their coats and beat those flames to black ash, while others ran to and from the cistern with buckets of water so the fighters could keep their beaters wet. All worked like he-men while the women watched, gabbed, made a fuss, and scratched because of Piddle's devilment.

The wind continued to blow.

"If only this God-damned wind would die down!" cussed Tod.

Old man Buck Smiles got after those flames with his wet sheepskin coat like a wampus cat.

Scatterwhiskers lay in the yard, not knowing what it was all about.

"What happened to him?" Virgie Smeet asked one of the men who passed with a bucket of water.

"That feller from Albuquerque hit him and laid him out," said the man, hurrying by.

Virgie looked fondly at Scatterwhiskers. "The poor boy," she sighed. Then she thought of Bob. "That beast! Oh, Lord, that wicked infidel!"

Marvin tapped her on the shoulder and beckoned her to their parked Oakland car, where Earlene sat with tear-swollen eyes. Marvin and Virgie crawled in, hoping no one would see them.

"Hey, where you-all goin'?" said a man with a water bucket. "We need you, Mr. Smeet, the sacaton's afire."

Marvin stepped on the starter, for he aimed to go home.

"I ain't fightin' no fire that Satan started," said Marvin as he drove off.

"Son of a bitch!" said the man with the bucket.

So when the Smeets had gone there wasn't a Christian left on the place, for the Mudgetts and that old dirt farmer had beat it when the alarm was given.

The fire moved eastward from clump to clump and soon reached the spot where Tewp had sold his whisky. One pesky flame hit the high grass where the keg was hidden and—

Oh, Lord!

That keg blew up like a barrel of gasoline. The flames from it were not red and fiery, they were pure blue. Lord, how that alcohol burned!

"Tewp," called Bob, fighting the fire like all get out.

"What?" said Tewp, a fire-fighting fool.

"Is that the kind of stuff you've been drinking?"

"Sure was," Tewp replied. "And that explosion was a damned good recommendation. . . . But it's all gone now."

"Too bad," Bob called back.

So at last they got the fire under control and finally put out. The sacaton patch was now just a flat of black ash. The tired men trudged to the yard, each carrying a burnt fragment of cloth which only a short while before had been something to wear.

Bob and Tewp walked over to the smoldering wooden keg.

"It was good while it lasted," said Tewp.

Bob reached down and picked up a charred piece of felt—Scatterwhiskers' hat. Only the brim was left, the crown was completely burned off.

Cletus walked over to where Scatterwhiskers lay in drunken slumber. The big farmer picked up his pal as easily as a sack of beans, threw him on his shoulder and, clad only in shirt and longhandles, strode into the darkness and down the road.

The last of the community folks to go were the McClungs.

"It was a grand occasion, Miss Simonson," said Tod, "and thank you-all for askin' us to play. . . . Sometime you-all come over."

Faybelle was worried.

"Where-all is Sudie and T. J.?" she asked everybody.

Roddy spoke up. "I seed the Reo parked down the road a piece of a ways. I reckon they wanted to let be. It's gone now."

They drove away in their strip-down Cadillac, and only Bob and Mary were left. The lights still blazed in the schoolroom, the air outside was thick with smoke. They went inside to douse the lights and call it a day.

Mary was tired, and Bob had to be on his way to Albuquerque. It was a long drive.

"I'll see you next week end in town, Bob," said Mary, as her young man fixed to drive off. "I think I'll have Lyndel with me. . . . I'm not certain yet, but I think I will."

Then she broke into tears.

"Oh, God," she said, half laughing and part crying, "what a finale to my career as an educator of the children of the earth! What a send-off party for the little community schoolteacher! Horsehair and fire, drunkards and hypocrites!"

The parting was brief, and Bob drove off. Mary went wearily to her room, locked her door, sat down in her big armchair, and laughed and laughed and laughed.

Then she laid her head back on the soft upholstered chair and fell asleep.

"Fire and brimstone—horsehair—flowers and the damned," she muttered as she dozed off.

When she awoke, the sun was shining and there was a rapping at the door. Someone fumbled with the knob and at the same time gave the door a kick, so whoever it was wanted in for sure. Mary yawned, stretched, smoothed her clothes, and went over to see who had come.

Who had come was Craze Rufe.

Mary let him in, and the half-wit stood there; his lips puckered because he was going to speak, his eyes fixed on the teacher.

"My, Rufe!" said Mary. "You *are* an early riser. Have you come to see *me?*"

"I ain't been asleep, by crikey."

He held a grease-stained package in his hands, tied with a dirty piece of string.

"Mama's asleep; so's Tennis, but I ain't done it, by crikey."

He stood for a minute in silence; his mouth twitching, his eyes staring at Mary.

Then he spoke.

"You won't tell Mama I come to see you?. . . I mind my mama, by crikey, and I don't devil nobody. I don't want to fuss with nobody in this whole wide, wicked world, by golly."

"That's what you should do, Rufe," said Mary.

"What would you-all do if you had a mama? You'd mind her, wouldn't you?"

"You bet I would, Rufe."

Rufe laughed in a crazy sort of way.

"I got a Santy Claus present for you-all," he said, "but don't tell Mama I give it to you, by crikey. She'll git mad. . . . You won't tell Mama?"

"No, Rufe, I won't tell your mama."

"You were sure good to me, teacher," said Rufe. "You made that man quit when he aimed to whip me. . . . You did, by golly."

"Forget that, Rufe. You and I are good friends, and I wouldn't let anybody hurt you." That was what the teacher said.

"So I bring you a Santy Claus present," said Rufe, giving Mary the package.

And then—

"I gotta go home now and he'p Mama. . . . You-all will sure like that Santy Claus present. . . . I'd give you thirty cents, but I ain't got it. I'd buy candy if I had thirty cents."

Then Mary said: "I'm sure you would, Rufe. And I tell you what! I'll give you fifty cents, and then you can buy some candy."

Rufe held his hands up in horror, like as though Mary aimed to give him a live rattlesnake.

"No, by crikey," protested Rufe. "I ain't takin' thirty cents from you! I'm givin' you a Santy Claus present, but you won't tell Mama, will you?"

"No, Rufe, I won't. But I am anxious to see what you have given me. Thank you, Rufe, thank you so very much."

The half-wit started off, and Mary watched him cross the yard to the gate by the road. He sang and yodeled as he walked.

Over by the McClung land, on that Santa Fe Railway, a freight train roared and whistled and sent black smoke upward. Rufe caught the sound, and his song came shrill like an old engineer twisting the tail of the whistle:

> *"Blow, freight train, blow.*
> *Comin' on down the line.*
> *Yew-eeee! Yew-eeee!*
> *Blow, freight train, blow.*
> *Got a ramble on my mind."*

But Mary knew that the only ramble on Rufe's mind was to go home and help his mama.

She closed the door and laid the greasy package on the table.

A gift. A Santa Claus present. Some small token of gratitude— something as simple as Rufe himself. It could be a hunk of stone or a precious gem. It was something wrapped up in paper by the half-wit and given to her, so she could see and feel his appreciation.

"The earth," she said to herself, as she fumbled with the dirty string and opened the package. "The sweet, kindly earth! . . . The wheat and the tares that spring from your humus. . . . But what a puzzle you are, Earth! Which is your wheat and which the tares?"

On the table Rufe's present came before her eyes.

It was a raw Irish potato; a piece of dry soil still clung to its brown skin.

## Chapter Six

THE election day of 1928 came and went, Al Smith, so the folks reckoned, was a mighty sick man, because he had got himself out-voted and the people of the United States aimed to put Herbert Hoover up in the White House. And the community was right pleased because Dick Dillon, a Torrance County man like them-selves, had been re-elected governor of New Mexico—and because Dillon was a dirt farmer's friend they reckoned they were all set.

Come election Tod and Faybelle got a hurt to their feelings that they couldn't get shed of, because it was on that day Mary Simonson made it public that she aimed to quit school teaching at Christmas time—that she would be married, by God! And the McClungs fig-ured, even if their kids did not attend the community school, that they would never get another teacher like Mary.

"You-all 're gittin' a gentleman for a man," Tod told Mary one day when she came over to say howdy, "and a man who can use his mitts and still be a gentleman when he ain't usin' 'em."

Faybelle thought: "Even if my Sudie didn't git a gentleman she's done married up to an honest-to-God tool dresser in the oil fields, and a man who'll stand up to anybody who don't treat Sudie like a lady."

For—

On the night of the dance, when they all came home, they found the can of Brer Rabbit syrup sitting on the kitchen table and on the lid was a cup—and between the lid and the cup was a letter from Sudie. The letter told all the folks that she and T. J. had started off to Artesia where they would get married, and where T. J. would find him a job of work in the oil fields, and how she aimed to hash in a restaurant.

" 'Dear Mama, Pappy and all,' " Tod slowly read from the letter, because Sudie's scribbling wasn't too plain. " 'I will try and write you a few lines. T. J. and me have done gone to Artesia to git married. I love T. J., and we cain't wait no longer. Don't worry about us 'cause T. J. will git a job in the oil fields tool dressin' or roustaboutin'. I aim to hash. Lord bless you all. I sure hope Lyndel can git a man when she gits old like me. I've took most of my clothes, and if I've forgot some you can send them on. I will read the Bible every day and be good. Your lovin' girl, Sudie.' "

"Lord, Lord, what a blessin'!" cried Faybelle.

"Wait," said Tod. "There's a P.S."

Then Tod read: " 'P.S. Tell Tewp to tell old man Buck that T. J. is gittin' married up with me.' "

That happened on the night of the dance.

The next day, being a Sunday, Tod killed a chicken and Faybelle fixed a mulligan to celebrate Sudie's wedding.

"To think that our girl," said Faybelle, "is Mrs. T. J. Smiles of Artesia, New Mexico, makes me want to holler praises to the Lord."

So they ate chicken mulligan for dinner, and when Roddy had all he wanted he got up and washed his mouth out with a dipper of water. Then he fixed to go over to the Juan Largo and talk with Earlene.

Now, because Earlene had a worry on her mind and was real anxious to talk to Roddy, she was there when he got to the Juan Largo. She was down in the deep brush where they had met for months past—down on the soft grass, now dry and yellow, where they had talked love just like the boys and girls in the magazines.

The poor girl had been crying; so Roddy said, "What the hell?"

Earlene didn't answer but just lay down, buried her head in her arms, and went to bawling. Roddy sat on his hunkers and rolled him a cigarette before he said "What the hell?" again.

The girl just went on sobbing.

There was nothing tender about any of the McClung boys: if Earlene expected Roddy to reach down, take her in his arms, and soothe her trouble, she could go to hell and stay there. That was what Roddy thought. He was not the kissing kind; he had only kissed Earlene when she asked him to; to him, having a woman was a necessity, kissing her was a luxury he could do without.

He took a puff on his cigarette, then he said: "What-all is ailin' you, Hon? How come you bawlin' so?"

Earlene lay silent for a minute, she didn't even sob.

Then: "Roddy," she said.

He puffed on his cigarette, but the damned thing wouldn't draw. He thought, To hell with the white papers they give free with the tobacco—wheat straws are the best.

"What, Hon?"

"I'm goin' to have a baby," sobbed Earlene.

Roddy threw down his cigarette and stared ahead of him, at nothing particular—just stared.

"Me?" he asked.

"Sure, you. Who-all else do you reckon!"

To Roddy this was a bad fix to get into—a woman on his hands, by God! To Earlene it was a page from *True Romances* magazine, and she was the poor unfortunate girl wondering as to what happy end would come about.

"Well," said Roddy, "you'll have to git rid of it."

Then the girl burst into tears for sure.

"I'll git the money from my paw," Roddy said, as though that was all there was to it.

He lit another cigarette because he felt better. He felt better while Earlene lay there making a fuss over nothing at all. But Earlene figured she was a true Christian girl who had strayed off the righteous path, and now she had to have her say-so.

"I'm a sinner," was Earlene's say-so. "Lord knows I am. But I ain't as much a sinner as all that."

A buzzard circled over the water hole farther down the Juan Largo—it smelled a critter dead and stinking, thought Roddy. Then he got his mind back to Earlene.

"There's a doctor in Albuquerque, I reckon," he said. "I don't know for sure, but I reckon there is. . . . Did you tell your folks?"

"Lord, no!"

"Better not."

"They'd kill me. Better a murder in the family than me the way I am."

That was what Earlene said with her head buried in her arms. Then she sat up, brushed her hair back, and looked Roddy straight in the face.

Lord, did that poor girl have a worry!

"Roddy."

"What, Hon?"

"We've got to git married. We've got to run away. . . . Right quick."

Now Roddy was not the loving kind; he was not the kissing kind, nor was he the marrying kind. He was a boy who aimed to ramble, gamble, and get in on big talk; he wanted to pull into the cities back yonder on the rods because he was built that way. He didn't need a woman to cook his vittles for him because money, and he aimed to have money, would buy all he wanted ready-cooked at the hash houses. His socks were not the kind that needed darning, so no girl could talk sock-darning to Roddy.

He wanted no female dragging in his tracks as he rolled along, because she would only slow him up. He didn't love Earlene. He loved no woman or anybody else. He liked Earlene down in the Juan Largo, for a fact, but outside of that deep, brushy draw she could go plumb to hell and stay there. That was what Roddy thought, and nobody was going to tell him different.

"We cain't." That's what Roddy said to Earlene.

The girl sat and thought and said nothing.

"We cain't," Roddy told her, "because you-all folks is Christian and we's plumb heathen. Your old man would track us down with a pack of hound dogs and put me in jail and give you worse than a cussin'. A Smeet gal cain't marry up with a McClung man 'cause it's agin good sense. . . . You've got to git rid of it, Hon, and I'll git the money from my paw."

So Earlene made a fuss. She made such a fuss that Roddy got rattled.

"Where-all could we go?" he asked her, mad-like.

"North, south, east, west," Earlene cried. "Anywhere away from my folks, 'cause I'm scared of 'em. Lord, I am! . . . God's wrath will follow us, but I ain't so afeared of the Lord as I am my maw and paw. They're so righteous they ain't forgivin' to anyone who ain't so good as them. You don't have to be bad to git my folks agin you—you just got to be not so good as them. . . . Lord, Lord!"

Then Earlene lay down and sobbed and made a fuss for sure.

But Roddy was part Tod and part Faybelle—he would spit tobacco juice in the eyes of mules when they made him mad, to ease
his temper; and he would cause the womenfolks to tickle at the under-
pinnings just to satisfy his devilment. But now when he saw Earlene
with the heartsick she had, a mite of Tod and Faybelle's sympathy
came alive in him. He reached down and gathered Earlene in his
arms, and he kissed her right smack where the tears were rolling
from her eyes.

"Roddy. . . . Honey!" Earlene whimpered.

Then she remembered what a poor unfortunate girl said to a handsome man in a love-story magazine: "Dearest, my own beatin' heart.
This scarlet sin is great Nature's cruel but thorough scheme to bring
our lives together, so that no blight shall wilt the roses round our
cottage door."

That's what she said to Roddy.

She remembered it was a girl named Rosalind who said those
beautiful words to a man called Alfonso, and Alfonso was a full-
blood Spaniard or Portuguese—she couldn't remember which.

Earlene lay in Roddy's arms happier than she was a few minutes
before, and under his breath the boy said: "Bear's ass." He didn't
say it aloud because he had no aim to hurt Earlene's feelings.

So that was how come Earlene told Roddy that he would be the
daddy of her baby, and how Roddy reckoned she ought to get rid of
it, and how Earlene wouldn't say O.K. because she figured it wasn't
the right thing to do. She was a Christian girl who had strayed from
the righteous path just a mite, and she didn't want to get too far off,
for then she would be lost for sure.

Earlene just lay with her head buried in Roddy's shoulder—the
sleeve of his shirt wet with tears. But she was not sobbing, and her
arms held him so tight that he wished she would let up; but he figured
if he told her to straighten out and let him roll a smoke she would
go to bawling, and that would be too much for a feller to abide.

Roddy didn't have too much of a kick coming when Earlene hung
onto him down in the Juan Largo; but he reckoned she would want
to do the same when he rolled along between Dallas, Texas, and
Knoxville, Tennessee. She wasn't very big, but she could be a heap
of a drag on a rambling man.

He had heard folks tell that a man had cussedness on his hands with an ornery horse, a hounding law, or a rambunctious woman. A feller could wear a horse down, he could dodge the law, but he couldn't get shed of a pesky woman, try as he might.

Earlene looked up and spoke.

"Preacher Flowers sure told us sinners an earful this mornin'," she said. "He told us all about the Devil and how he hangs around the big cities, like Albuquerque, and makes the folks his demons because they ain't got enough to do, and have to take up sinnin' so's to be energetic. He said the men who wear suits and white shirts make the best demons 'cause they's educated fools and git paid for what they know and not for what they do. . . . He sure is a good preacher and knows his onions."

That was what Earlene said about Mr. Flowers.

"Big cities," said Roddy, far-off-like, and with a ramble on his mind.

Right then, as though the Devil had come to light a spark to Roddy's rambling mind, the roar and rattle of a freight train came down on the Juan Largo—a tantalizing, beckoning call that seemed to say: "Come on, Roddy, hook me in the middle and I'll give you a free ride plumb to Texarkana."

And as the train pulled closer the roar and rattle became louder, and that old engineer saw a crossing ahead and he pulled the whistle. It blew shrill like a thousand coyotes on a hill at sunup; then deep as a hundred bulls pawing the earth and roaring for cows; then shrill again, until the sound straddled the wind and rode it over the prairie.

"I aim to roll around, Hon, and git me a job of work for a spell. . . . I want to hit 'er up to the big cities back yonder."

"I'd be happy with you just anywhere, Roddy. I love you so."

"I aim to gamble."

"If a gamblin' man is my man, then I'm his woman and I'll do for him. Honest, Hon."

"I ain't got no money."

"But you'll gamble and git you a job of work. . . . We'll have love, darlin', and that's all that matters. The magazines say that love is all a body needs to keep goin'."

Roddy thought, To hell with love; he liked rambling free and eating ham and eggs at the hash houses better. He wanted breakfast, dinner, supper, and passing miles. He wanted to hear those old freights hoot and toot as they carried him over the steel and ties—and he wanted no woman trailing on his tracks.

Now he had one for sure, hanging on to him where she aimed to stay. He had to get shed of her. Lord, Lord, what a pickle!

So before those two parted at the Juan Largo for that day—before Earlene took out south for the Smeet farm and Roddy north for the homestead by the tracks—the boy kissed the girl and laid her on the grass. She said she had to have marriage, and Roddy said O.K.

It was O.K. with him because he was seventeen years old and a free man. And on the way home the girl walked spry while a song came from her mouth. The boy reached the McClung farm and smelled the tar come down from the tracks, and watched the steel rails stretch eastward—east beyond Vaughn, past Clovis and through Amarillo; to Chicago and Pittsburgh and all the places on the map. To the big blue ocean that washed a coast line over two thousand miles away.

It was during that week that Mary Simonson came over to the McClungs to say howdy. They heard her honk her automobile horn outside, and Faybelle called "You-all come in" from the window. Mary wanted to know if it would be fitting with Tod and Faybelle if she took Lyndel with her to Albuquerque over the week end.

Tod said, "I reckon," and Faybelle seemed right pleased, so Lyndel got all fixed up on the Friday night when Mary called to pick her up. She had on the nice new dress Faybelle made for her from the cloth she bought out of the Sears, Roebuck catalogue. It was Lyndel's best dress, just as fine as anything Sudie had, and she was right proud.

They all watched the teacher and their youngest girl take off for Albuquerque.

"Seems kinda empty around here with the girl young uns gone," said Tod, more times than one during that week end, "—Sudie gone south and the baby north. The baby'll come back, though; she'll come back to the farm."

Sure enough, late on Sunday night they all heard Mary's car drive up and go away, and into the house came Lyndel.

The little girl stood before them.

Faybelle said, "Glory be!" Tod asked, "What you-all done to yourse'f, Hon?" And Roddy said, "God damn!" Piddle didn't say anything, but he thought: "Jesus!"

Lyndel looked as though she had stepped clean out of page 63 of the Montgomery Ward catalogue.

Pretty!

Lord God!

Faybelle carried the kerosene lamp over to the center table, and Tod took hold of Lyndel and led her into the light. All gathered around to see what had happened to this little girl.

She was so clean that Tod asked her how come, and Lyndel admitted that she had been in a bathtub big enough to lie down in, and that Mary had given her plenty of soap and a fuzzy towel.

"I ben to the beauty shop, too," Lyndel told them.

Faybelle felt of the girl's hair, and it was softer and prettier than she had ever seen it before.

"What-all did they do to you, Hon?" That's what Faybelle asked her. "You look pretty but natural."

"She sure looks natural," said Tod.

So Lyndel told them all how after she got out of the tub Mary took her down to the beauty shop where a woman gave her a big card with pictures of pretty girls on it, all with their hair fixed different, and how Mary looked at it, too, and said: "I think this style would be most becoming."

Then, Lyndel told them, the woman worked on her hair and curried out the kinks; and when it was all cleaned and pretty she made her sit under a big floomagadunjet that had dry air in it, and all she had to do was look at a magazine and sit.

"The chair was sure comfortable," Lyndel said, " 'cause it had stuffin' in it."

Faybelle was all aflutter.

"Then what?" she asked.

"Then Miss Simonson took me to a store where there was girls' dresses, and they were most becomin'. She picked out this here dress and two more, and some underthings and stockin's of I don't know what."

Then Lyndel opened up a bundle and showed them all what she had. And when Faybelle saw those pretty things, she said: "Samuel, sing praises to the Lord!"

"Then what?" asked Tod.

"Miss Simonson had to go see some kinfolks, so Bob took me to a pitcher show. There were cowboys and horses in it and two men got shot dead. . . . It was sad, 'cause a girl's feller got killed; but it was only a pitcher show, and I didn't bawl."

Tod looked at Faybelle, and Roddy said, "Hell." Jay Boy and Buster figured they would like to have seen that picture show. Tewp was over at old man Buck Smiles' and wasn't there to see Lyndel come home, and he wouldn't have given a damn anyway. Piddle had gone to sleep in the wood box with his quid in his mouth, and all reckoned they had better wake him because if he swallowed it it would make him sick.

But they were all too interested to hear of Lyndel's doings in Albuquerque to wake Piddle.

"And Bob," asked Tod. "What kind of a job has Bob got?"

"He cleans and presses suits for dudes. He's got a shop with a pipe comin' out of it, and every time he presses a suit it makes steam like an engine on the Santa Fe Railway."

"Boy, howdy!" cried Buster.

Then they all went to bed, and Tod and Faybelle figured the trip to Albuquerque did Lyndel good; and they aimed to say "Thank you" to Mary Simonson.

When Tod and Faybelle were together in the blankets, the man said to the woman: "Do you-all reckon the city will git that young un?"

"I reckon," said Faybelle.

"She's rooted to the farm but she ain't yit taprooted. Mebbe we cain't hold her."

"I reckon," said Faybelle, half asleep.

"Do you-all think she'll take up with them fancy doin's now that she's seen 'em?"

But Faybelle was asleep and didn't give Tod no mind; so he just rolled over and said to himself, "I reckon she will," and figured if the Lord ordains it that that was all there was to it, and nobody could do anything about it.

The next day Tod cranked up his old strip-down Cadillac and drove into town. He came home with the store vittles he had bought and a letter from Sudie. The letter said that she and T. J. were married and living in a rooming house. And when Faybelle read that part of the letter she said, "Lord bless them young uns." Then the letter told the folks how Sudie had had a job hashing but quit because she didn't like the Greek, and that T. J. was offered a job in the oil fields but didn't accept it because of the wages. T. J. was idle—they were both idle—and didn't like Artesia nary a bit. They had sold the Reo truck and aimed to take east for Oklahoma. Because T. J. would work in the oilfields if he could find a boss who would treat him right, and Sudie would hash in a restaurant. And Oklahoma was God's own place on the map for oil-field folks.

Sudie wondered if Tod would loan them twenty-five dollars so they could get to Tuskahoma. They aimed to travel the cushions because T. J. didn't think it right to take his wife out on the bum. Tod thought so, too, so he went back to town and sent Sudie a money order for twenty-five dollars.

Then came Wednesday.

Then came the Wednesday that Roddy had fixed with Earlene for their runaway—she to meet him down in the Juan Largo, where from both would head for the tracks and catch an eastbound freight out of Lucy. He would have a bundle—she too—and he would get fifty dollars from Tod.

Through all the days and nights past, Earlene had felt herself mighty happy. She sang while she worked about the house; out in the corral, when she milked the cows and threw fodder to the stock, her voice carried a song. And Marvin and Virgie wondered how come.

"You-all's tooth ain't hurtin' no more, daughter?" asked Marvin.

"No. It's all gone."

After, when Marvin spoke to Virgie in the kitchen and Earlene was outside singing, he said: "Our daughter's a reg'lar mockin'bird today. How come she's so doggoned pleased about somethin' all of a sudden?"

And Virgie said: "I reckon it's the Christianity in her comin' out."

Come the Wednesday, Earlene got her bundle together. She tied up a dress or two, and face powder, and soap; she hid it back of the barn where her *True Story* magazines were cached in the straw. Then she looked at the clock anxiously until the hands told her it was time to get to the Juan Largo.

Roddy would be waiting for her, she thought; she must not keep her man waiting at the church, as the feller says.

Lord!

All this while Roddy sat out by the McClung woodpile whittling on a stick. He whittled and thought and had a weary song on his tongue.

> *"Goin' down the road feelin' bad.*
> *Goin' down the road feelin' bad.*
> *Lordy, Lord!*
> *And I ain't gonna be treated this-a-way."*

Tod heard him, so he said to Faybelle: "That's a lonesome song our boy's got on his mind today."

"I reckon," said Faybelle, busy with something to do about vittles.

All this while Roddy was thinking—he thought of the big cities back yonder. He daydreamed of all the rounders like himself who pulled their chairs up to the tables where the poker chips were stacked high. Where they handled the cards and laid their money down.

He thought how the Red Ball freights—on that Santa Fe, that Rock Island, that Burlington, and that old T. & P. road—rattled and tooted from town to town keeping the gambling rounders on the roll. He figured he wanted no pesky woman on his tracks.

So he went to the house and gathered up his extra pair of bib overalls. He put his razor and comb in the pockets and made a roll and tied it with a string. Then he opened the drawer of the table where Tod kept his business doodads and tore him a blank check from Tod's checkbook, because he knew doggone well how to forge his daddy's signature.

Then he hunted down Piddle.

"I'm tellin' you-all and nobody else," Roddy told Piddle. "I'd write 'em a letter, but I cain't write for no good at all. After I'm long gone, long enough to hook me a freight and git out of the way, you can feed 'em the news. For I'm off on the ramble and I'm gonna lay my money down."

All Piddle said was: "Good luck to you, son. When you git to Little Rock hunt up my old friend Suggs. Tell him I'm feelin' of the finest kind and I aim to see him some day. But mebbe he's dead and long gone. That was a heap of a time ago."

"You-all will let 'em wonder till I'm far off on the road?" Roddy said, anxious-like. "You won't tell 'em so's they can catch up on me?"

"I was a rounder myse'f in my younger days," Piddle said. "I'll treat you right, son."

Piddle shut up and went to chewing, while Roddy took up his bundle and lit out for the highway across the tracks.

Then, just about the time Roddy flagged down a truck and hooked a ride east to Vaughn, that division point where the long freights stop and roll out again, Earlene hummed happily and walked spry to the Juan Largo with her bundle under her arm. She was going to her man, and she was happy. Roddy was breaking away from her, and he was happy, too.

While the truck bumped and backfired and got to percolating, Roddy carried on his weary song.

> *"Feed me corn bread and peas.*
> *Lord, feed me corn bread and peas.*
> *Lordy, Lord!*
> *And I ain't gonna be treated this-a-way."*

The truck driver didn't aim to stop at Encino, so they passed it on the fly. Roddy thought it best to forge Tod's name to a check for fifty dollars.

> *"Mama won't buy me no shoes.*
> *Lord, Mama won't buy me no shoes.*

> *Lordy, Lord!*
> *And I ain't gonna be treated this-a-way."*

At Vaughn he wrote and cashed the check. Then he bought ham and eggs before he headed for the freight yards. In the yards he met a rounder named Dutch who was waiting for an eastbound freight on the Santa Fe.

"Here," said Dutch, "you can git the Santa Fe out for Amarillo or the Southern Pacific to Tucumcari—both roads'll take you east. I aim to head for Dallas. The Santa Fe is best."

So Roddy decided to head for Dallas with Dutch.

While Roddy was eating a hamburger over at the Harvey House —and Dutch was eating the steak and onions the boy had bought for him—he felt a dizzy spell come over him. He rested his head on the counter, and the waitress asked him what ailed him.

"I don't know," said Roddy. "I git these spells often. A pain comes in my chest and a dizzyin' in my head. I cain't figure it out."

"It must be your heart," said the waitress, who knew all about ailments because her sister was a nurse. "You'd better see a doctor."

When the dizzy spell passed over, Roddy went to eating his hamburger.

That night Marvin and Virgie got a worry on their minds because of their girl. Earlene went to sobbing again, and Marvin said he didn't care what, he would take her to Vaughn to the dentist, even if he had to drag her. She lay on her bed and bawled her eyes out, and all the praying they could do had no effect.

Marvin would take her to the dentist, and that was all there was to it.

At that time, too, a Santa Fe freight rolled east between Hereford and Amarillo. The black smoke from the engine rose high, and it screened the star-lit sky from the trailing cars. The whistle moaned, and the wheels clattered on the rails. And from an empty gondola, nigh in the middle of the train, came a weary song.

> *"Down in the jailhouse on my knees.*
> *Lord, down in the jailhouse on my knees.*
> *Lordy, Lord!*
> *And I ain't gonna be treated this-a-way."*

The brakey came through and passed by the two bums in the gondola, giving them not one mite of mind. For, way back at Clovis, Roddy gave the brakey a dollar bill; and the brakey said: "All right. You two bums are colored pink. I'm color-blind, and I can't see pink. Watch out for the dick in Amarillo, though."

The brakey walked by.

The freight rolled east.

Dutch slept while Roddy sang.

He sang because he was happy and free. He was happy because he had no woman to drag him down and make him stay put. Because he was a rounder heading for the cities back yonder—where there was gambling and big talk a plenty—and where all good rounders ought to be.

*Chapter Seven*

WHEN Christmas Day of that year came around and the folks of
the community got real brotherly and sisterly, they went around to
each other's houses to shake hands and say, "Christmas gift." After
the womenfolks got themselves settled in the warm kitchens and
sleeping rooms, and the men squatted themselves outside by the
woodpiles and went to smoking and whittling, they all started in
chewing the rag and put their talk to the things that took up a heap
of the folks' minds at that day and time.

One, for a fact, was that Mary Simonson had quit the school
and had gone to Albuquerque to get married. The new teacher would
be a man, it was heard tell.

"Praise the sweet Lord," said some folks, while others argued,
"We'll never git another teacher so good at education as Miss Simonson, by golly."

And among those who had the latter idea were Tod and Faybelle
McClung.

Mary came over to say howdy and goodbye to the McClung folks
just before she packed up to leave. Tod and Faybelle liked her better
than any other neighbor; and they didn't aim to let her get away
without a word of regret and to tell her how sorry they were that
she was high-tailing it for the big city. And the thought of her going
made Tod cuss like a he-man; and Faybelle, although she wasn't
the crying kind, felt a knot in her throat the size of a turnip.

One of the reasons Tod and Faybelle took such a shine to the
teacher was because she always had right smart of an interest in the
doings of their kids. And even now, when she was all set to light out
and perhaps never see them again, she asked, anxious-like:

"Do you hear from Sudie and Roddy?"

"We got a card from Sudie last week," Faybelle told her. "It had
a picture of Tuskahoma on it, and Sudie says she and T. J. are feelin'
of the finest kind. Sudie's goin' to git a job hashin', she reckons, and

T. J. aims to go to roustaboutin'. We ain't heard from Roddy yit, but he cain't write for nothin'."

"He's on the ramble," said Tod, "so he's gittin' along all right. Ain't nothin' goin' to git in the way of a boy on the ramble."

Tod was pleased about Roddy's rambling, even if the boy *did* forge his daddy's name to a check and do him out of fifty dollars. The check was forged so well that the bank didn't know different; and because Roddy was Tod's own son Tod didn't raise a kick. Roddy was covering miles, and when the miles roll under a boy he is getting somewhere.

"He'll ramble and come home," Tod told Mary. "His trail will lead back to the land."

"Maybe," said Faybelle.

"It will," said Tod, yet he had a worry on his mind.

Now, because Sudie and Roddy were long gone and the balance of the kids were out in the yard away from hear-say, Faybelle spoke her mind to the teacher.

"You're gittin' a right gentleman for a man, teacher, and one that will *do* for you. He might not make a hand in a field of beans, but he will provide for you in his own citified way—a way mighty furrin to us'ns."

Faybelle sat silent for a minute; then she continued her thoughtful talk.

"I'm thankful to the dear Lord for the man Sudie got. I wouldn't have asked for one better, for a fact. T. J.'s her kind, and that's all there is to it. And the Lord wills it. . . . We're too low down in the dirt to hope Lyndel gits a man like your'n."

Mary heard Lyndel then, outside, laughing as Buster chased her about the yard.

"Us folks who live in and by the dirt," said Faybelle, "raise kids like our mammies and daddies grew us: like potatoes pulled out with the earth all over 'em—some grown to be cooked down and do good to folkses, some to rot, and others to go back to the soil and make more of their kind. . . . The best always go back to the land."

Again silence. Tod said nothing, Faybelle said nothing. Mary waited for one of them to speak. Then:

"She's rooted," said Faybelle. "Lyndel's rooted to the land."

"But she ain't yit taprooted," Tod told her. "She can still be got off without much pullin'. And don't you-all forget it, wife!"

Faybelle said: "We cain't stand in her way. Because what the Lord ordains must be."

Mary breathed easy and started in on her say-so.

"Before I go," she said, "there's something I would like to ask of you. . . . It will be worth a lot to you."

"What? Fire away," said Tod.

"About Lyndel and Buster. Their future."

She's speakin' her mind, thought Tod, sitting there quiet-like.

"Tod ain't gittin' rattled," were words that came to Faybelle's head.

"I've been thinking about it for a long time," went on Mary, "but I've said nothing because the time hadn't come. Now it has."

A pause. The McClung folks waited for her to continue.

"Roddy and Sudie have left the farm and gone off to where they think it is best for them, and Tewp and Jay Boy are still with you. All the book learning in the world wouldn't do *them* any good. They are best as they are. But Buster is different. He's only ten years old and has time to get started and finished. He'll improve the worth of your farm, Tod, if you'll only give him a chance."

"I make my own farm," said Tod. "Buster can only he'p me."

"Look about you," said Mary. "The people of the land are coming out of the homespun and are treating the dirt as it should be treated."

"I've always been kind to my dirt, and it's paid me back in crops and cash and a chance to raise a family on it. There ain't another man in Torrance County's as had as much luck as me at farmin'."

"That's the honest God's truth," put in Faybelle.

"How come Buster can do better'n me?" Tod wanted to know.

"Because he's young enough to be taken off the land, just for the time it takes to put reading, writing, and arithmetic into his head. So that he can help you meet the competition that's coming your way in the future."

"Nobody can compete with me at farmin'," bragged Tod.

"Marvin Smeet can," said Mary.

"That bastard!"

"And Mr. Mudgett."

"He's another."

"They keep up with the times, Tod, and are prepared for what's coming. . . . When Buster is your age farming will be mighty different, more complicated, than it is now. It's only fair to him—"

Faybelle tried to say, "What is good enough for us is—"

Mary cut her off: "And that exactly is the thing that is holding you people down in the dirt."

"Where we're satisfied to stay," Faybelle told her.

"But where you won't be allowed to stay," said Mary. "In time the neighbors will be so far ahead of you, you won't be able to catch up—and you'll want to catch up. . . . They'll progress, go forward with the time, while you will still be turning the soil as your father did; just old-fashioned folks willing to let be—what's good enough today is all right ten years from now. . . . Darn it, Tod and Faybelle, don't let the Smeets and Mudgetts drive you off your land and send you rolling over the prairie like a dry tumbleweed. Don't—"

"I'm here to stay put," said Tod.

"Don't let those pesky neighbors get ahead of you in the big-scale farming that's only a few years away from this valley—scientific farming that will need brain as well as brawn. Buster has the brains. He wants to feed them, as you eat to build up your muscles so you can handle a four-mule plow. He wants education, Tod—book learning with all the trimmings."

"I'll teach him to handle mules."

"And when you buy more land, plow up more fields, invest in modern machinery—which you will surely have to do to keep Marvin Smeet down where he belongs—you will need brains to work your farm as it should be worked. You will need someone to help you figure overhead and profit by pure doggone arithmetic. Someone who can farm by lamplight at night with a pad and pencil after all of you have spent a hard day in the fields. Big-time farming's going to take brains to operate it, Tod, or the banks will get all you've got."

"Them sons of bitches!" said Tod.

"A patch of land and a one-furrow plow is not enough for a

farmer in a country as broad as this, Tod. Those Smeets and Mudgetts will get ahead of you if such is good enough for your youngsters
because it suits you. Think big. Think in terms of McCormick-Deer-
ing, of gang plows and four-row middlebusters, and plan to spread
your land to sections instead of just acres. . . . All that will take
careful thought and figuring. Above all, it will take—"

"Strength, and the love of the land my kids have got in 'em
right now," interrupted Tod.

"And book larnin'," said Mary in Tod's own language.

Then: "*Please*, Tod and Faybelle, *please* send Buster to school!"

So Tod thought for half a minute; then he said: "I reckon a farmer
handy with figures will be useful about the place—but with me to
boss him, by God! I reckon it's all right to send him to school, even
if I *do* hate the bastardly things and you ain't there to give him the
learnin'."

"Promise?" asked Mary.

"Promise, God damn it," said Tod.

But Faybelle just sat and thought.

"And what about Lyndel?" she asked the teacher, after all that
citified talk. "You didn't say nary a thing about Lyndel among all
them kids."

Mary braced herself for the tussle she knew she was in for.

"Lyndel. Well . . . Bob and I have been thinking that we would
like to have her in Albuquerque with us. We could care for her, and
send her to school. Then we could teach her a trade so that she could
earn for herself. She fits in with us like a bean in a pod."

Faybelle felt an argument coming on and set herself ready to
defend Mary's good intentions.

But—

Tod rose and faced the teacher. His voice was loud and de-
termined. It was also kind.

"Then git her out of here, for Christ's sake!" he cried. "Git her
out before she taproots and cain't be pulled loose. . . . She's too
soft for the land, anyway. When the mud sticks to her skin it chaps
and welts and makes her cry. She's a sissy. She wasn't never meant
to be a daughter of mine, so help me God! Git her out; take her

away, and don't bring her back till you've made a woman out of her somethin' like yourse'f."

That was all Mary needed to make her so doggone happy she could hug Tod and Faybelle—but Tod and Faybelle were not the hugging kind.

"Praise the Lord for all his manifold blessin's," muttered Faybelle.

So Mary told them that she and Bob would come for Lyndel right after they got themselves married. She told Faybelle not to do any fussing about getting the kid slicked up for city life, because she herself knew how to go about all those kinds of doings.

Also, Mary told Faybelle, she had a carful of things that she couldn't use in Albuquerque and figured the McClungs could use them to advantage. There were lots of nice dresses and underthings, even silk stockings and high-heeled shoes, and all these she brought over and had parked outside in the yard.

There was a stack of clean aluminum pots and pans, too, that Faybelle could use for cooking her vittles and canning up garden stuff. Lord, if Faybelle wasn't tickled silly to see all those shiny doodads!

Mary had offered the pots and pans to the Widow Burge first, but her kind intentions were turned down because the pots were made of aluminum and the Widow Burge was a full-blood Jehovah's Witness.

"Land sakes!" said the Widow Burge to Mary—Mary loaded down with all those shiny doodads. "I'll declare it's through the Lord's godness that you ain't dead and rotten. Don't you ever read what Judge Rutherford says about aluminum cookin' doodads? We Russellites know it for sure, and it plumb grieves me to think how the millions of folks who ain't Witnesses die every year from eatin' vittles cooked in 'em. Cancer in the stomach, that's what the poor critters git from their ignorance. Lord! The Judge should tell folks about it on his phonograph records. He has written enough about it, Lord bless him."

So Mary put her pots and pans back in the car.

"I always say," went on the Widow, "that a body couldn't *give* me an aluminum pot, and here the nicest woman in the community is handin' me a dozen! Git thee behind me, Satan."

And because the Widow said "Git thee behind me, Satan" in a joshing way, Mary didn't get sore and aimed to take the pots and pans over to Faybelle McClung.

So all that sort of thing made fine gossip for the community folks while they sat about on Christmas Day; after they shook hands with each other and said, "Christmas gift." But the food for talk that really got tongues a-wagging was not so much that Mary Simonson had done quit, Lyndel McClung's going to Albuquerque, or Buster's aim to take up book learning—but the news that the Reverend Luke Flowers and Earlene Smeet had gotten themselves married.

The word went from house to house like the Rawleigh man peddling patent medicine products. As soon as it went into a neighbor woman's ear it was all set to come out of her mouth further down the line. When the womenfolks heard it they stood for a second with open mouths, like somebody had biffed them, and then they said, "Well!" and "Do tell!" or "She didn't marry him for his money, 'cause he ain't got none but what goes into his hat."

It had them all buffaloed; it made them scratch their heads and wonder—wonder why a girl of sixteen, still in school, should want to marry a man fifty-eight years old.

"Earlene Smeet's got a man of God for a husband. It's the Lord's doin's." That's what the Christians said.

"In breedin' stock, like gits like. Their young uns will be sure enough hypocrites," the infidels gossiped.

"That first kid of theirs will be the spit and image of Preacher Flowers," laughed Tod McClung when he heard, " 'cept he'll have the long face of Marvin Smeet, too. He'll be half Smeet and part Flowers. Lord God! What a combination!"

That was the kind of talk which went around the community when Mr. Flowers got himself settled with Earlene over at the Smeet farm. The Christians said it was the Lord's doing, so it was O.K. with them; the infidels said it was all right because they reckoned old Luke and young Earlene were two beans in a pod— except that the husband was a little crustier than his wife.

Some of the folks round about said that Luke Flowers would

never be a daddy; but as time passed by it let them know different. The women looked close at Earlene when they met up with her, and when they went their way and got to chewing the rag among themselves they figured she was in the family way. And although the women never said it outright, they looked at each other as though to say: "They must 've been carryin' on before holy wedlock. And him so agin lovin' and huggin'!"

That was what the neighbors thought.

That was what the McClungs thought.

But Marvin and Virgie Smeet knew different.

Because just after Roddy took out on the ramble Earlene's spell of the blues got worse. She wasn't in fit shape for school, and *it* so close to the Christmas vacation. She couldn't help clean the house or cook the vittles; Marvin had to milk the cows by himself and throw fodder to the stock; and it all left Virgie with little time to study the Bible and do other such pleasant things.

So Marvin put water in the radiator of the car, asked Virgie what-all she needed in town, and went into Earlene's room and said: "Quit your cryin', daughter, for I'm haulin' you-all to the dentist in Vaughn."

Earlene just lay on the bed crying and didn't make a move to get up.

"My teeth don't ache," she said between sobs. "It's worser'n that."

"Does your in'ards hurt?"

"They don't hurt."

"Then what-all you blubbin' about?"

Virgie came in the room to see what-all.

"Nothin' ails her," said Marvin to Virgie.

Virgie thought for a minute.

"Maybe you got a tapeworm, Hon," she said.

"I got worser'n a tapeworm," sobbed Earlene.

"What-all?"

"A human bein'," cried Earlene, going into rambunctious tantrums.

Marvin understood.

Virgie understood.

Their girl!

Marvin clenched his fist as though he aimed to pick up a horse-whip, but his mind said, "Let be." Virgie didn't scream as when she saw Bob and Mary making love on the night of the dance; but her Christianity came out all over her, and she stood there as though a bolt from heaven had struck her and she was fixing to drop.

Then she sat down on the bed, gathered Earlene in her arms, and said to Marvin: "It's just about time to do up the chores, ain't it, husband?" And after Marvin left, Virgie kissed Earlene. She dis-remembered exactly the time she kissed her last; it was when the girl was a little mite—a long time before. And it was in Virgie's arms that Earlene quit crying and fell asleep.

Virgie found Marvin outside. He had his head buried in his arms and leaned his long body against the bars of the corral. He wasn't doing anything particular except think. He was thinking hard.

Virgie stood silent for a minute; then she braced herself for her say-so.

"Marvin Smeet," she said. "You are my lawfully wedded husband and I am here to tell you what's what."

That's what Virgie said, all braced up.

Marvin still rested his head in his arms against the corral, and he seemed as though he gave Virgie no mind. But Virgie had lived with him these many years and she knew he always listened when she spoke.

Then he said: "Who-all is the man?"

"Search me. She never said, and I didn't ask her. She's gone to sleep and don't bawl no more. We'll git it out of her, though."

Marvin looked up; he seemed relieved a bit because Virgie didn't have a trace of anger in her talk. He expected rambunctiousness, but his wife was calm.

There was more human being in Virgie Smeet than the neighbor folks knew about—more of the ordinary, everyday woman on the street and in the kitchen. That part of her she had kept hid by sanctimonious airs and pretending high-up religion; a part she had acted so as to boost her in the preacher's sight—to make the neigh-bors seem small fry and not on par with her in a godly way. But Virgie was human, and it took a turn such as had come about to bring the real goodness out of her where all could see it. No more pretending. No more making fake shame such as she and Marvin did even to themselves, such as happened on those nights before Earlene was born. And because Marvin had lived with Virgie for so long he was the same as she—the same as before, changed as now.

"Marvin," Virgie said, "I reckon we're gittin' punished for our sins, and the Lord is goin' to pour it on till we holler 'Calf rope' if we don't stop transgressin'. We've been hypocrites, husband, and that's all there is to it. You've been a scribe and I've been a Pharisee. And because the Lord don't like them kind of folks he's goin' to lay it on a plenty till we git meek and righteous enough to suit his holy taste."

"I reckon," said Marvin.

"And what I mean by meek and righteous ain't the variety we've been livin' up to for so long. From now on, to git on good terms with the Lord, we'll have to change our ways right smart; we'll have to give up all this petty sinnin', such as makin' folks think God shines his countenance on us more than others.

"We ain't goin' to sell Tod McClung another worthless male animal and then pray for a bolt of fire to strike us down if the Lord thinks it ain't good business tactics. Because them fiery bolts never come and we always figgered we were mighty safe in askin' for 'em.

"Now the Lord lets us have punishment a plenty, so we're ahollerin', 'Calf rope.' But He's merciful, is the Lord; He's doled out His wrath upon us in a way in which we'll have time to make amends as true Christians should. He's left you and me to go on with our lives, without an ache in our bodies except in our hearts, and sent worser'n a bolt of fire on that little critter we love more than anything else in the world."

Although Marvin didn't speak, Virgie knew he figured what she said was good preaching.

"Come on, husband," said Virgie. "Let's go to the house and fix our girl a nice supper to eat when she wakes up. She ought to be mighty hungry, poor young un, 'cause she's been off her appetite these last few days. She's a-feelin' better now, Lord be praised, and so are we."

Marvin put his arm around Virgie's waist—for the first time in many a day—and together they walked to the house. They aimed to fix Earlene some supper.

At suppertime Earlene up and told them that Roddy McClung was the man who got her the way she was. Down in the Juan Largo, she told them, it happened. She felt doubly sinful because she had lied to the teacher, said she liked to go home by way of the draw because there was nature there. Nature! Earlene didn't give a hoot for nature so long as Roddy was at the Juan Largo waiting for her. She didn't love the acre patches of wild verbena that bloomed along the draw. If a paisano bird scampered over the prairie as she took her trail down she didn't notice it. The mockingbirds in the box elder by the water hole had no music for her. It was Roddy she loved with all the heart she had; still loved him and always would.

"I'm a sinner," said Earlene, after she told them who-all was the daddy of her baby.

And Virgie said kindly: "Ain't we all! You, your daddy and me, and Roddy McClung. Some folks is worse sinners than us, and we ourselves are a little shy of what the Lord calls high standards, and as such we're not as good as others. But we can be thankful, husband and daughter, that we've got a mighty merciful and forgivin' Judge to reckon with before each of us comes to our buryin' day."

Then Marvin and Virgie got to thinking about what they should do, and because it was the Lord they had to reckon with they thought about the preacher.

The next day Marvin and Virgie went over to call on Mr. Flowers, and the preacher met them at the door.

"Welcome to the house of the Lord, Brother and Sister Smeet," said Mr. Flowers. He had a knife in his hand; he had been peeling potatoes like an honest-to-goodness bachelor. "Welcome; and make yourselves at home under His righteous countenance."

Virgie sat down quietly, but Marvin remained standing so he could speak his mind.

"Brother Flowers," said Marvin. "I've heard you preach from the pulpit many a Sunday mornin', and your words have always hit home among your congregation. You always ask some of us to prove we're good Christians and how we follow the path of righteousness.

. . . Now, Brother Flowers, I'm goin' to ask you if you-all practice what you preach."

Mr. Flowers laid down his knife and looked his most reverendest.

"Fire away," he said.

"Do you honestly believe, Brother Flowers, that Christ died to save the world? . . . Do you believe He looked down from the cross on all them Jews and centurions and said to Himself, 'I suffer this for your benefit'?"

Mr. Flowers looked Marvin straight in the face.

"I do," he said.

"That was a long time ago. . . . Nigh onto two thousand years."

Mr. Flowers figured in his mind that Marvin was mighty handy with arithmetic.

"Then," said Marvin, "I've come to see you prove to your two most earnest followers, my wife and me, that you're willin' to save one lone sinner from hell and damnation, and from the critical words of a lot of pesky neighbors."

"That's my stock in trade—savin' sinners," said Mr. Flowers solemnly.

"And you won't need to die to do it," said Marvin. "You can stay alive and healthy—better off than you've ever been before."

"What sinner? . . . What do you aim for me to do?"

"My daughter Earlene. Marry her."

Luke Flowers gasped; it was a very reverend gasp.

"Are you-all craze?" he said.

"We ain't craze," said Virgie. "We're askin' you to marry our daughter."

So it was made known to the preacher that Earlene had sinned and was in the family way; that Roddy McClung was the daddy and he had skipped out leaving the girl to hold the sack; that both Marvin and Virgie craved a son-in-law now more than ever before—and that it was their Christian hope to have their girl love, honor, and obey Mr. Flowers. He could claim the baby as his own and nobody outside the family would know different.

Mr. Flowers thought how young, soft, and pretty Earlene was; what a good cook she had already proved herself to be by the countless messes of fried chicken she had served him; how Marvin's fields and herd brought money to the household; how he could enjoy all the benefits of the Smeet farm by still being a man of God, still conduct his Sunday meetings in that fine house, and not have to do one lick of work except marry the girl and claim the baby.

He said: "I promise to marry the girl and make her a lovin' husband, and if the baby's a boy we'll name him Luke after me."

Marvin gave Mr. Flowers some money, and the preacher and Earlene went off and got married by a justice of the peace; because that bridegroom didn't want any truck with a regular Baptist minister.

So on that Christmas Day, while the neighbors were going around shaking hands and saying, "Christmas gift," Luke Flowers sat down to dinner at the Smeet farm a married man. Virgie and Earlene had fixed him fried turkey and mashed potatoes, but because the preacher loved corn bread and clabbered milk better than any other vittle, he said he wanted that too. Earlene fixed her loving husband a bowl of corn bread and clabber.

## Chapter Eight

FAYBELLE was always mighty particular around Christmas time to remind Tod to get her one of those pretty picture calendars for the following year, which the store gave away free. So when Tod cranked up the Cadillac strip-down, ready to gun her into town, Faybelle would call just as he was about to pull out:

"You-all git one of them pretty pitcher calendars—them that's got cows on 'em."

For a fact, the calendars *were* pretty. They always had a nice colored picture of some kind; sometimes Mary holding Jesus when He was a little mite, sometimes cows walking down the road, and sometimes a naked, or nigh naked, woman.

And under the picture was the name of the mercantile company, and always an invite to do business with them.

*General Merchandise*
*Farm and Ranch Supplies*
*We Buy Hides and Pelts*
*Your Trade Is Appreciated*
*Thank You*

If the picture was religious, or had cows on it, or lakes and trees like up in the mountains, Faybelle would say: "Gosh! Hon, looky here how pretty!" But if it was of a naked woman, or a nigh naked woman, she would say, "Pshaw!" and make some flour-and-water stickum and paste last year's picture over that shameless critter.

When the old year was gone and the new calendar was hung on the wall of the sleeping room, over the sewing machine, Faybelle would cut out the old picture and put it in her trunk—where she kept the family album and the photographs of kinfolks; and where she even had a snapshot of the folks who came to Uncle Tally's funeral, back there in Atoka County. The picture was faded, but all the faces were familiar—all standing around the coffin in which Uncle Tally could be seen, lying dead and looking natural.

As each month passed, Tod, or some of them, would tear off a leaf and crumple it up and throw it away, until the whole pretty calendar was used up and another year come around.

January, February, March.

Those long, cold months when the heater in the sleeping room kept blazing from the first glint of daylight until all folks were well under their blankets at night. The cold nights when the frost would creep through the cracks in the walls, and even through the window panes, and form a crust of ice on the water bucket and make the coffee grounds in the pot look like little brown hailstones. Those short winter days when the folks looked out from the windows on the snowy whiteness of the prairie—the snow that forced them indoors from their labor, but was a gift from God to the farmer and his thirsty land. And when the land wasn't white it was a tawny brown—a brown dry and cold—asleep because it had nothing to do until it was awakened by Tod's plow, June warmth, and July rain: an earth so rich that it could lie asleep while the poor folks who lived on it had to be up and about to keep old starvation away. There were the chores to do, there were always the chores.

April, May, June.

Spring came to the prairie with the wind out of the west. No April showers here; no May flowers in this country. Wind, dust, sunshine a plenty. Snow could be expected up to the last of May; and one year Tod broke ice on the horse trough on the twelfth day of June. The mules were hooked to the middlebuster and furrows were chiseled in the fall-plowed field. The land took the seed, and by the time Tod tore the June leaf from the calendar the crop had sprouted, was making leaves and stems.

July, August, September.

Lord, those were busy months! Long days of sunshine and then the first rains of summer—or the rains of any account, as the feller says. Days of churning the field with the riding cultivator and the swinging hoes; making hash of the tumbleweeds, careless weeds, verbena, and thistles—nuisance plants that figured they had as much right to the field as the beans, corn, and sorghum cane. And while Piddle, Faybelle, and the kids—Buster out of school and Lyndel back from Albuquerque for the summer—chopped the weeds

around the stalks of the crop, Tod rode his cultivator and sang his
weary song.

> "I loved you, honey,
>   Till the poleece ran me down.
> Sweet Lord!
> I loved you, honey,
>   Till the poleece ran me down.
> Git up, you hard-tail mules!
> You kicked me round and round and round,
> Till the poleece came and ran me down.
> Lord God, take my weary blues away!"

On a day during those months the menfolks corralled the cattle
and Tod built a fire so as to heat the branding irons. When all the
cattle were rounded up and penned and the irons hot, Tewp got
among them on horseback and fixed to heel the calves with his lariat
rope and drag them to the fire, while Piddle and Jay Boy flanked
them and held them down. Then Tod would run the iron over their
slick hides and cut a swallow fork on their left ears.

## TOD —

T-O-D Bar, that was the brand Tod McClung recorded with the
Cattle Sanitary Board, and the critters that carried it were Tod's
own and nobody else's. And with the end of September came bean
harvest—that big chore of the year on the success of which depended
the amount of vittles to go into the McClung bellies, the clothes for
their backs, the debts to be paid at the bank, and the improvement on
the worth of the farm.

October, November, December.

Corn and cane harvest. Fall plowing and beating old man Winter
to the draw. Weaning calves and making deals with the cattle buyers
who came around. The precious bean fodder stacked away in safety;
the speckled beans themselves off to the elevator and more good
dollars and cents in Tod's name at the bank. Then Christmas, and
the folks of the community getting right neighborly. And again
Faybelle called to Tod as he cranked up to go to town:

"You-all git one of them pretty pitcher calendars—them that's
got cows on 'em."

So Tod brought home another calendar, and on the first day of January he pulled off the last leaf of the old one and called another year done quit.

Now three years had gone by since Roddy took off on the ramble, Sudie married T. J., Mary Simonson quit the school for Albuquerque and took Lyndel with her, and Buster started learning education from Mr. Ralls, who took Mary's place teaching kids. All that happened in 1928; now the start of 1932 had come along.

Those three long years had given Tod McClung right smart of time to study on what Mary Simonson told him about competition from the neighbors, how he would be left with a one-horse outfit if he didn't look spry.

Lord!

Tod cranked up his Cadillac and drove into town to see the banker; and because Tod was a farming fool and knew what it was all about the banker let him have money to get more land, buy more cattle, and put improvements and machinery on the place. So Tod bought and worked, and soon he had one of the prettiest little ranches in Torrance County.

He leased two sections of land adjoining his homestead—two sections, which together with his own six hundred and forty gave him a ranch of nineteen hundred and twenty acres, and around it all he strung up a boundary fence.

He had the well driller come out with his rig and sink him a cased well; three hundred and fifty feet under the surface of the ground they struck water, and over this Tod put a brand-new Stover windmill with a sixteen-foot wheel, and right by it a galvanized storage tank to catch and hold the water. And near by he built a water-lot corral in which he put cement troughs for the stock to stick their snouts in.

Lord, Tod had him a ranch from way back!

Tod reckoned his pasture would run thirty head of cattle to the section, and together with his stubble, bean hay, and corn fodder his ranch would carry a hundred head without going to broom weed. And he ran a herd of the finest kind—high-grade Hereford cows, and enough registered bulls to keep them finding calves right along.

In time he sold the old Cadillac strip-down to the junk yard and bought him a new Ford pickup that really got to moving and covered miles. And for Faybelle he got a washing machine and an iron that heated itself with gasoline; and for Buster he bought all kinds of schoolbooks.

Was Buster a smart kid!

He came home each evening to tell the folks how much learning Mr. Ralls had crammed into his head. He could recite poetry and figure arithmetic; he could name all sorts of places on the map, and he knew all about George Washington and Abraham Lincoln. And what surprised Tod was that all this book learning didn't hurt the kid nary a bit for farm work in the summer months, or slack him up for his home chores—those he had to do before setting out for school in the mornings and after coming back in the evenings. He was a kid who could keep geography and George Washington in his head, where they belong, and properly slop hogs with his hands.

And Lyndel!

If any man said Lyndel wasn't a smart kid, too, Tod would have smacked him in the eye. Because she was right there in Albuquerque with Mary Simonson, whose name was now Mrs. Bob Alcorn, and Mary was sending her to school in the daytime and having her help around the house at night. But it wasn't all work and school with Lyndel, because she wrote Tod and Faybelle often and told what she was doing. School and housework, going to picture shows and the beauty shop, taking baths and going for walks to the park and zoo with girls her own age. And it was a good zoo, too, Lyndel wrote, because it had snakes in it.

On Saturdays she helped Bob in the cleaning and pressing shop. She liked that kind of work, but she aimed to be a beauty operator and give fancy women permanent waves and facials and make good money. That's what Lyndel wrote the folks; she told of all those fine things in her letters, and when Tod and Faybelle read her handwriting they figured she was a sure enough scribe and nobody could tell them different.

It came a day in 1929 that word went through the community that Earlene had found her a baby boy. She aimed to call him Luke —Luke Flowers, just like the preacher.

And the word came among the people: "Earlene done got her a

big boy last night. . . . Gonna name him Luke after his daddy."

The neighbor-women said: "Well!"

Or "Do tell!"

Or "I swan!"

But Tod McClung said: "I still say he ain't goin' to be nothin' pretty. He's goin' to grow up and look too much like his daddy. He's goin' to be another Luke Flowers."

And Faybelle said: "Shame, Hon! To say such a thing about a poor little old innocent babe!"

Tod didn't get a chance to see Earlene's baby until it was nigh six months old, but Faybelle had, and she said it was right pretty. When Tod finally *did* see the baby and take it and dance it on his knee he was satisfied it wasn't ugly like old Luke.

"Give him time," Tod said to Faybelle after Earlene had taken her kid and gone home. "Give him five years and he'll be the spit and image of Luke. Luke Flowers is born in him, and you cain't take it out of that baby if you soak him in kerosene for a week."

That's what Tod said about Earlene's big boy.

Somehow when Marvin Smeet came to Tod's mind the thought of Silas Domino, the bull, popped up with him and got Tod rattling-mad.

Lord! Did Tod cuss when he found he had bought a bull not fit to be the daddy of his calf crop!

"A dirty coyote's trick," Tod had said to Faybelle. "And to think I could fall sucker to his game. Me! The best judge of a critter in the valley."

"I reckon Marvin thought you was such a powerful good farmer you-all'd see Silas wasn't no account," Faybelle said, like as though she was standing up for the Smeets against her own loving man.

That got Tod plumb riled.

"It's the principle," he cried. "Agin the doin's of an honest Christian. Even Luke Flowers don't preach favor of dealin's like that."

For a fact, Tod found Silas to be no bull at all and had to ship him off as a beef critter with his steer calves—over a hundred dollars' worth of young bull gone to be cut up for steaks and roast beef in Kansas City.

But that was long ago and nigh forgotten. Marvin had become a changed man since then.

What a change had come suddenly over Marvin and Virgie Smeet now that Earlene had a loving husband!

Cakes!

Magazines with pictures in them!

All kinds of things such as that the Smeets sent over to the McClungs just to show they were neighborly. And one fall, at bean harvest, Marvin offered to lend Tod his new bean thresher, because Tod didn't have one.

"How much you-all want for the use?" Tod asked him.

"Nothin'. We're neighbors, ain't we?"

Now the McClungs and Smeets kept visiting each other and chewing the rag, and always Faybelle would brag on Earlene's baby.

"You know," Tod said once while he was dancing Luke Junior on his knee. "I sure hope Sudie and T. J. will git 'em a big boy or girl. I got me a hankerin' to be a granddaddy."

When Tod said that Virgie looked at Marvin, and they both went red; and Earlene glanced over at old Luke and they both lowered their heads to look at the floor. And after, while Tod was alone with Faybelle, he got rambunctious.

"Pshaw!" said Faybelle. "They didn't mean nothin'."

But Tod was all het up. "Jesus Christ," he said. "The way they looked, it seemed they figgered I couldn't be a granddaddy if I wanted to."

During those three long years letters from Sudie came mighty infrequent. Sometimes a card would come from Konawa, or Pruitt City, or Borger, and say, "We are fine, hope you are the same;" and when a letter came it would say that Sudie was working as a hasher in a restaurant, and that T. J. was or was not working in the oil fields. Sometimes he was tool-dressing, or roustabouting, or on a pipe line, and sometimes he was idle and gambling. But Sudie, she was always hashing for some Greek in a restaurant.

"Them pesky young uns!" Tod said to Faybelle after reading one of Sudie's letters. "They'll git along better when they git older."

But toward the end of the third year Sudie quit writing altogether, and when Faybelle got herself into a worry Tod would say: "What-all you squawkin' about! She's all right, God damn it. She's got a man, ain't she?"

Roddy!

Roddy didn't write one lick of a line to the folks back home since the day he left. None of them knew where he was or where he had been; but because he hadn't shown himself back on the farm Tod figured he was still on the ramble, and if he was getting around he was doing all right.

In spite of Roddy and Sudie, Tod was right pleased with the way the Lord and the elements were treating his farm, his family and himself. He got a kick out of Lyndel's letters and felt she was making strides in the city; Tewp and Jay Boy were honest-to-God ranch hands and ignorant of everything else, except that Jay Boy was right smart of a guitar picker; and Mr. Ralls was making a scholar out of Buster.

At nights when Buster worked on his homework at the sleeping-room table, Tod would get up from where he sat to look over the boy's shoulder and see for himself what he was doing.

"What's that?" Tod asked, putting his finger on a pink place on the map in Buster's geography book.

"That's Portugal," Buster told him. "That pink country is Portugal."

So Tod figured that the feller who did the lettering on that map was an honest-to-God scribe, and the guy that made Portugal pink sure knew his onions, and that he would whip any man who said different.

## Chapter Nine

IT WAS a big turn in Tewp McClung's life the day he threw down his hoe in the field and said, "The hell with it." That was in the summer of 1932, while the family was battling weeds along the bean rows—all hoeing except Tod, who rode the cultivator and got those old hard-tails to perambulating and scratching up the earth.

That was the day Scatterwhiskers, the cowboy from over at Dan Blakey's, drove up in his Ford car, right to the field fence, and honked his horn to attract attention. And when he saw that nobody gave him mind he said, "God damn," and got out and walked over to where Tewp swung his hoe over some pesky tumbleweeds. Scatterwhiskers told Tewp that Floyd, Dan Blakey's second cowpuncher, had quit his job and gone to Texas, where he hoped to land a job with the Matadors—their Hartley County ranch—and that Dan was sure in need of a cowboy to take Floyd's place. Scatterwhiskers reckoned Tewp might like the job, so Dan had sent him over to see about it.

When Scatterwhiskers said that, Tewp didn't even give the matter extra consideration, because he just threw down his hoe and said, "The hell with it."

Tewp didn't say that about the job at Dan Blakey's, for a fact; he meant the beans and the hoe and the plowed-up field—because he now had the chance to become an honest-to-God cowpuncher, and he was shed of bean-chopping for life.

To the folks working in the rows he said, "So long." That was what he said, just "So long." Then he and Scatterwhiskers walked over to where Tod was driving the mules and calling them bastards. When Tod pulled the lines to the team and said, "Whoa," Tewp opened up and told his daddy he was going to work for Dan Blakey.

"All right, son," said Tod. "I reckon I can spare you. Main thing is if you-all think takin' the job is worth your while. How much is Dan goin' to pay?"

"Forty a month and chuck," Tewp told him.

"For a fact," agreed Scatterwhiskers.

"Then take it, son," Tod said, taking up the lines. "There's money for you, and I can spare your he'p." Then he smacked the mules on their butts with the lines and went to cultivating beans, while Tewp and Scatterwhiskers drove to the house to get the riding out-fit and bedroll together.

Tewp shed himself of his field shoes and put on his cowboy boots, which he aimed to wear for the rest of his life. He had a brand-new saddle which was made in Amonett's shop in Roswell; it had a nickel horn, wide swell, double rig, low cantle—and it cost Tewp ninety dollars. Scatterwhiskers said he reckoned it was a sweet little saddle in which to ride those old bronc's down.

So Tewp tied up his blankets in the canvas tarp and loaded the roll in Scatterwhiskers' car, along with his saddle, bridle, Navajo blanket, chaps, and spurs. Then they two drove off to the Salt Lakes country and Dan Blakey's ranch.

As they drove into the ranch yard Tewp noticed a girl—a damn pretty girl—walking toward the house.

"Who-all?" asked Tewp.

Scatterwhiskers winked. "That's Carol," he said, "Dan Blakey's daughter. She's got right smart of a bee in her heart for me, but she won't say nothin' or admit it. But I can tell by lookin' into her sweet little old eyes."

"She sure's good-lookin'," said Tewp.

"You're damn whistlin'; and, boy, she thinks a heap of me, too. She don't say nothin' and treats me like dirt. Sweet lil ol' mama!" The whiskery cowboy swept his paw over the scene about him. "See this spread? . . . See that girl? . . . Boy, why do you think I've been punchin' cows for old Dan these last five years and toleratin' his crowbait horses? When the Babbitts in Arizona, the Matadors in Texas, and even the Prince of Wales up in Canada have been writin' me to go and work for 'em at double wages! I won't quit old Dan, though, 'cause he's the only son of a bitch who gives a damn about me."

"I thought you just said Carol did," said Tewp.

"Carol who?"

"Carol. Dan's daughter."

"Sure she does, but she won't admit it."

Tewp remembered reading quite a few stories in the western love magazines about cowboys marrying the boss's daughters, but somehow he couldn't see Carol taking any sort of a shine to Scatterwhiskers.

"She won't brag on me," said Scatterwhiskers, as they drove to the saddle shed beside the horse corral to unload Tewp's riding outfit, "but deep down in her sweet little old heart she loves me and adores the very ground the bronc's I ride lope over. Why? 'Cause I'm a man of ideals, that's why! . . . She won't let on, though; she'll cuss me out and order me around and treat me like I was a greasy Mexican—but it's just a *pretend*. Don't pay her no mind."

Tewp McClung thought he was some punkins that night when he put his riding outfit along with Scatterwhiskers' in the saddle shed and threw his bedroll on the floor of the bunkhouse. He was now an honest-to-God cowpuncher, and he didn't have to look up to any man except Scatterwhiskers and Dan Blakey, and no woman but Carol, Mrs. Blakey, and old lady Snyder, the cook. He was working for wages on a sixty-section outfit with no farm about it but a hay meadow, and no more would he have to hoe beans in Tod McClung's field—that field on the two-bit McClung ranch. Tod might be Tewp's daddy all right, he thought, but he wanted no more truck with any two-bit outfit now that he was drawing wages from old Dan Blakey.

That's what Tewp thought, and he thought like an honest-to-God cowpuncher.

While Scatterwhiskers was in the bunkhouse fixing himself up for supper, washing his hands and combing kinks from his hair, Tewp took a walk in the yard.

There he met Carol.

"Hullo," said Carol. "Is he drunk?"

"Who?" asked Tewp.

"That louse."

Tewp thought she was a hell of a pretty girl. She was brown-headed, and most of the boss's daughters in the magazines were blonde. He knew because he saw their pictures on the covers all colored up. But he could go for her, he thought, brown or blonde.

"Listen," said Carol. "You're working for Dad, and you will find he will treat you right. Don't let that skunk lead you into trouble."

With that Carol walked away.

Tewp returned to the bunkhouse where Scatterwhiskers was all fixed up ready for chuck. On the way he got to studying on Carol.

She thinks a heap of him, he thought. That rough talk is only a *pre*tend. Scatterwhiskers is an honest-to-God bronc'-peeler and a good old boy. No girl could resist falling for a cowpuncher, Tewp figured.

Old lady Snyder, the cook, fixed the boys beans, fried potatoes, and steak—and biscuits far better than Faybelle knew how to make. The cowboys ate in the kitchen along with her; but Dan Blakey, his missus, and Carol did some fancy dining in the ranch living room, eating jelly-bean chuck at a table covered with a white cloth.

Mrs. Snyder was fat and always joshing; she had a red face and talked a plenty. She had only one eye; the other, folks said, she lost up on the Texas Panhandle because she got into a fuss with somebody; but it didn't keep her from doing a lot of talking and cooking.

"I've cooked for cowboys all my life," said old lady Snyder to the boys while she chewed steak, "and I've always found 'em windy and full of hot air. They're always blabbin' off about somethin' they don' savvy. They're smart-alecky and ignorant. They ain't no good. But, Lord, I love 'em better than any other humans, and I like 'em to call me 'Mother.' "

"Mother," said Scatterwhiskers, eating beans and trying to satisfy the old lady.

"Yes, and you're the sorriest of the lot. You don't know nothin' and you blab a plenty."

"I know all about cattle and horses, and that's all I need to know," Scatterwhiskers said. "I've follered the chuck wagon all my weary life."

"Yes, and I reckon you have!" said the old lady Snyder, real rambunctious. "You follered it all the way from Texas out here into Mexico; and whenever the wagon stopped you caught up with it and got your whiskery chin into the bean pot. . . . The good Lord knows I've cooked for some mighty big outfits in my day and time, but I never thought I'd come down to cookin' for a doggone no-account bean-eater."

When Tewp and Scatterwhiskers lay down on their beds to smoke after supper, Dan Blakey's top hand said: "All the women hate me. I'm just a poor lonesome cowboy."

"Even Carol?" asked Tewp.

"She treats me rough, but it's only a *pretend*," Scatterwhiskers told him. He had forgotten Carol among all the women who hated him.

They puffed on their cigarettes.

"But by God there was a sweet little old mama down in Roswell who thought I was the cat's eyebrows," continued Scatterwhiskers. "She thought enough of me to send me her pitcher and a lovin' note on it, by golly. . . . Sweet lil ol' kitty cat, doggone her!"

He lay there looking thoughtful for a minute, then he went to his war bag and brought out a picture of a girl to show Tewp.

"There's my sweet mama, and she thinks a heap of little old me," said Scatterwhiskers, with a heap of pride in his voice.

Tewp looked at the picture. It was one of those three-for-a-dime three-minute photos you get at carnivals, and the girl wasn't so hell-fired pretty. She was bleary-eyed and sort of worn-out looking; she seemed as though she stayed up late of nights, and was no spring chicken at that.

"Where'd you-all find this sweet mama?" asked Tewp.

"In Roswell, one time I went down there in my Ford car," Scatterwhiskers said, fixing to give Tewp all the romantic details. "She worked in a sportin' house."

"She looks kind of that way," commented Tewp.

"You bet. . . . I had a heap of money on me at the time, and I was out for fun, so I asked a feller at the pool hall where a nice respectable sportin' house was that would cater to the likes of me, and he said there was a pink-colored house on Virginia Street that was first class. The landlady had four chippies in at the time, he said, so I got me down there to look 'em over."

Tewp listened to Scatterwhiskers tell about this sweet mama.

"The landlady met me at the door and I said, 'Howdy,' and she said, 'It's a fine day,' and I said, 'It sure is,' and then she trotted out the whores. . . . And boy! Right there is where I met that sweet little kitty cat you-all are lookin' at in the pitcher."

Tewp still thought she didn't look like much.

"So I said to the landlady: 'I got me some money and a Ford car, and I'd like to take this little old gal here out for a ride and some eats, because I'm a poor lonesome cowboy come to town.' Then she and the whore got to whisperin' to themselves, and finally the landlady said to me: 'It will cost you fifteen smackers which you'll give me right now.' So I said, 'All right,' and after dolin' out fifteen bucks me and the sweet mama went for a ride."

"God damn!" said Tewp.

"But wait," went on Scatterwhiskers. "That ain't all that sweet thing cost me. 'Cause I took her into a restaurant and bought her chuck, and she ordered the best they had 'cause she figgered I had the cash and knew how to spend it."

Tewp figured that Scatterwhiskers was a he-rounder and had a way with the girls.

"Then she said she wanted to dance, and we went to a place where there was a dance; and every time she wanted a dollar, or two dollars, or five dollars to put in her stockin', I gave it her without a fuss; and all the time I knew she was takin' a sure enough shine to me."

"If I had a sister like that," said Tewp, "and knew she was a chippy, I'd hunt her down and kill her. But I've only got two sisters, and they're both in good keepin'."

But Scatterwhiskers wasn't finished. "So that night I slept at the sportin' house and it cost me another twenty-five smackers, and the next mornin' when I was fixin' to go home, I figgered that that sweet mama altogether cost me damn near a hundred dollars; and I had another hundred left, by God."

Tewp studied on the brand-new saddle he could buy at Amonett's for a hundred dollars.

"So when I was just fixin' to pull out," said Scatterwhiskers, "that sweet mama asked me how much money I had left and I said: 'A hundred smackers.' And boy, howdy! Did she take me 'round the neck and tell me never leave her as long as she lives! She said she loved me better than any other feller in all the world, by golly."

"I still say," said Tewp, "that if I had a sister like her I'd take her out and kill her and leave her to the buzzards."

"Then," continued Scatterwhiskers, "she made out like she was bawlin'; but I couldn't see her eyes gittin' wet like women do when they bawl. So she asked me for my name and address so she could write to me, 'cause I was sure enough her sweet daddy. And then I came home and worked for about two weeks before she sent me the pitcher."

"This?"

"Sure, it came in an envelope and all I saw was her little old sweet face and that note on the back."

Tewp turned the picture over and read what Scatterwhiskers' sweet mama had written.

*Sweet daddy, come to town. Your mama is suffering.*

That's what the picture said.

"I cain't figger out," said Scatterwhiskers, "what that little darlin' saw in a big whiskery son of a bitch like me."

"Maybe she liked you because you are so doggone generous," suggested Tewp.

"And there you have it, boy! *Generous*. That's me all over."

Scatterwhiskers took the picture from Tewp and looked at it fondly.

"Did you ever see her again?" Tewp asked.

"Never more. Just as soon as I got the pitcher I cranked up the old Ford and drove down to Roswell to see my sweet mama; but the landlady told me she had took out for Amarillo the day before. She'd gone off with her pimp."

Scatterwhiskers put the picture back in his war bag for safe keeping.

"Little darlin'," he said fondly as he tucked it away. "The only woman in the world that loves this whiskery big-hearted cowboy."

"What about Carol?" said Tewp.

"Oh, her! She says disrespectable things about me but it's only a *pre*tend."

And that night Tewp slept sound and happy, because he was a sure enough cowboy drawing wages from the boss of a sixty-section outfit.

When the alarm clock buzzed the next morning it was plumb dark outside; but after Tewp and Scatterwhiskers pulled on their boots and levis and tucked their shirttails in, and had gone out to the corral to do up the morning chores, they saw a light in the ranch-house kitchen where Mrs. Snyder was rustling up some breakfast, and over the east horizon of the prairie the morning star was rising.

While Scatterwhiskers went to the kitchen for the milk pail, Tewp hung around the corral and scrutinized the two saddle ponies held there for horse wrangling. The morning chill was in the air, and the steady breeze that gets up just before dawn in New Mexico turned the wheel of the windmill to a lively hum. The rooster in the chicken house crowed as though he aimed to tell the hens it was nigh time to get out and scratch, lay eggs, and do other things becoming to the poultry tribe; and in the shed the calf bawled like it had a hanker to get its snout among the old cow's tits. There was the smell of hay, manure, and horseflesh in the air—a mighty pleasant and sweet smell when it hits a feller's nostrils before sunup, when the freshness of night still hangs over the prairie.

Tewp McClung drank it all in, and his heart beat happy—ahead lay a day of hard riding on the open range, the feel of a horse with action under him, the prairie breeze smacking his face as he galloped along. It was working up to be a great day for Tewp McClung.

But the peacefulness of it all was broken when the door of the kitchen opened and Scatterwhiskers came out with the milk pail on his arm, when he stood in the light for a moment to argue with Mrs. Snyder.

"Git out!" the cook was yelling. "Git out and don't devil me with your high-up notions!"

"But that's the kind of feller I am," Scatterwhiskers yelled back at her. "I've got me some high ideals, by God, and nobody's goin' to tell me different. . . . I've got high ideals, and it's gonna take more'n a fat cook to tell me not to spit in the milk bucket. . . . Dan will tell you-all, 'cause I've worked for him for five years, that I'm the best—"

"Git out!" hollered old lady Snyder. "You're windy like the rest of 'em. They're all blowhards and you're the blowhardest of the bunch."

The door slammed shut, and Scatterwhiskers came out to the corral with the milk pail.

"What's up?" Tewp asked.

"The old bitch told me not to spit in the milk bucket. Me, with high ideals!"

Scatterwhiskers milked the cow, and Tewp hunkered down as he listened to the squirt hit the pail and silently took in all Scatterwhiskers said as he bragged on himself. And after that chore was done and the milk taken to the kitchen, the two cowboys got out their lariat ropes and fixed to catch them a pony apiece to wrangle horses on.

Tewp's rope sang out and caught the grulla* around the neck, while Scatterwhiskers snaked down the sorrel.

"That's Sunburn," said Scatterwhiskers, as they were saddling the ponies. "Don't cinch him up too tight 'cause he's got a mean streak in him. He pitched with Floyd and ruptured him, but Floyd didn't savvy horses like me. I can handle 'em, by God. Wait, you'd better ride the sorrel 'cause he's gentle, and let me have the grulla. I know more about horses, and that son of a bitch cain't—"

"No, by God!" said Tewp, like he meant business. "I'm ridin' this horse."

"All right," said Scatterwhiskers. "But don't cinch him up too tight. He's got a pitch in him."

Sunburn humped up when Tewp pulled on the latigo.

"I'm the best hand with horses," bragged Scatterwhiskers, "as ever had a gut."

Tewp's heart thumped with pleasure as they rode off into the darkness of the horse pasture, for this was his first day of work for old Dan Blakey—that boss of a sixty-section outfit—and he aimed to hold the job for years to come. He enjoyed the feel of Sunburn's gait under him; he liked the smell of the dewy grass that the wind lapped up to smack him in the face; he liked to listen to the pad of hoofs, the creak of saddle leather, and the jingle of spurs—he even enjoyed

---

* A mouse-colored horse. Pronounced: *grewya.*

listening to Scatterwhiskers tell of what a bronc'-stomper he was.

This was freedom—clean honest-to-God freedom—elbowroom freedom that the cowboy alone knows above any other cuss in the world.

Out of the darkness came the nicker of horses. Tewp's body thrilled as Sunburn answered the call, chewed on the bridle-bit, pranced and ducked his head to loosen the pull on the reins. Sunburn came alive because his pals were near, and Scatterwhiskers' sorrel was acting up the same.

"All right," said Scatterwhiskers, as his horse danced under him. "Let's git 'em. Give that horse his head or he'll pitch for sure. Let's go!"

They put their spurs to the ponies and rode onto that horse herd like hawks on pullets. Scatterwhiskers rode on one side of the band, and Tewp on the other.

God, what a feeling!

Horses running like hell for high water with no tight rein to hold them back; spurs urging them on; the saddle's smooth armchair comfort on a horse at full gallop.

The hoofs pounded as the horse herd high-tailed it across the flat in the direction of the corral. A hundred and sixty hoofs beating the prairie sod—four hoofs to each of forty head of horses. Horses of all colors common to their kind—sorrels, bays, grullas, grays, buckskins, palominos, paints and blue-roans—horses white as the cleanest calico, horses black as the bottom end of a bean pot.

When the horse herd was penned and the big gate closed on them, Tewp felt the silence fall heavy on him after all that action. They unsaddled the wrangling horses and went in to breakfast.

It was daylight by the time breakfast was done with. Mrs. Snyder fed the boys coffee, steak and fried potatoes, beans and cane syrup—and biscuits! Lord, the biscuits that old lady could make!

Tewp ate mostly in silence except for a steady "You-all pass the biscuits," or "I'll thank you-all for the meat"; but Scatterwhiskers fussed with the cook and complained about the chuck.

"Watch out for that windy feller," said Mrs. Snyder to Tewp, who was still wrangling a biscuit with syrup on it after Scatterwhiskers had washed his mouth out and left for the corral. "He's a blowhard and he's mean, too. He's got into more trouble, I've heard folks tell, than I don't know what. He's a sneakin' coyote from way back, and his daddy ain't got no credit for raisin' such as him, though *he* might be a good Christian for all I know, Lord bless him."

Tewp said, "I reckon."

Dan Blakey was out at the corral telling Scatterwhiskers what the boys should do that day.

"Where's the other boy?" asked Dan.

"In the kitchen with the cook roundin' up biscuits. Eats more'n he's worth. Looks like he's goin' to make a sorry hand. Lazy, that's what he is. But, by God, I'll make him come out of it and make a hand. Just give me the sorriest horses and the most worthlessest cowboys; and by golly, when I git done with 'em they'll be top horses and top hands. Damned if they won't, Dan."

"All right," said Dan, "but what you boys can do today is ride out the Red House pasture. Next week, when we round up, we'll make the drive to Red House and brand in the corrals there. Miguel is herding his sheep in the pasture now, but he'll have to move his camp to Yellow Lake before next week. He's watering his herd at Red House, and I told him to do so. If you find him there, leave him alone."

"All right, all right," said Scatterwhiskers, building a loop in his catch rope.

Tewp came through the corral gate and took up his lariat.

"Mornin', Mr. Blakey," he said.

"Morning, Tewp," said Dan. Then to Scatterwhiskers: "And both of you boys stay together."

The ropes sang out again and the day's mounts were caught.

"And leave Miguel alone!" said Dan to Scatterwhiskers, and the way he said it Tewp figured he meant it.

Tewp was feeling fine as he rode with Scatterwhiskers out to Red House.

"Is Miguel still makin' them horsehair quirts and ropes like he used?" asked Tewp.

"Sure," said Scatterwhiskers. "That's all the sorry greaser's good for. You-all heard Dan tell me to leave him alone?"

Tewp nodded.

"Well, Dan knows my favorite sport is whippin' sheepherders, even if they work for Dan, and I've whipped Miguel a plenty."

Tewp didn't say anything. He wished Scatterwhiskers would shut up. He would rather listen to the creak of the saddles, the pad of the horses' feet on the grass, and the snorts they gave every so often.

"Next week we round up and brand at Red House," said Scatterwhiskers. "Dan will git some extra hands to help with the job. You and me will have plenty to do the next few days. There's about thirty head of horses in the remuda that'll need shoein'."

That familiar thrill ran through Tewp.

Roundup!

Branding!

Dust and the smell of burning hair!

Riding hard and chousing critters!

More dust, bellowing, and changing horses three times a day!

Sweating in the saddle with his shirttail out!

He was grateful to Scatterwhiskers—sorry as that whiskery cowboy was—for the good fortune that had come to him. He'd treat Scatterwhiskers like a friend and a man.

"Old Dan knows I've got more qualities than the average feller," said Scatterwhiskers. "He trusts me to run this outfit properly for him. And, by God, I'd take the end of a rope to any man who don't treat Dan right. I would, by golly."

The prairie was broad and wide open, and Tewp felt better now because Scatterwhiskers had shut up for a while and seemed to be studying on something.

Tewp got his mind on Carol and tried to remember if he ever had read about a girl exactly like her in the magazines.

He had, by golly!

The girl was a blonde, not brown-headed, but she was the same girl to Tewp. The magazine girl's name was Viola.

He thought how fine it would be if some rustlers tried to steal Dan Blakey's cattle like they did in the magazine; and how he, Tewp, would save Carol from being taken along with the cattle, just as that cowboy, Brazos, saved Viola in the story. There wasn't much difference between Brazos and himself, he thought, except that Brazos always carried a six-shooter with him wherever he went and

Tewp didn't; and Brazos had a lot of fancy doodads on him and Tewp just wore plain levis and leather chaps. And the only difference between Viola and Carol was that Carol was brown-headed, but she was born that way and couldn't help it. So Tewp saw no reason why the rustlers couldn't come and steal Carol along with Dan's cattle and he, Tewp, ride out and save her.

Of course, Viola's old man owned over a hundred thousand head of cattle and Dan Blakey only had fifteen hundred, but Tewp knew that Dan would be right pleased if he knew he had a cowpuncher working for him who would save Carol from being rustled along with the cattle. He would do some fancy shooting and riding while he was taking after those rustlers, and he'd make sure not to let a bullet hit Carol who would be gagged and tied over a rustler's saddle fork; and it would sure be a heap of fun and he'd get to marry Carol and live happily ever after.

Tewp came out of his dream just as they were rounding the hill by the Red House well. The big galvanized wheel atop the tower of the windmill glittered in the sunlight. Below, in and about the corrals, rested a large herd of sheep.

"There's that sorry greaser now," said Scatterwhiskers.

"Miguel?"

"Sure. Miguel."

Miguel rose from where he was sitting in the shade of the storage tank when the two cowboys approached. There were no friendly greetings exchanged between Scatterwhiskers and the Mexican; those two had no love for each other, and Tewp knew it. He wished he had first met Miguel alone. It would have been better for him. He had no hard feelings toward the sheepherder.

"Git the hell out of here with them snotty-nosed sheep," hollered Scatterwhiskers, sour-like. "I've told you not to water them here any more, ain't I? Or don't you-all savvy English talk?"

He fumbled with his rope strap and untied the lariat from his saddle fork. Miguel knew what he was in for, but that didn't faze him nary a bit from giving Scatterwhiskers his say-so.

"Dan say I can water the sheeps here," said Miguel, like he wasn't scared of Scatterwhiskers or didn't aim to move at his orders. "He's boss of this sheeps, by gar."

That's what Miguel said, and it made Scatterwhiskers mad.

Scatterwhiskers said nothing but took the end of his rope to the sheepherder. He lashed him over the shoulders and across the face, and when Miguel tried to duck and break away that whiskery cowboy spurred his horse on him and let him have it the harder.

"Now scatter them sheep," he called to Tewp. "Chouse 'em out. Scatter 'em."

Scatterwhiskers was boss, so Tewp choused the sheep out of the corral and onto the flat. He figured if Dan should raise hell he would put the blame on Scatterwhiskers and make that ornery cowboy like it. He wasn't afraid of Miguel, if the sheepherder took it into his head to get even; but he had a heap of respect for Dan Blakey, and he would spill the works if Dan should get on his high horse.

After the two cowboys had done their devilment they loped off over the prairie.

Miguel sat nursing his bruises and grieving over his scattered sheep.

"*Tejanos cabrones!*" he cried. "Texas son-of-a-bitch *cabrones!*"

The cowboys rode over to Miguel's camp but stayed only long enough for Scatterwhiskers to dismount, kick over the sheepherder's bucket of beans, pour out the water from the keg onto the ground, and pick up a newly made horsehair quirt.

"You-all don't aim to take that quirt with you?" asked Tewp, still up in the saddle and thinking all this devilment was a dirty trick on Miguel.

"He shouldn't leave valuables layin' around," said Scatterwhiskers, looping the quirt on the horn of his saddle.

Although that top hand found time to dump Miguel's bag of dried peaches on a near-by anthill, he had to make it short because they heard the roar of a truck going toward Red House. Scatterwhiskers swung into the saddle, and the two galloped across the prairie like as though the law was after them.

Where the two ruts that is called a road makes the bend a mile from Red House, the pair of Dan Blakey's cowboys rode up on Cletus Woods driving hell-bent for the windmill in his truck. Cletus was looking for Scatterwhiskers and reckoned he would find him at Red House.

"I didn't aim for you-all to come today," said Scatterwhiskers, as Cletus stopped the truck. Then he turned to Tewp. "You'd better ride up the draw a piece of a ways and see if you can find any cattle the other side of the ridge. Just look at 'em, that's all. I'm anxious about 'em."

"What you-all so hell-fired anxious about of a sudden?" said Tewp. "Dan told us to stay together."

"To hell with Dan. Me and Cletus have got to talk business matters. Somethin' that ain't your God-damned concern."

Tewp reined his horse ready to lope away.

"Wait a minute, Tewp," called Cletus. "Wait a minute while Scatterwhiskers gives you an idee of what's our business." Then to Scatterwhiskers: "You damned fool, maybe you-all couldn't talk Floyd into doin' some work, but here's Tewp and he's a damned good sport. Let him in on it and we can make double. . . . I sold that sorry little critter out before dinner yesterday, and I could have got shed of a couple more easy. All we need is help, and Tewp's the right guy."

Scatterwhiskers looked as sour as stale vinegar.

"Dan didn't see you come in the pasture?" he asked Cletus.

"Hell, no! Dan's gone to Encino. I passed him on the highway east of Lucy. That's why I thought it was safe to come over now."

"Nothin' doin' in daylight, by God," said Scatterwhiskers. "If you-all want Tewp to work with us, and if he can see reason without augerment, me and him will work by daylight and you finish the job at night. Just like me and you's always done, but none of this daylight stuff for you."

"All right, all right, God damn it," said Cletus. "But with Tewp's help we could handle bigger stuff and maybe two or three of them little ones."

Scatterwhiskers said he reckoned they could, and Tewp slouched in his saddle, wondering what-all this business deal was about. He smelled something dirty.

"Then let him in on it," said Cletus, mad-like.

So Scatterwhiskers faced Tewp and told him what's what.

"Look here, Tewp," he said. "We're given you-all a hint that ain't goin' to do Cletus and me no good if you don't see reason. But

you're a smart boy, like I've always told everybody, and I'm here
to tell you that I ain't goin' to have no trouble gittin' you around to
seein' reason."

Cletus let Scatterwhiskers talk. Tewp rolled him a cigarette and
listened.

"I'm a man of ideals, and I treat a pardner right; but when the
feller I treat right don't see reason I treat him rough. . . . You-all
saw what I did to Miguel, didn't you? Well, I did that 'cause I don't
like sheepherders, and Miguel's a sorry son of a bitch."

Tewp nodded like he understood.

"Of course, I only use a rope on a sorry Mexican, but when a
pardner I treat right don't see reason I use this."

Scatterwhiskers unbuttoned his shirt and drew out a blue-steel .45
six-shooter from a holster under his armpit. Cletus grinned and
figured how Scatterwhiskers talked and acted like a real man.

"All right," said Tewp. "What the hell's your business?"

"Tell him," said Cletus.

"Dan's got a heap of cattle, ain't he, Tewp?" said Scatterwhiskers, fixing to let Tewp in on the business deal. "More cattle than
he'd ever miss if a few of 'em should go off somewheres. You and
me work for flunky wages, and it ain't right. Dan ain't treatin' us
right, Tewp."

"Go on. Tell him our business," prodded Cletus.

"Me and Cletus here, and now you too, are in together on a little meat-market business. We—"

"No, by God!" cried Tewp. "I ain't doin' nothin' like that!"

Scatterwhiskers flipped his six-shooter around his finger.

"As I was sayin', me and Cletus and you are goin' to butcher some
of Dan's yearlin's whether you like it or not. All me and you've got
to do is cripple 'em and let 'em lay, and we do that in the daytime
while we're workin' for Dan. Cletus will be around somewheres so
we can let him know where the critters are at; and Cletus will come
out at night, kill 'em, skin 'em, and haul 'em off in the truck. Maybe
we'll have to come out sometimes and give Cletus a hand with the
butcherin'; it wouldn't be a business of high-up ideals if we didn't.
And I'm here to tell you-all that Cletus is the best meat peddler in
Torrance County."

"There's money in it, Tewp," said Cletus. "We'll split the profits in three parts—one part for each of us."

"You bet," said Scatterwhiskers. "And, Tewp, all me and you has got to do is cripple 'em and keep quiet—except to Cletus—and Cletus will do the dirty part."

"It's all dirty," said Tewp.

Scatterwhiskers spat, because he was plumb disgusted.

"He ain't seein' reason," Scatterwhiskers said to Cletus, putting his six-shooter back in its holster. "But we ain't got time to talk, 'cause we're workin' for old Dan Blakey, and we treat him right if he don't us. So me and Tewp have got to tend some cattle up by the Long Water Hole, and they're big cattle, Cletus. . . . Do you git me, Cletus? Big cattle up by the Long Water Hole. And nothin' by daylight, do you savvy? . . . By the Long Water Hole!"

With that Cletus drove off, and Scatterwhiskers and Tewp put the spurs to their horses.

There were a score or more of slick Hereford cattle lying around the Long Water Hole when the cowboys rode up. They consisted of cows with unbranded calves, and a half-dozen long-yearling heifers and steers.

"What you-all aimin' to do?" asked Tewp.

"Attend to them critters."

"Which?"

"Just one of 'em," said Scatterwhiskers, unconcerned-like. "But I'll bet you ain't cowboy enough to tie your rope on that big yearlin' there."

"Hell! He ain't nothin'," said Tewp.

"It takes a he-man and a good horse to rope and hold as much beef as that. You've got a good horse, but I've got my doubts about the cowboy ridin' him."

Tewp thought Scatterwhiskers was crazy; the steer wasn't so hell-fired big.

"He ain't no sucklin' calf," said Scatterwhiskers. "You're on the best ropin' horse on the ranch, but I'll bet you ain't cowboy enough."

"I'll bet I can," said Tewp, like an honest-to-God cowpuncher.

"I'll bet you cain't."

"I can show you, by God."

"All right, go ahead and rope him around the neck, and I'll catch him around the leg so's you-all can git your rope loose. Try it, Tewp, and I'll hold him so's you won't lose your rope."

That's what Scatterwhiskers said, and he talked as though he thought Tewp wasn't cowboy enough to tie onto that heavy steer.

Tewp unhooked his lariat and tied the end around the saddle horn with a strong figure-eight knot. The cattle scampered when the boy rode onto them, crowding up to the old steer with a swinging loop. But he didn't aim to let that yearling get away, because he gave his loop a wide swing over his head and let it fall to catch the high-tailing critter around the neck. While Tewp's horse stood firm on the ground, and the steer danced and bawled at the end of the rope, Scatterwhiskers rode up and roped that hunk of live beef around the leg, just below the knee; and after giving the rope plenty of slack that whiskery cowboy spurred his horse away at a full run. When he reached the end of the rope his horse came to a sudden stop, the tight rope nearly pulling the saddle from the cinches, and the yearling fell to the ground kicking and bawling.

"By God," said Scatterwhiskers, concerned-like, after they dismounted and were loosening the ropes. "We've crippled him."

"God damn," said Tewp, scared to think what Dan Blakey would say if he found out.

Now Scatterwhiskers was ready to talk!

"So you see, pardner," he said. "You-all 're just as much in this business as me and Cletus. And what's more, you ain't goin' to say nothin' to Dan or nobody. . . . You're a damn good hand at ropin' and help cripplin' steers. . . . Tonight we're goin' to see what kind of a hand you are at butcherin' 'em; 'cause you're ridin' out with me to the Long Water Hole, right here, after the sun goes down."

They mounted and coiled their ropes as they rode. Tewp figured Scatterwhiskers had pulled a good one on him, but he was right pleased because he had tied onto that steer.

"Cletus will git around forty-five dollars for that critter cut up into meat," said Scatterwhiskers, "and that means fifteen bucks apiece for us. Fifteen smackers for you, Tewp, not countin' the wages old Dan is payin' you."

As they fox-trotted along, Tewp thought of what he could do with fifteen dollars, and what a dirty trick they had played on Dan Blakey.

They rode the Red House pasture until sundown and then loped for the home ranch corral to unsaddle their horses and do up the chores.

And just about the same time, at sundown, Miguel was driving his sheep to his camp; and as he passed the Long Water Hole he noticed a crippled steer-yearling lying beside it, and he figured Dan Blakey ought to know about it.

When Tewp and Scatterwhiskers finished eating their supper that night, after Scatterwhiskers had got Mrs. Snyder's dander up by fussing with her, they both lay about the bunkhouse waiting for darkness to come around. There would be no moon, they decided, but the night would be bright with starlight. And when blackness fell on the country they saddled their horses and took out for the Long Water Hole. As they rode through the yard on the way out they heard old lady Snyder rattling the dishes in the kitchen and singing "Onward, Christian Soldiers"; and they could see through the lighted window of the ranch living room, and there was Dan sitting in his armchair reading some high-toned newspaper, and Mrs. Blakey at her knitting, and Carol playing the piano.

Now was Scatterwhiskers getting even with Dan Blakey for not treating him right!

By this time Miguel, at his camp out in the Red House pasture, had gotten his sheep bedded down for the night, and he had his kerosene lantern burning in his tent. And although he was mighty sore— as anyone would be, Mexican or American—when he got to his camp at sundown to find his bean bucket kicked over, his water keg emptied, his dried peaches dumped on an anthill, and the new horsehair quirt which he had spent days making swiped, he felt better now that his pal, Ismael, had come over to call on him with a pint of white mule. That made Miguel feel better, by golly, because he had good bootleg whisky to get drunk on and a friend to tell his troubles to.

Ismael had walked every foot of five miles to bring the sheep-herder the whisky and keep him company, so Miguel didn't lose any time in opening up and telling him what happened that day.

"*Cabrones!*" said Miguel when he had done finished telling.

"Their mothers are whores," said Ismael in Spanish. "They are

*Tejanos,* and we cannot expect anything but mischief from such people, I think. They speak too much with their big mouths, those people, and their hands work with the Devil for no good at all."

Miguel shrugged his shoulders and took a slug of white mule.

*"Verdad,"* he sighed, "but what can we do about such people?"

"Kill them!" cried Ismael. "Kill them as our grandfathers killed them for their impudence. There was such good killing of *Tejanos* in those days we do not see any more. My uncle, who lived in Lincoln when it was Las Placitas, met a man on the street one day. That man was from Texas, and my uncle killed him for his impudence. They hanged my uncle, but he is now a saint in heaven, I think."

"They were very beautiful, those days, or so my father told me. New Mexico was more for the *people* then," sighed Miguel.

Miguel held the white-mule bottle tightly in his hands. He hated the thought of it getting empty!

"It tastes like garbage juice, this whisky," he told Ismael.

Ismael shrugged his shoulders like an honest-to-God Mexican.

"They say Billy the Kid was killed by a *Tejano* but he killed many *Tejanos* himself before he died so young. That is what the people say. He was not of them, that boy, but was a good friend of the people, I think."

*"Yo creo,"* said Miguel, who was getting thirsty for a drink of water, "and I would like to see with my own eyes he with the *bigotes* die of a bullet, and I would enjoy it much if the buzzards pick his meat and get fat because of him. . . . But now I would also enjoy a cup of water, for the whisky has made my throat hot and dry."

"The nearest water is at *Casa Colorada,*" said Ismael, "but you will require it before you set to work tomorrow, and if you have a pail we can go. The night is bright, and the sheep will lie bedded until dawn, for there is no moon or wind to disturb them. Which way is nearest to the windmill?"

"By way of the Long Water Hole."

*"Vamos,"* said Ismael, as Miguel picked up an empty lard pail.

It was but a mile and a half from Miguel's camp to the Red House well; the sky was starlit, and the prairie level—and the two Mexicans walked along with plenty jabbering. Miguel was *that* thirsty he had a hanker to stick his mouth down in the muddy brine of the Long

Water Hole when he came to it, which was now only a short distance away, but he figured he could tolerate his dry tongue until he reached the clean water of Red House which was only a half-mile further on.

"Are you not afraid of the coyotes, leaving your sheep alone this way?" Ismael asked him.

"No," said Miguel. "The smoke from my fire will keep the coyotes away; also such animals do not like the smell of me about the camp. The sheep are safe at the camp because of the smell of me."

Ismael laughed.

"And how many sheep are in your herd?"

"More than a thousand."

"*Chee-la!*" Ismael laughed loudly. "Your smell must be great to outdo that of a thousand sheep."

Miguel laughed, too, because although his mouth was dry the white mule had gone to his head right smart.

They kept on walking.

Then Ismael said, "I see a light."

"It is at the Long Water Hole," Miguel told him.

"It is a car, I think."

"*Verdad,*" said Miguel.

They turned their course directly to the water hole.

"*Jesús y María!*" said Miguel, as they quickened their step. "I know who it is. It is Dan Blakey come to see about the crippled steer that lies beside the water. I had it in mind to tell him when I should see him, but I suppose the *bigotes* told him first."

They walked to a point about a hundred yards from the water hole; they could plainly see the three men working on the steer in the light of the head lamps. Then Miguel grabbed Ismael by the arm and held him back.

"Wait," he said, quietly. "I see the *bigotes* and the new *Tejano,* but that other man is not Dan Blakey. . . . That is not Dan's car, I think. . . . *Cabrones!* They have killed the steer, and Dan is not there. He is too fat for Dan, that other man."

So Miguel and Ismael lay low on the prairie and watched those three crooks cut up Dan's steer.

Now what happened was that Cletus had driven his truck around on the bald prairie by the water hole until he found the steer that Scatterwhiskers and Tewp had crippled that day. He had gotten there first—ahead of the two cowboys—and had already killed the critter with the blunt side of an ax. The steer had fussed and kicked but couldn't get up, so Cletus let him have it with the ax. That was how Cletus worked, by golly. And when Tewp and Scatterwhiskers finally rode up Cletus was cutting its throat and fixing to skin it.

"What you-all can do," said Scatterwhiskers to Tewp, "is dig a hole with that there shovel so's we can bury the guts and hide."

So Tewp got out the shovel and dug him a hole.

"*Ladrones,*" whispered Ismael to Miguel, watching from the darkness.

"*Cabrones,*" Miguel whispered back.

So when those three crooks had the critter cut up and loaded in the truck, the guts and hide buried in the hole, Tewp and Scatterwhiskers said "So long" to Cletus, mounted their horses, and rode for the ranch at a lope. Then Cletus gave that old truck the gun and headed her straight for town.

Miguel rose to his feet and he meant business; his thirst was gone and any white mule that had got tangled up in his head was no longer there.

"*Por adonde vamos?*" Ismael asked him. "*Qué ahora?*"

"To the ranch," said Miguel. "I know that other man, I think. He is a farmer who peddles meat about the country. This is where he gets that which he sells. *Cabrón!* Dan Blakey knows nothing of this business, I think, but he will be glad to hear. . . . *Vamos, compadre!*"

"The walk is far."

"If it were at the other end of New Mexico," said Miguel, "I would walk that far to tell him. If that one with the *bigotes* goes to jail, I can herd my sheep in peace. *Vamos!*"

So that was how come Tewp and Scatterwhiskers and Cletus got themselves into trouble. That was why the two Mexicans woke Dan Blakey up from his sleep that night and told him of what they had seen at the Long Water Hole. How they saw the three of them butchering the steer, and how it was with their own eyes they watched Tewp bury the hide and guts.

After Dan heard them tell about it he piled the two Mexicans in his car, and they drove out to the Long Water Hole; and sure enough, there was the blood on the grass and the dug-up earth where the hide was hidden. And Dan was so mad he took the Mexicans with him and drove into town to fetch the law.

The law went with them back to the Long Water Hole, and they dug up the hide and guts. The skin was still soft and bloody and right on the side of it was Dan's officially recorded brand. It was enough evidence to jail any cattle thief in the whole state of New Mexico.

Now Tewp and Scatterwhiskers were sleeping soundly in the bunk-house—Tewp anxious for the alarm clock to go off, because they were going to shoe horses the next day and Tewp sure liked to shoe horses.

But it wasn't the alarm clock that awakened Tewp. No, by golly, it was the law. A law with a shiny badge and a six-shooter. And the law didn't say: "Come on, boys, let's shoe horses." He didn't say nary such a thing. He said: "Come on, fellers, you're goin' to jail." And when the law said that, Tewp and Scatterwhiskers went to jail.

The law hauled them off and then hunted down Cletus. He found Cletus and his truck, and the truck was loaded with freshly killed beef; and when the law told how he had Scatterwhiskers and Tewp in jail Cletus just opened up and confessed all. He told how he and Scatterwhiskers were in on that meat-market business for a long time, and how old Dan Blakey always supplied the beef, unbe-knownst to himself. So that got Dan Blakey as mad as a wet hen, and he aimed to send them to the State Pen if it was the last thing he would do on earth.

The State Pen was exactly the place where Tewp, Scatterwhiskers and Cletus went.

So Tewp didn't get to work on Dan Blakey's roundup as he hoped. He went up the line to Santa Fe, instead, and they cooped him like a rooster in the State Pen. And when Dan Blakey and the law told Tod about Tewp's doings and where he had gone, all Tod said was: "If my boy played that coyote's trick on the man he drew wages from, he deserves a life sentence, and that's all there is to it."

After Dan and the law had gone, Tod said to Faybelle: "Another failure in the kid harvest, Hon. Another pesky tare in a sparse crop of wheat. Why-all cain't I raise kids like I raise beans? . . . Lord, Lord! It takes more than plain dirt farmin' to raise kids."

Tewp didn't get a life term in the State Pen as Tod told Dan and the law he should. He got five years along with Scatterwhiskers and Cletus, and Tewp reckoned five years would pass soon enough. He reckoned the governor would parole him in time, and then he would go back to cowpunching on some big outfit and have no more truck with a bean field. He figured the bean field was the whole cause of all his trouble, because if he hadn't hated the bean field he wouldn't have quit it to go off with Scatterwhiskers, and if he hadn't gone off with Scatterwhiskers he wouldn't be in the State Pen. That's what Tewp reckoned.

When Tewp got himself all set up and comfortable there in Santa Fe, he sat down and wrote the folks a letter. He wrote the letter on a piece of paper with all sorts of regulations printed on it, and in red ink was stamped a number.

Tewp told the folks that he and Scatterwhiskers and Cletus were all set for five years. How Faybelle was not to worry about him because he had a good job making bricks. How he wore a striped suit, and how when he asked the warden if he could wear his cowboy boots along with his striped suit the warden said, "No." And how he had his picture taken front ways and sideways with a number on it. How he was feeling of the finest kind, and how Scatterwhiskers said to tell all the folks howdy.

## Chapter Ten

IN AN oil town on the Texas Panhandle a side alley running south from Main Street gives a short cut from the center of town to the railroad tracks; but most folks avoid it—particularly the field bosses, their wives and youngsters—because it is just not considered right for anyone with a lick of decency to be seen on it.

It is only one block long, and the houses that line its sides are low and squatty; with painted board walls and steel roofs, windows curtained with dirty muslin, doors that open and close seldom by day and often at night.

Just about in the center of the block is the only two-storied building on the street: a false-front outfit of painted gray—gray paint weather-worn and cracked—with a rusty steel roof. It is a ramshackle affair.

On the high false front is painted in dirty white:

*BLUEBONNET  HOTEL*
*Clean Rooms 50¢   Cots 25¢*
*Cash in Advance*

Although this short cut down to the tracks is named Rose Street, the oil-field workers call it "Chancre Alley"; and the Bluebonnet Hotel, they dub "The Old Whores' Home."

Always on warm days an old darky named Abel—a big black one with blue lips and kinky hair—sits on a chair at the door of the hotel, and when nobody seems to be passing that way he tilts his chair back and hums to himself, but when an oil-field man comes by Abel gets up and says, "Howdy."

Maybe the man will go by and give Abel no mind, and then the darky will go back to sitting and humming, but sometimes one will stop and chew the rag and ask Abel what-all he has upstairs.

"Thar's a new un in," Abel told a driller one afternoon in the summer of 1932. "She jes' come in and, boy, howdy! Is she a sweet gal!"

"White?" asked the driller.

"Sho' white! . . . Slim like a movie queen; brown-headed."

"New to town?"

"No, suh! She ain't new to town. She knows how to treat you-all boys right," said Abel.

"Have I ever seen her?"

"Reckon you have. She's kinda thin-lipped; knock-kneed sorta, too. And I tell you-all, boss, dem knock-kneed ones—"

"What's her name?"

"Name's Toots."

The driller got to using his thinker. He knew most of the wild ones in town, but he just couldn't place this one.

"She sounds like that girl that hashed for the Greek on Main Street. . . . But *she* has a man."

"Dat's de gal," said Abel, "but her man's done quit her."

The driller remembered the thin-lipped, slightly knock-kneed hasher.

"And you say she's upstairs?"

"Yas, suh! And she's waitin' for boys jes' like you-all," said Abel. "Lonesome and waitin'."

The driller was dirty and greasy and had whiskers on his face. It was his day off and he was well on the way to getting drunk. He had a pint of bootleg in his pocket, a stink on his breath, and a hankering to get a sweet mama to do some loving on. He had stopped at the right place.

"You say the girl's name's Toots?" the drilled asked Abel.

"Yas, suh. Toots."

"That girl down at the Greek's, they called Sudie."

"Dat's what dey called her down at de Greek's, but upstairs she's called Toots. But Toots or Sudie, she's one mighty sweet lil ol' gal."

The driller had seen Sudie hashing behind the counter down at the Greek's and had often sized her up to be a trim package.

"And you say her man quit her?" The driller remembered her man, too; a lazy lout of a would-be rounder, who let his wife feed him while he two-timed her and did her wrong—and drank and couldn't take it, and gambled and always lost. "That no-account bastard. Where did he go?"

So Abel told about Sudie's man taking out and leaving this poor girl to make a living as best she could.

Upstairs in the Bluebonnet Hotel, Sudie McClung's room was small and had a low ceiling. The window had a torn blind but worked up and down like it should; the pretty flowers printed all over the wallpaper had faded; it was torn in places and showed stains where some tobacco-chewing oil-field man had spit and hit it.

Her bed was a double one, made of iron, and the mattress sagged in the middle—and spread over it was a pink counterpane. When she wasn't working she lay on it just to read love and detective story magazines. She liked the bed then. And when she slept in it by herself—there were nights when she did—she liked it then, too. But often during the day, and most nights of the week, she hated that bed with all her heart.

She liked the golden-oak dresser that was part of the furniture. It reminded her of back home, because Faybelle had bought one just like it out of the Montgomery Ward catalogue after bean harvest one year—one like it exactly, with a mirror and three drawers. And all through the day, when she didn't have company, Sudie would sit in front of it and look at herself in the glass. She would comb her brown hair, and fix up her face with rouge and lipstick, and wonder how long she would stay pretty. She had lines on her face like a girl of thirty-five, caused partly by the worry over T. J. and partly by the company she kept from the time he quit her until now.

She liked to look in the mirror, though.

There was the washstand, too, and the slop bucket sitting beside it. And the stack of clean towels on top of the dresser and the heap of dirty ones down by the slop bucket. And the bottle of Lysol; and the stink of Lysol about the room. Lord God! Sudie hated the washstand.

Now, on that afternoon, she sat at the window looking down on the street—on Rose Street, the alley that decent folks just didn't have any truck with. And she saw the driller standing below talking to Abel, and she figured they were talking about her.

It was hot outside, and the room was not only hot but stuffy—even with the window wide open. So, partly because of the heat and partly because of the company she kept, Sudie wore only a cotton dress, black stockings, and house slippers. She put on more when she went down to the Greek's to eat, three times a day, but up there in the room the dress, the stockings, and the slippers were enough. She needed no more.

While she watched from the window she ran her hand through her hair, and under her dress she felt her body. It was *that* that the driller and Abel were talking about, she thought.

Soon she would see them enter the hotel, and she would hear them climb the stairs. While they were on their way up she would go to the dresser, light a cigarette, and hold it in the corner of her mouth so she would look tough. And when the driller would come to her room she would say: "Howdy, Butch, how's my sweet papa today?" And the driller would give her two dollars, or more if she could get it out of him, and she would take off her cotton dress. And after he had gone she would give two bits to Abel, six bits to the madam who ran the hotel, and keep a dollar for herself. It was the same old routine with every caller she had. She hated herself for acting that way, but what else can a poor girl do!

A week ago, she thought, she would have been sitting there wondering if the driller would be coming up to see her or Mildred. But now Mildred had gone to Amarillo, where Sudie would meet her in three weeks' time, and she was the only girl left in the joint.

Mildred had been good to her and had taken her away from the Greek's when that dirty restaurant man had cussed her out, got fresh with her, and made her work extra time just because she no longer had a man to tell the Greek to lay off. That was after T. J. had quit her, by golly. So when Mildred was good to her she brought Sudie to the Bluebonnet and broke her into the racket and gave her some advice because Mildred had been at the game a long time.

"Never work a town more than a month," Mildred told Sudie just before she left for Amarillo. "Stick here another four weeks, and then foller me up. You'd better foller me close till you're broke in. I'll make the circle, and you'll be back here in six months, and you'll see *more* swell burgs on the way. First to Amarillo, then Dallas, then Houston and on to El Paso. You cain't stay more'n a month in one place 'cause of the law. There's always the God-damned law."

So when Mildred said "So long" she gave Sudie the address where she could find her in Amarillo.

Mildred was heavy and blonde and talked with a husky voice. She was over forty and coming to the end of the rope, as the feller says. But she had saved up a heap of dough and had bought a rooming house of her own in El Paso, and she promised to give Sudie a job any time she pulled into El Paso. So Sudie felt sort of fixed up and had nothing to worry about.

Did Mildred give the Greek a cussing when she found him treating Sudie rough! That was when Sudie kept on hashing after T. J. quit her and just before she was rescued and taken to the Bluebonnet. And the more Sudie bawled the rougher the Greek got, until Mildred came along and told him what was what.

T. J. quit Sudie all over a hasher at the Greek's named Moselle. Moselle—that was the hasher's name.

Sudie was happy with T. J. at the start—when they left the valley in that old Reo truck and took up living together in Artesia. That was when Sudie wrote Tod for the loan of twenty-five dollars so they could get to Tuskahoma by riding the cushions because T. J. had sold the Reo truck and didn't want to take his wife hitch-hiking if he could help it. And when Tod sent them the money they left Artesia and went straight to Tuskahoma, and as soon as they got there Sudie sent her daddy and Faybelle a postcard with a picture of Tuskahoma on it.

Lord, that was a long time ago! Over three years.

They left Artesia because T. J. didn't get along with the oil-field bosses and the Greek for whom Sudie was hashing treated her rough. And because the Greek cussed Sudie, T. J. threatened to whip hell out of him; and then Sudie got herself fired.

T. J. was a real man to her then.

Artesia.

Tuskahoma.

Konawa. Where T. J. gambled.

Pruitt City. A little place close to where Sudie was born.

Tulsa. Lord, what a big town was Tulsa!

Borger. Tough and sassy.

Mexia. T. J. got in jail in Mexia.

Then they landed in this Texas Panhandle oil town.

They lived in a rooming house on Main Street and registered as Mr. and Mrs. T. J. Smiles. Sudie hooked a job with the Greek right off, but T. J. sat around a long time before he went to roustabouting in the oil fields. And besides Sudie in the restaurant were two other hashers—one's name was Moselle.

Moselle was blonde and older than Sudie. She knew more about hashing and had a knack of handling the men that came there to eat. She had a deep voice and was a real hand at calling the orders.

When an oil man ordered half a dozen fried oysters Moselle drew in a heap of air to her lungs and then let it out with: "Six in the grease!" And the cook in the kitchen called back: "Six in the grease, comin' up!" But he couldn't shout it half as loud as Moselle.

It was just *that*—that beautiful way Moselle called "Six in the grease"—that made T. J. fall in love with her. But every time Sudie called "Six in the grease!" or "Eggs, fry two, sunny side up!" she sounded like a wet hen in a thunderstorm and made T. J. dislike her the more.

That was only one side of the counter, as the feller says—T. J.'s side where the customers sit and eat. On the hasher's side Moselle was fast taking a shine to T. J. Most folks thought that T. J. was just a low-lifed no-account; a guy who would lay around for long spells and let his woman feed him and pay the rent. But not so Moselle, because she looked him over and figured him out to be a real man.

Then, too, T. J. figured Sudie didn't have any guts.

One evening he came home shaky all over and badly in need of a drink. He was white in the face like he had seen a haunt, so Sudie went down to the Greek's to borrow enough money out of her wages to get T. J. a pint of bootleg. That was when he was working as a roustabout in the oil fields for a short time, and they gave him a job to do way up on the derrick—high up on the crown block, by golly. And while there T. J. looked down and got him a hanker to jump. But one of the workers saw what he aimed to do and he grabbed T. J. and held him down until he got over his spell. Then T. J. climbed down the ladder and went home.

When he told about it all to Sudie that night she got a fear. While he talked she could see what would have happened to him if that worker hadn't grabbed him and held him down until his spell had passed. She saw in her mind T. J. toppling off the crown block and falling through the air until he went splosh on the ground. And when she saw all that, her loving husband dead and squashed, she got the shivers and went to bawling.

Then T. J. quit talking and went to swigging the likker, and he said to himself, "She's chicken-livered."

All that time—those years—Faybelle kept writing to Sudie and telling her how the home folks were getting along: how Lyndel was doing right well in Albuquerque and how Mr. Ralls was making a scholar from way back out of Buster; how they hadn't heard from Roddy but both Tod and Piddle figured he was O.K. because he was on the ramble; how Jay Boy was feeling of the finest kind and always picking on his guitar. And because Tewp hadn't yet got himself into trouble and gone to the State Pen, Faybelle wrote that he was getting to be an honest-to-God cowpuncher. She told how Earlene Smeet had married Mr. Flowers and got them a big boy, and how Marvin and Virgie came over to see them often; and she wrote about all the new improvements Tod had put on the place.

So Sudie wrote back to say how she and T. J. were getting along as best a husband and wife can, and for the dear Lord to bless all the home folks, and for Faybelle to say howdy to old man Buck Smiles from T. J., and how they aimed to get back some day.

Then Sudie stopped writing and Faybelle heard from her nevermore.

That's when Tod said to Faybelle: "What-all you squawkin' about! She's all right, God damn it. She's got a man, ain't she?"

That, too, was the time T. J. nearly got killed while working on a pipe line. The time the pipe burst and his two partners were blown to hash and he went to the hospital with cuts and bruises but no serious hurts.

When Sudie went to see him all laid out on a clean bed and done up in bandages she asked the doctor if he would live or die. She was *that* anxious.

The doctor said: "He'll be all right. We'll fix him up so that he will be as good a man as he was before. Not more than three weeks at the most."

Then Sudie felt better and said, "Praise the Lord."

Moselle came to see T. J. at the hospital, too. She brought him cigarettes and magazines and talked loving words to him when nobody was around. And when T. J. asked her to yell "Six in the grease," just like he loved to hear it, she filled her lungs with air and let fly so you could hear it way down the passages of the hospital. Then the nurse came and told her to shut up because there were sick people around.

When the doctor let T. J. out of the hospital he told him he could go back to work because he was just as good a man as he was before. But when T. J. came back to the rooming house he told Sudie that he was a crock from the heels up and would never be able to work again. Then Sudie hugged T. J.'s neck and told him not to worry about nary a thing, because she would *do* for him as a loving wife should.

Shortly after T. J. left the hospital the same doctor came to the restaurant for an order of ham and eggs, and after Sudie had called "Ham and—sunny side up!" he asked her if T. J. had gone back to work.

"No," said Sudie. "He cain't; he says he ain't fit."

"That's funny," said the doctor. "When I dismissed him from the hospital he was in first-class condition. He ought to be working."

"He cain't," said Sudie.

The doctor seemed to be thinking for a minute while Sudie stood there and chewed on her pencil. Then he said:

"I think I know his trouble."

"What?" Sudie asked.

"Chronic inertia."

"What's that?"

"A very common complaint," said the doctor. "Particularly in the southern states. An epidemic has been raging for generations among the mountain people of Georgia. The patient has a feeling that he must lie on his back when normal people are up and doing something; and the mere thought of work gives him a pain in the pit of his stomach."

So Sudie told the doctor that what he said was wrong with T. J.

was the honest God's truth, because that was just the way T. J. acted.

Then one morning she came to work and the Greek told her that Moselle had quit. Sudie was glad to know that because she didn't like too well the attention T. J. was giving that hasher, and figured Moselle was the cause of a lot of the cussings her man was giving her lately.

And because Moselle had gone Sudie felt a heap better that day at the restaurant.

When she got home to the rooming house after work that day she found the room empty of T. J. She figured he would be down at the pool hall gambling, so she didn't give it any more mind. But it wasn't until she went to the dresser to do her hair that she found the letter stuck in the corner of the mirror.

The letter was from T. J.

> Mrs. Smiles
> Dere Frend
> Goodby forever. I am quitting you all for Moselle. We luv each other derely. We ar going way. I aint telling the foks back home I quit you all. But if you want to tell the old man I am a sun of a bich you can.
>
> Yours truly
> Your Husband
> Mr. T. J. Smiles

That's what the letter said. So Sudie bawled and fussed, but went on hashing for the Greek.

When the Greek heard tell that T. J. had quit Sudie he began to get fresh. One time when Sudie finished up her shift for the day she went to the side room to change from her uniform into her street dress, and while she was there in her slip the Greek walked in on her and got fresh. Only when Sudie told him she would scream and raise a fuss did he go away because there were customers in the restaurant and he figured any kind of a racket might hurt his trade.

He went back to his place by the cash register and let Sudie be.

From then on he treated Sudie real mean; and once, after he had cussed her out and she was bawling, Mildred came in and asked Sudie, "What's up?"

So that night Mildred went over to talk with Sudie at the room-

ing house, and she said how she had had the same kind of trouble
with men herself, a long time ago, but there wasn't a single man on
earth could get her down in this day and time.

"You'll find," Mildred told Sudie, "that wherever you go the men
are low-down and no-account and will treat you rough just because
you're a poor country girl tryin' to get along in a wide wicked world.
But I cured that, and I don't mean maybe. I learned to take their
cussin' and lovin' together and make a *pre*tend to like it. But all the
time I aimed to make 'em pay for the pleasure with the coin in their
pockets earned by the sweat of their brows. When I was young and
green like you I bawled a plenty when a man got done havin' his
fun with me, but I dried my eyes with his dollar bills. Now I know
enough to take his money and cuss him out for change. You'll get
the same as me in time, kid, and that's all I can promise you."

And Sudie looked into Mildred's eyes and saw they hadn't any
worry or care in them; and Mildred's mouth was hard and ready to
open any time and call a man the things he deserves.

"I threw heart love and teardrops down the sewer with my virginity. In time you'll get the same as me, kid," Mildred promised, so as
to cheer Sudie up.

Sudie packed up and quit the Main Street rooming house for the
Bluebonnet Hotel; she quit the Greek, too, and figured that if he
wanted to get fresh with her now he could come around to where
she stayed and pay for it.

"From now on your name is Toots," Mildred told her.

So on the afternoon in midsummer she looked down on the driller
talking to Abel. And over their heads, and over the roofs of the
town, she saw the plains stretch out flat and unbroken except for
oil derricks along the sky line. And the sky line reached out to the
southwest where the Rock Island Railway followed it to New Mexico
and the bean country.

As it was midafternoon she reckoned how all the folks back there
would be out chopping weeds in the bean field. How Tod was riding
his cultivator and singing to the mules; and how all those hoeing in
the rows would be listening to Piddle telling windies of his past
doings, or maybe Piddle had taken it into his head to shut up and
say nary a word. She figured how she would like to be there with

them, but had promised herself she would never see those folks again. She couldn't go back on a promise to herself and Mildred. Because she was to meet Mildred in Amarillo in three weeks and follow her to the big cities beyond; and how she would make the oilmen, the cowboys, the farm hands, the rounders, and the pimps pay for their pleasure.

When she looked down on the street she saw that Abel and the driller were no longer there and talking; then she heard them climbing the stairs.

"The dirty low-life is comin' now," she said to herself.

She lit a cigarette and put it in the corner of her mouth so she would look tough when the driller came in.

When Abel rapped at her door she opened it to let the driller in. He sat down on the bed with her and acted real friendly. She felt in his pockets to see if any money clinked or there was a billfold about him, and he squirmed and giggled because he was plumb goosy. She said she thought he was real handsome and looked like a good sport. She held her hand over her nose because he stank of oil and sweat and grease and whisky. But after he gave her two dollars and she had stuck the bills in the garter of her stocking she let him kiss her.

"I'll bet you're just a sweet, generous old papa come to his sweet mama," she told the driller.

And, by golly, she hit the nail right on the head that time—because that driller was just a big lonesome sweet daddy out for a good time.

## Chapter Eleven

IT WAS getting nigh time for bean harvest on Tod McClung's ranch. That is, September had come around and frost was just a mite over a month away, and he had to get his crop pulled, threshed, and sacked before the cold hit, or the season's work would come to nothing but a heap of grief. And so far Tod had harvested no grief from off the soil.

Why?

Because Tod was an honest-to-God dirt farmer. That's why.!

So it came a day early in the month that Tod decided to take Faybelle and drive to Vaughn in the pickup so he could get the machinery parts needed for the harvest—new parts to replace those worn on the row binder so that the corn crop could be gotten in without any fuss, rivets and bits of spare leather to patch up the harness for the mules, things Jay Boy said he needed for tinkering on the tractor so he could make it percolate like the Case people aimed for a Case tractor to percolate.

Piddle and Jay Boy said they would hold down the ranch while Tod and Faybelle were gone and not let anybody run away with it. And because Lyndel had gone back to Albuquerque after her summer vacation and Buster was off for the day getting education from Mr. Ralls, only Piddle and Jay Boy were left to hold down the ranch and do up the odd chores there were to do.

So Tod said to his old lady, "Let's go," and they got in the pickup and headed straight for Vaughn.

The Ford skidded over the prairie like no man's business until it got a couple miles southwest of Vaughn, when Tod had to slam on the brakes at a grade-crossing on the railroad because he heard a train hoot and toot to the north, telling him that he had better stop or it would make hash of the pickup, Faybelle, and him too.

He stopped and waited for the train to pass; because it was that old Golden State Limited on its high horse, and the engineer was twisting her tail on to Carrizozo, and on and on plumb into California.

While they waited for the train to pass by, they sat there saying nary a word. In fact Faybelle had kept her mouth shut as tight as a jailhouse for five miles back; and Tod had kept looking at her and reckoned she was thinking about something and decided it was best to let her be. If she wanted to think—well, hell, let her think. That's what Tod reckoned.

So that Golden State came on.

Just before it came to the crossing the engineer gave the whistle a toot—and it kept on tooting until the big black engine came right in front of Tod and Faybelle sitting there in the pickup. The engineer leaned out of his cab and waved to them as he passed.

Lord, Lord! Did those drivers roll and those side rods clank!

Then went by the big tender, on the side of which was written plain, so you could see it way off, SOUTHERN PACIFIC LINES.

Then came the baggage cars, the coach, the chair cars, the diner, the Pullmans, and the observation. And right at the end of the observation platform, the very tail end of the train, was the big glass do-johnny that had "Golden State" written on it, and in the middle of the circle was a bunch of oranges in a picture that made Tod plumb hungry just to look at them. Standing on the platform were some dudes. They wore suits.

When the train passed on Tod stepped on the starter to get the pickup going, and at the same time he looked at Faybelle.

"What you-all so quiet about, Hon?" he asked.

"Thinkin'," said Faybelle.

"What-all about?"

"Just wonderin'."

"What?"

"Wonderin' where our boy is. How he feels and what he's doin'. Roddy."

"I wonder, too," said Tod.

If they only knew it then, the answer to their wondering had something to do with the train that had passed. For, at that very minute, six hundred or so miles down the line, in a desert town west of Tucson, Arizona, a sort of dressy-looking hobo slid down from where he had been sitting on the freight platform of the Southern Pacific station, and walked toward the waiting room and ticket window. It was Roddy McClung.

The door of the waiting room squeaked as Roddy opened it. It could do with a touch of oil. And the room itself smelled of stale tobacco smoke, and the seats along the wall were shiny with wear. It wasn't passengers sitting in them that had made the seats shiny— only a few came to or left the one-horse station—but loafers who came to sit and gas. And inside the ticket office the agent was tapping away at the telegraph and the light from his electric lamp shone on his face below the eyeshade, and he seemed as though he would give Roddy no mind until he had the message he was sending done finished with.

Then the agent got up and said, "Hullo."

Roddy said, "Howdy," and the agent waited for him to speak his wants.

"When does the Golden State git in—westbound?" Roddy asked.

"You'll have to wait all day for that train—Number 3," said the agent. "Right now she's way back in New Mexico somewhere. Where you going?"

"To Los Angeles. I aim to see that old Pacific Ocean."

For a fact, Roddy *did* aim to see the Pacific some time before his dying day, and he figured he had better do it while he was young and spry. He had seen the Gulf and the Mississippi River, the Arkansas and the Sabine—now he was going to look on the Pacific Ocean, and nothing was holding him back.

The agent was real anxious to sell Roddy a ticket to Los Angeles because he didn't do that kind of business every day in that two-bit depot in a one-horse desert town. He would like to write a ticket for Roddy plumb into California.

"There's other trains," the agent told Roddy, "the Californian, the Sunset Limited, the Apache, the Argonaut. Why don't you let me sell you a ticket on one of those?"

"No," said Roddy. "I'll wait for the Golden State. I ain't in no hurry."

"Want a ticket?"

"No. I'll wait."

So the agent went back to his telegraph tapping and Roddy walked out in the hot sunshine to loaf about the town.

Now Roddy was not the kind of feller who bought tickets to go riding on trains. He wasn't going to pay out money to the Southern Pacific when the Golden State Limited had a blind to hang on. And although the railroad company didn't know it, freight trains, and passenger limiteds, too, were just made for the convenience of Roddy McClung.

And because the Golden State always stopped at that town, as all the limiteds did, Roddy would hang it as it pulled out, and hell or high water couldn't stop him. Nothing could stop Roddy from getting to see the Pacific Ocean.

He had pulled into Tucson on a freight from the east that he had hooked out of Lordsburg. Then a truck on the highway brought him from Tucson to this dinky town. All that freight-train stuff was too slow for Roddy, by golly, and it got his suit and jelly-bean hat all sooty and mussed up. He liked to grab the limiteds best, he thought; with the high moguls—although they sat in the Pullmans talking high-up business and about Shakespeare and such, while he, Roddy, hung on the blind. But he was on the ramble and getting around, and he was doing of the finest kind.

But, as the agent said, the Golden State was way back in New Mexico somewhere and he would have to kill time around that hot, dinky main-line town until it rolled in. So he just walked down to the pool hall where he would feel at home.

In the pool hall two Mexicans sat on a bench by the wall, with a spittoon in front of them. And what they talked about didn't interest Roddy because they talked in Spanish and Roddy couldn't talk Spanish nohow. But there was one guy practicing shooting pool by himself who Roddy thought looked like a good old boy. And after the guy put up his cue on the rack Roddy went up to him and said, "Howdy." The guy said, "Hullo."

"Where you from?" asked the guy.

"First Oklahoma, then New Mexico, then here and everywhere," Roddy said.

"It's a big scope of territory," said the guy.

"Where *you* from?" Roddy wanted to know.

"Right here. Been here all my life," said the guy.

"Sorry sorta country," said Roddy.

"Isn't bad when you get used to it."

"How'd you make a livin'? I don't see no grass or water. No farmin'."

"No farmin', but there's always the railroad. I work for old daddy S.P.," said the guy.

So Roddy figured the guy must make a heap of dough if he stayed in one place all his life and worked for the Southern Pacific.

"I'll match you-all for a game of pool," said Roddy. "I'm killin' time. I've got a heap of time on my hands, and I need somethin' to do to kill it."

"I'll shoot you a short one," said the guy. "Then I've got to go to work."

Work!

Lord! Roddy was sorry for that feller.

"Where you headin'?" asked the guy while he was chalking his cue.

"Beyond Yuma," said Roddy, taking a shot.

"L.A.?"

"Sure L.A. Then the whole God-damned world."

The guy laughed.

"Takes a long time to see the world."

"I'm young," said Roddy. "Got to kill time livin' my life, just like I'm shootin' this here game while I'm waitin' for the Golden State."

"Pullin' out tonight?"

"I reckon. On the Golden State."

"Won't be in for a long time. Be dark when the Golden State comes in."

"So I reckon," said Roddy.

The billiard balls hit and clicked over the green cloth of the table.

"Better stick around," said the guy. "You're a good pool shooter."

"No. Life's short." Roddy's ball clicked another and sent it into a pocket.

"Thought you said you had to kill time livin' it," said the guy as he took a shot. "It's a crime to kill a short life."

"There's goin' to be plenty to do in it before I croak. I can take it easy." There were just a few balls left on the table, Roddy was pocketing them fast. "I can kill time just ridin' the blind baggage. I've rode more baggage cars on the railroads than you can heap in a month of Sundays."

"And you're pullin' out on the Golden State tonight?" laughed the guy. "I guess that's what the S.P. builds baggage cars for."

"You bet. And when I'm ridin' 'em I'm as happy as a pig in the slop."

The game finished, and the guy put up his cue.

"Then good luck to you, son," he said. "Hang on the Golden State and it will haul you right up to the Pacific Ocean."

That, exactly, was what Roddy aimed to do.

They were switching a freight over in the yards when Roddy walked out in the street. It was westbound, but he let it be because he didn't want any more truck with those creeping turtles. That freight between Lordsburg and Tucson was the last he would ever hook, and he didn't mean maybe.

He remembered how he rode the blind on the Sunshine Special, on the T. & P. road, between Abilene and Sweetwater only a few weeks before. That was a real ride; and he dropped off while the train was slowing down and he walked out of the yards without a dick on his heels, feeling fine and like he had been covering miles in a hurry. That was the way Roddy liked to feel. He liked to kill time when he was stuck over in a town, and to travel fast between them.

Then he thought of the hitch-hike on the highway between Sweetwater and Sierra Blanca; how comfortably he rode in that salesman's new Chevrolet sedan and how he helped smoke up the salesman's tailor-made cigarettes; and how the salesman had to stop at all those stores in the towns between and made him yawn and cuss and want to be going. It was comfortable, all right, but it wasn't traveling. He didn't feel the wind smacking his face or hear the clicking of the rails under him. No, by golly, Roddy was built to follow the railroads and no other doggone vehicle.

Then he thought of how he caught the Argonaut out of Sierra Blanca and into El Paso—how he ditched her right in the Union Depot and anybody would have thought he had stepped out of a Pullman—how he walked through that big waiting room like a high mogul and headed for the back of town.

He wasn't feeling good after he ditched the Argonaut, though—felt like pure honest-to-God hell. A feller in a sporting house in the back of town told him he had better see a doctor because he was white around the gills and looked ready to croak.

He, Roddy, got scared when the feller said that, and he *did* go to see a doctor and the doctor thumped his chest and sounded his heart.

"You'd better stay in the low altitude country," the doctor told him, "and don't do any strenuous work."

Strenuous work! Roddy laughed and promised the doctor he wouldn't do any strenuous work.

"Live here?" the doctor asked.

"No. I'm goin' to the coast."

"That's better," said the doctor. "But don't exercise too much. You have a bad heart."

So Roddy thought the doctor was a hell of a gyp when he got paid for thumping his chest and telling him not to exercise and to get down to a low altitude. Piddle would agree with him, by God! Because Piddle had told him when he was just a kid that doctors were no account for anything on earth and got paid for what they knew and not for what they did.

"Son of a bitch," Roddy said when he left the doctor's office.

Then that slow turtle out of Lordsburg! That switching, creeping half-mile of rattling boxcars that dirtied up his suit and jelly-bean hat! That brakey who cussed him out for riding it! Insult to injury, by God!

That's what a guy gets for riding a freight anyhow.

But tonight!

Tonight he would ride the fast Golden State Limited westward to the Pacific, and hell or high water wasn't holding him back.

So as Roddy walked down the hot street, just walking and thinking, while the sun over the desert was plumb roasting him in his fine suit, he smelled food cooking in a house not fifteen feet from where he was. He suddenly felt hungry and got to thinking of steak and onions or something. Coffee, too. Then he saw the sign over the door of the house.

## HOME COOKED MEALS
## MRS. BUSSEY, PROP.

Now Roddy wasn't the kind of hobo who walked up to a house and asked for a handout or offered to chop wood or mow lawns for a feed. He wore a suit, and gambled for money, and always had cash in his pocket. That's the kind of rounder Roddy was. He gambled and rambled and didn't like to muss up his suit. He wouldn't pay out fare to the Santa Fe, or the Southern Pacific, or the T. & P., because those big companies were rich and didn't need his trade. But when some old widow woman or somebody was serving meals to make a living, Roddy always laid his money down and helped them out.

So, hungry as he was, he went in to see Mrs. Bussey about some vittles.

Mrs. Bussey took right smart of a shine to Roddy because she figured he was a nice young man who took good care of his appearance and manners. She told him she had spareribs that day and asked him if he liked that kind of eats.

Lord! Did Roddy like spareribs!

For fifty cents you could eat all you wanted at Mrs. Bussey's. She supplied meals to the railroad men—because that town was too small to have a beanery—and so she made her living by feeding the Southern Pacific. She was a kindly old lady and liked the boys to call her "Mother."

"Where you from?" she asked Roddy.

"New Mexico."

"What part?"

"Just about the middle of the state."

The old lady said, "My!"

Then she said, "Got a mother?"

"Sure."

"Brothers and sisters?"

"Plenty. My old man—his name's Tod McClung—is right smart of a hand at raisin' kids."

The table was well laden with food, and Roddy had a good time eating. He liked the spareribs cooked just the way Mrs. Bussey had them; the creamed cauliflower was better than any he had had before. And all the while Mrs. Bussey sat there talking and asking questions.

From the middle part of New Mexico.

His father's name is Tod McClung.

That's how much the old lady had found out about Roddy so far; but before he left she would get his whole history or her name wasn't Mrs. Bussey.

"What's the name of the town you come from?" she asked.

"Ever been to New Mexico?" Roddy asked back.

"No. I came to Arizona from California."

"Then you wouldn't know the town anyway."

Wait! Mrs. Bussey would get it out of him yet. His whole history. She always had before, with boys just such as this one, whom she would like to be a mother to and get his regular trade. He wouldn't leave the house without giving her the name of the town if she had to coax him with a piece of blueberry pie.

"And what's your name?" she asked.

Roddy suddenly felt sort of funny; it wasn't the food, he reckoned, but he *did* feel sort of funny. So he helped himself to some mashed potatoes.

"You look white," said the old lady. "Are you sick?"

"I ain't sick."

"It can't be the food, you know. That's not what's making you sick."

"I ain't sick."

Roddy got up; his head felt like it was reeling around unusually bad—worse than when he ditched the Argonaut in El Paso. His plate was heaped with food, but he didn't give it any mind.

He reached in his pocket for fifty cents, found it, and laid it on the table.

"So long," he said.

Mrs. Bussey got up and followed him to the door.

"Are you going? . . . It isn't the food, you know. All the S.P. men say—"

Mrs. Bussey was nice, but Roddy felt so bad that all he could say was:

"So long."

Then he put on his hat and walked out on the street. But before he had taken ten steps he fell to the ground.

"Lord, Lord!" Mrs. Bussey cried as she went over to where the boy lay. "I hope this doesn't spoil my trade."

When she shook Roddy to make him get up and come inside for a nice cold glass of water she found him to be dead.

So the law came, and he got to figuring and shaking his head over the body of Roddy McClung. He asked Mrs. Bussey who-all this dead boy was and where he came from. But Mrs. Bussey was plumb ashamed to admit that she didn't get his history before he died because it sure would come in handy now. Roddy didn't have a scratch of anything on him to tell where he came from or who he was.

"He said he comes from the middle part of New Mexico," Mrs. Bussey told the law, "and his father's name is Tod McClung. I tried hard, but that's all I could get out of him."

"What were his last words?" asked the law.

"'So long.' . . . He said that and died."

The law figured he would have to hunt up the whereabouts of Tod McClung, but that would take time and before he found him the boy would be pretty well stinking. So he called a coroner's jury, and had a box made for the body and aimed to ship it to the county seat, west along the railroad, by the Golden State that would come through that night. The County could bury it, and that's all there was to it.

So Roddy McClung rode out of that little desert town that night. He went west. He rode the Golden State—that same train that passed Tod and Faybelle at the crossing way back in New Mexico that morning. And Roddy didn't have to ride the blind, as he aimed to do; because they loaded him in the baggage car itself. But before he got to the Pacific Ocean the County took him off and buried him in a graveyard out where the desert crept up on that county seat town.

And when the law found the whereabouts of Tod and Faybelle he wrote them to say how Roddy was dead and buried, and told them what Mrs. Bussey had said about the way he died. It was his heart that killed him, not Mrs. Bussey's vittles.

The law wrote that Roddy ate spareribs, creamed cauliflower, and mashed potatoes; and how Mrs. Bussey talked with him while he ate. And how Roddy got white in the face and got up and died, and how that was all there was to it. How he had a nice grave out in the cemetery, and if Tod would like to reimburse the County for burial expenses it would be greatly appreciated.

So Tod sent the law the money the County was out for having Roddy die in it.

And while Faybelle cried and fussed she wrote to the law and asked him if he knew what Roddy's last words were. And the law wrote back to say that they were "So long," and both Tod and Faybelle reckoned that "So long" were just about the nicest last words their dying boy could say.

## Chapter Twelve

MRS. BOB ALCORN—Mary Simonson of earlier days—lived in a little stuccoed frame house in Albuquerque, a couple blocks off Central Avenue on the way to Old Town. The house had a living room, and a kitchen with a dining nook on the sunny side, and two bedrooms. And there was a bathroom with a white tub that looked as though it came right out of the floor, and all kinds of doodads to turn and make water come and go.

The living room was fixed up right pretty and had a fireplace in it. There was a big stuffed davenport along the wall and two comfy armchairs to match. Bob sat in one, and Mary in the other—or sometimes Lyndel would sprawl in a chair reading a book while Mary stretched out on the davenport. Or maybe Bob would get to the davenport first—and go to sleep on it and snore—with his shoes off and his feet stuck up on the arm. But Bob's feet didn't stink, so it was all right with Mary and Lyndel. But of course, if any of the menfolks back on the ranch did that, and took off their shoes to lie and laze—Lord, that would be different!

Mary had a radio in the living room, too—a much better one than she had at the community schoolhouse—and lots more books, all of which she kept neatly lined up on a shelf. And there were two Navajo rugs on the floor, and a table with an electric lamp on it, and a rack for Bob's pipes, and even a canary bird in a cage in the corner of the room.

In the kitchen was a gas range that came alight by turning a handle, and a refrigerator that kept vittles fresh and cool. And whenever Mary or Lyndel washed the dishes they didn't have to pack in water from a well, lugging buckets through the dust or mud outside, because there was a sink in Mary's kitchen all shiny and white. And, too, the sink had a faucet for both hot and cold water, and over it all was an electric light so folks could see every speck of dirt on the unwashed dishes. And when the dishes were all done and dried all Mary or Lyndel had to do was put them in a built-in cupboard with doors on it that kept them away from the flies. But there were no flies in Mary's kitchen; and that, too, was a mighty different matter from the ranch back in the valley.

So on an afternoon in September, when Bob was down at the shop and Lyndel off at school, Mary came home from downtown; and after putting the bundles of things she had bought on the kitchen table, went to the living room and threw a book she had borrowed from the library on the davenport. She had seen the book in the library, liked the title, and borrowed it.

After Mary had lit a cigarette she went back to the kitchen and sorted out the bundles she had brought from town. Some were vittles which she put in the refrigerator and the cupboards, others were dry goods that had to go in the closet in the hall. Among these was a package for Lyndel. It contained a brand-new store dress and a pair of shoes.

Because, only the day before, Lyndel had said: "It's getting close to bean-harvest time in the valley. The folks will be up to their necks with chores. I'd like to be there to help them and stay in Albuquerque at the same time. But I suppose that's impossible."

"Quite impossible," said Mary.

Every year when Lyndel said, "Bean harvest will soon be here," Mary knew that the girl's birthday was just up the line.

Now Mary cast her mind back a few years and got to studying on how much Lyndel had learned in that short time and how she had got to speaking like an honest-to-God city girl. Mary had a hard tussle with her at first, but soon the *ain't*'s and the *cain't*'s slipped away from her tongue, as well as the *you-all*'s and the *what-all*'s, and in time the kid learned that the *g* on the end of the *ing* was there to be sounded. But try hard as Mary might to citify Lyndel's talk, the sound of the soil still lingered in her voice that through her long weary life she would never get completely shed of.

Those years. Those four years.

1929. . . . "The folks 'll be missin' me this bean harvest. I reckon Maw can git Buster to he'p her with the odd chores."

Lyndel was ten then. So while the bean harvest was finishing up and the beans getting sacked, the kid had a birthday party in Albuquerque and Mary gave her a pair of roller skates.

1930. . . . "I guess Buster can take time off from his schoolin'
and help Mama with the chores."

"School*ing*," Mary corrected her as she had been doing all year,
"not schoolin'."

So Lyndel said "school*ing*," and Mary gave her a birthday present.

1931. . . . "Bean harvest again. But Dad has bought the machinery that will make things easier for him."

Lyndel was talking like a born city girl now.

And now.

1932. . . . Bean harvest in the valley. Thirteen years had passed
since Lyndel was born in the tent by the railroad tracks. Thirteen
years since Faybelle fainted in the bean shock and Piddle ran to get
the old neighbor woman with the doctor book. September, 1932.
Lyndel's thirteenth birthday was right up the line.

That's exactly what Lyndel had said the day before: "September.
Bean harvest. I'm now thirteen years old."

Mary got to thinking and replied: "September, and the harvest already in swing down in the valley. But your birthday will not be until
October."

"I know," said Lyndel. "The frost stayed off a long time the year
I was born. That's why I was born in bean harvest and October together. That was the first season Dad had on the land, and I suppose
God thought he needed the extra time for planting till harvest. So
he held the frost back and Dad got the beans gathered in time. It
was short enough at that. . . . But even then we made a crop—the
very first year on raw land. Even with me to come in the middle of
the harvest and lay Mama up. Other years the frost came earlier,
but Dad was a real farmer and always got the beans in before they
were nipped. Nothing is going to get Dad down, because he's Tod
McClung and was just born lucky. The land won't, and he's smart
enough to know the tricks of the climate—only maybe us kids."

"Oh, I don't know," Mary said. "Tewp has maybe gone to the
bad, and Roddy. . . . Poor Roddy!"

Lyndel had learned of Roddy's death earlier in the month. As
soon as Faybelle heard of it from the Arizona law she wrote Lyndel
about it. Also Tewp in the State Pen. She wanted to write to Sudie,
too, but try as she might she couldn't think where Sudie was. That

oldest girl of hers should keep her informed as to what she was doing, Faybelle thought. And Lyndel cried and fussed for a day or so and then eased up in her feelings like a real McClung. Roddy's time had come, and when his time came he went, and that was all there was to it.

"But Sudie has her husband, and I suppose both are doing well," Mary went on. "They are perhaps so busy they just haven't time to write home. Jay Boy is still on the farm and Buster is doing exceptionally well. . . . And as for you—well, Tod McClung has reason to be proud of you."

"Jay Boy will go; he will leave the land. . . . You just didn't get him in time. It's only Buster and me you saved, as Mr. Flowers would say."

"Oh, I didn't *save* anybody," Mary said. "You two would have gone that way of your own accord if I had never come to the valley. You would both have gone to the community school in time even if you had to sneak there like you did to your tin-can-label school under the railroad tracks."

"It isn't so much what you did to *us,* Mary," said Lyndel. "It's how you made Dad come out of the —"

"Homespun. The good old mountain homespun."

"I was going to say 'hogpen.' "

"No. Homespun. The hogpen doesn't apply to farmers in America. Out of the soil, maybe; but the soil is clean and rich, and the life of us city people, too."

"Jay Boy is still that way—he'll ramble off," said Lyndel, sadly. "And Tod McClung won't stop him."

That's how Lyndel talked the day before Mary bought the new store dress and shoes for her coming birthday. And now Mary thought of the girl again as she closed the closet door and went into the living room to sprawl out in one of the armchairs.

A gawky kid now—thirteen—the gawky age. But the brain was there, the looks would come later. Later—looks, clothes, boys, marriage.

"But she'll come back to the land. . . . She's rooted, but she ain't yit taprooted. . . . She'll come back to the land." That's what Tod McClung had said. "Git her away before she taproots, and don't

bring her back." That's what Tod hollered at Mary, rambunctious-
like.

"She'll come back to the land."

"She's rooted."

Mary, resting and thinking in the chair, nodded her head and fell
asleep.

She awoke when Lyndel came in. Lyndel back from school blew
into the room like a fresh prairie breeze. She had her friend Winifred with her—of all her friends, Lyndel liked Winifred the best.

The thump of Lyndel's schoolbooks on the table awakened Mary
out of that afternoon nap. When she looked up the kid was beside
her—tall, but with that doggone thirteen-year-old gawk, clean as
an after-rain wind, all het up about something that excited her.

"Oh, Mary!" she cried. "Winifred went to the movies last night,
and they have a picture showing now that I want *so* badly to see. I
just *must* see it. . . . It's about a farm, isn't it, Winifred?"

"The feature's about a farm, and they have a short that shows
farming in all parts of America. There's even some farming scenes
in the newsreel."

"Oh, Mary!" cried Lyndel. "Just to see a harvest even if it's only
a picture. And folks like Dad and Mama and Piddle and all! To see
horses plowing up the ground and—"

"But you have been seeing that all summer," said Mary. "You
have just come back from the ranch."

"I know, but I *do* want to see that picture. Winifred says she will
see it again, just to go with me."

"Of course you can," said Mary. "Bob won't be home until seven
o'clock at the earliest tonight; so supper won't be ready before seven-
thirty. You have loads of time. Don't you want something to eat before you go?"

"No. We'll get a malted milk at the drugstore. But you won't be
lonesome, Mary?"

Mary picked up the book she had brought from the library.

"No. I have this book. I won't be lonesome. Run along, but be
sure and be home by seven-thirty."

Winifred grabbed Lyndel ready to be off.

"Wait," Lyndel said to Winifred. Then to Mary:

"What's the book, Mary?"

"Just a book I found at the library. The title interested me. It's a new one."

"Is it good?"

"I don't know. I haven't read it yet. The librarian says it is."

"What's it called?" Lyndel asked.

" 'Remakers of Mankind' by a man named Carleton Washburne. I'll tell you about it after I have read it."

"Has it got love in it?"

"I don't know yet. The subject interests me. It's about a pet hobby of mine, I think."

Lyndel hesitated.

"Oh, come on, Lyndel," said Winifred. "We'll get there in the middle of the feature if we don't hurry. I'll know what it's all about, but you won't. . . . Hurry!"

The girls turned to go, and Mary opened the book. While they were going through the front door Mary heard Lyndel say: "Has the picture got much romance as well as the plow horses, Winifred?"

But Mary didn't hear whether there was romance and plow horses together in the picture or not, for the door closed before Winifred answered.

"O God," said Mary, looking up at the ceiling, "just give me five more years of her. Then she can have her romance and plow horses. She can get her man and go back to the soil."

## Chapter Thirteen

"God damn."

That's what Jay Boy said.

That's what Jay Boy said when the wrench slipped and skinned his hand while he was tightening up the last bolt on the Case tractor, after he had done tinkered with it and had it just about ready to percolate.

He cussed like a man while he sucked at that hand—all bloody and black with grease—while Piddle sat on an empty orange box close by, chewing his quid and saying nothing until Jay Boy skinned his hand; then he opened up and said: "What the hell?"

"Aw, these God-damned wrenches!" said Jay Boy. "They ain't good for nothin' but slippin' from bolts and debarkin' hands."

Jay Boy was a first-class mechanic, and he knew he had that tractor ready to percolate. He got up and brushed the dust from his knees. Piddle sat there looking at him, and by the way he shifted his quid to his back teeth seemed as though he was going to open up and say something.

And that's exactly what Piddle did—he opened up.

"Foolin' around with them there tractors and engines, gittin' your hands skinned and cracked with grease, ain't goin' to do your artistics any good, son," he said.

"I ain't artistic," said Jay Boy, still sucking and making a nice clean wet place in the grease on the hand. "I'm a damn good mechanic, by God, but I ain't artistic."

"You're a guitar player, ain't you?"

"I reckon."

"Well, then, you're an artistic. That no-account Buster ain't no good for nothin' because all he knows is isms. But you, son, can tickle that old guitar and make sweet music. And that's better than all the isms on God's green earth."

Jay Boy took a chew at Piddle's plug now that he had the tractor done tinkered with and fixed, so he was ready to talk and spit. That old Case would get turning the belt when the harvest got to moving, and she would twist the pulley of Marvin Smeet's thresher like a tractor should.

"How old are you-all, son?" asked Piddle.

"Sixteen, and a damn full sixteen."

"When I was sixteen I was on the ramble and gittin' around. I'd seen oceans, and rivers, and mountains, and cities you've only heard tell of; and I had yit to do my mechanics and artistics."

"You ain't had any mechanics or artistics," Jay Boy scoffed. "You-all rambled and gambled and got shed of the D.T.'s, but for more'n that you weren't good for nothin'."

Piddle said a dirty word. Then: "You're a damn good mechanic and an artistic, too; but all that ain't goin' to do you-all any good if you keep sittin' here at the ranch. You've got to send your music rollin' in far parts, and the place to turn them tractor bolts ain't here. . . . But you cain't turn bolts and tickle a guitar too, cause your hands'll git stiff and the tune on your guitar will sound like a couple of fussin' alley cats."

Jay Boy felt like he needed to sit, so he got up on the tractor seat and looked down on Piddle all slouched over on the orange box.

"Where'd you-all do your mechanics, as you say?" asked Jay Boy of Piddle. "How come you had mechanics which spoiled your hands for artistics?"

"My mechanics didn't spoil my hands *for* artistics," said Piddle, like Jay Boy had handed him an insult. "They were spoilin' the artistics I done already had. . . . The mechanics was a motor boat."

"A motor boat?"

"A motor boat, by golly!" said Piddle. "And not on the damn Pecos or Rio Grande, neither. I had that old put-put on the daddy of all rivers—the Mississippi."

"Now I'm gittin' to see your augerment," said Jay Boy. "Go on, I'm listenin'."

"It wasn't so doggone long ago," began Piddle. "Just before the war; I'd say back in 1910 or '12. . . . It was when I had a house-boat."

"A houseboat, for God's sake!"

"Yes, a houseboat! And a big one, too. And don't look at me like I was a liar; 'cause I was the biggest bootlegger on the Mississippi."

"There wasn't no prohibition back before the war," said Jay Boy.

"Oh, yes, there was, by golly," Piddle said, and he said it in a way to tell Jay Boy to shut up and let the old folks do the talking. "There were plenty counties in the states along the river between St. Louis and Vicksburg that were plumb dry. Not a pint of beer or a shot of whisky could be bought in any of 'em, and a feller would have the law on him if he even had a sniff of booze on his person. And I tell you for sure the laws in them states were plenty tough—they had packs of hounds that could scent likker a mile off, and leg-irons to shackle him with when he was treed. The only safe place for a ramblin' man was in the middle of the river.

"And, son, I led an easy life on that old river. My houseboat had two rooms: one I ate and slept in, the other was where I did my preachin'."

"Preachin'!" cried Jay Boy.

"Preachin', by golly! I had that meetin' room fixed up with seats and even a pulpit; and a piano painted white, because it came out of a nigger church in Natchez. And under the platform from where I preached I kept the barrels of beer and—"

"Beer and preachin'!" yelled Jay Boy.

"Shut up, son. In all my long voyages I only had to preach once. The preachin' was just a blind for my bootleggin'. It was a damn good blind in that country, too."

Piddle was getting wound up.

"In them good old days I loaded up my houseboat in St. Louis. Lord, all the vittles I'd need for the voyage! And I'd git my black preacher's suit all cleaned up and made fresh. Way down in the hull I had stowed away barrels of beer, kegs of whisky, gin and brandy in gallon jugs. Lord God! I had me a cargo!

"Then I'd start down the river and take life easy. I had a little motor boat trailin' behind but I never used it only to run to shore when I had the houseboat anchored in the river close to some island or bar. . . . Lord! . . . I just sat and steered and the current carried me down. No power or sail on my boat. No, by golly.

"I had me an empty gallon jug floatin' beside the boat, with a line from it up to where I sat steerin' and most the time sleepin'. The jug had a hook, line, and sinker on it and was baited to catch fish. And all I had to do was watch it and when I saw it wiggle I knew I had some old catfish on the hook, and I'd haul it in and have me fish for supper.

"And soon I'd come to a sawmill on the river in one of them dry counties, and I knew all them sawyers and mill hands were spittin' cotton for a drink. So I just anchored my boat and put on my preacher's suit—just in case the law should come around—and looked my reverendest and hoisted the flag."

"The flag?" said Jay Boy.

"Sure the flag! And a bell, too," went on Piddle. "I'd ring the bell and hoist the flag, and the flag was a big white one on a pole and had 'Come Sing Praises' written on it in blue letters. Then the boys knew that old Piddle had dropped his anchor and was there to show them real hospitality.

"They'd come aboard, and we'd open the trapdoor behind the pulpit and git out the stuff that made 'em merry. I had the benches fixed so we could put six of 'em together upside down and sideways, and we'd have a gamblin' table. And there'd generally be one of the boys who could tickle the piano and we'd have a hell of a good time. I'd make me a heap of cash and the boys would go home drunk—dry as those counties were."

"Hell! That sounds all right," said Jay Boy.

"You bet. . . . Then I'd weigh anchor and start down to the next mill in a dry county, and so on down to Vicksburg. I'd never go beyond Vicksburg. By that time I'd have my beer sold out, and the boat would be gittin' top-heavy."

"Top-heavy?"

"I'd use the beer for ballast comin' down, and when it was gone it made the boat lighter for towin' up to St. Louis again."

"You'd git towed?"

"Sure."

"How much it cost you-all?"

"Cost, nothin'. A steamboat would always haul me up 'cause I was a preacher spreadin' the word up and down the river—and they're good Christians, them Mississippi steamboat cap'ns. And when I'd git loaded in St. Louis I'd start down again. That was the life, son."

"And you only had to go to preachin' once, you say?" asked Jay Boy.

"Once. That was the third trip down. . . . Did I have to go to preachin', and I don't mean mebbe!"

"The law came up on you?"

"Hell, no," said Piddle. "Worse'n that. It was a boatload of women."

"God Almighty!"

"We were all havin' a heck of a time. A big poker game was goin' on in the middle of the preachin' room. I was standin' over a hat chuck full of dollar bills and coins, and a guy up at the white piano thumped out music. The boys hadn't really got started yit and were only slightly likkered up. Then them pesky women sailed up on us."

"Did they come right in on all that gamblin' and drinkin'?" asked Jay Boy.

"No. Not quite. Somebody out on deck gave the yell that a boat-load of twenty, twenty-five females was pullin' up alongside to star-b'rd, and then we all got busy. I just opened the trapdoor and sent the booze and cards and poker chips down below. Then we turned the benches up straight and the boys sat down lookin' like a bunch of Sunday-school kids. The guy up at the piano changed his tune from 'Sweet Adeline' to 'When the Roll Is Called Up Yonder I'll Be There.' I got up on the pulpit and started preachin'; and I had the hat full of money there by me like it looked what the boys gave to the collection. Then the women came in."

"Then what?"

"Oh, nothin' much. We had a hell of a good meetin'. We did some prayin' and sang hymns. The old gals said they had heard there was a preacher on the river and aimed to patronize him, and they took in my talk like I was a reg'lar hand at spreadin' the word. I finally got rid of 'em by sayin' that I reckoned the men was worse sinners than the women, and that those on board were in need of some extra preachin', sorta private-like, and that I sure would be proud if the ladies would go home."

"Did they go?"

"They went, all right, but it took 'em most of an hour with all their jabberin'. But they were right generous, and each helped the size of the money pile in the hat. So I shook hands with them all as they were gittin' out, and some of 'em said, 'Lord bless you, reveren' brother,' and another said, 'May your good work see you plumb down to New Orleans,' and such nice things. And when they got out we hauled up the booze and cards and all had a good time."

"That must have been the honest to God's real life," said Jay Boy.

"I'll say," continued Piddle. "I made about a dozen trips and then got a hanker to take out for Oklahoma. I finally sold the boat in Memphis to a *real* preacher who would use it for legitimate purposes. Damn! Did I have a time paintin' and scrubbin' that boat so's it wouldn't have no stink of likker about it to offend his reveren' taste, him bein' an *honest* preacher. He looked it over and bought it, and I took out for Little Rock, on my way west, and there I met my friend Suggs. . . . You-all heard me tell of Suggs?"

"Sure."

"Then about a year later I landed back in one of them sawmills in a dry county on the Mississippi. Just sorta gamblin' and ramblin' around. And out there in the river I saw my old boat with the flag flyin' 'Come Sing Praises.' I went out with the boys, and I'm doggoned if that preacher didn't have the hull full of beer barrels and the benches upside down ready for a poker game. I felt like suin' him for stealin' my patent."

"Didn't the law ever catch up with you when you were in that racket?" asked Jay Boy.

"Never once. I was *that* good a preacher."

"I thought you said you got your mechanics from that old motor boat. How come?" Jay Boy asked.

"Oh, that damn put-put was only good for trailin' behind, and I used to tinker with the engine and git my hands all greasy and skinned and it spoiled my artistics."

"And what were your artistics?"

"Boy!" cried Piddle. "Look me in the face, and you're lookin' at the man who once was the neatest hand at dealin' cards and rollin' dice as ever rambled the whole country out. That, son, takes as nimble a pair of hands as you-all's are for ticklin' that old guitar. So I say, leave off the mechanics and git down to your guitar playin'. Did you know you could git a little canoe and paddle that river up and down just makin' music like an honest-to-God travelin' minstrel? You-all could . . ."

But Jay Boy wasn't listening to Piddle any more. Because an idea came to his head, and he was thinking hard, and the ramble bug had struck him right sudden.

"All you'd need," Piddle was saying, "is a bundle of clothes and your guitar; and you can buy a canoe in Memphis and . . ."

Jay Boy started humming that song he often played on his guitar:

> *And I'll float down the river*
> *In my little red canoe,*
> *And I'll never see my darlin' any more.*

Then he looked up and figured it must be about noon; because Clydey, Tod's new hand, hired just the day before, was driving in his team from the fields to the corral. It was dinnertime. Jay Boy slid down from the tractor seat and Piddle got up from the orange box, and they both walked into the house.

Now the reason Tod hired Clydey as a hand was because he was getting short of help on the ranch—all the kids but Jay Boy and Buster either married, dead, in the State Pen, or at a city school. And Jay Boy was now sixteen and a man ready to take off on the ramble as soon as the bug stung him. Buster, for most of the day hours, was getting education from Mr. Ralls—hours when he was needed most on the farm. And besides, Tod had right smart of a crop to handle, beef cattle to tend, and dairy cows bawling their heads off morning and night with a hanker to be milked.

All that required working hands; and as Clydey looked a likely feller with good manners, no outward sign of ailments, and corn-fed from the Texas South Plains, Tod said to Faybelle: "He ain't pretty, and maybe he's got a mighty inexhaustible appetite; but he comes nearer lookin' like us and the dirt we till than any button I know; so I reckon he's worth thirty dollars a month and vittles."

To that Faybelle said, "I reckon," so Tod hired Clydey on as a hand, and in one day the boy proved to be a team-handling and hoe-slinging fool.

Now late September had come around. The air over the high prairie was the kind that tells a feller's nostrils that frost is maybe only three weeks away, maybe two; and warns a bean farmer that he had better beat the oncoming nip of the first freeze to the draw, or all that sweat that he, his wife and kids and kinfolks, shed the past summer was only to make shirts and socks fit for laundering and nothing else; and that bean plants were tenderer than brass monkeys when the cold hit. So Tod McClung sniffed the air and looked to his matured and maturing crops and figured bean harvest was only a day or two away.

Lord!

Tod had a mighty harvest to handle this year. Because as time went on he broke more soil and fenced in big fields that only a couple years before were part of the cow pasture and in natural grama. Now he had half his original homestead—three hundred and twenty acres—in field stuff. Two hundred acres of that were in beans, the balance to corn, cane, barley, and wheat. And it was the cleanest crop ever grown in Torrance County, Tod reckoned.

Tod was a scientific farmer, too. Because he had a boy called Buster who could read like nobody's business and the biggest words didn't faze him. He knew what "legumes" meant; and "proteins" in stock feeding—words Tod had never heard tell of in the early days. And then, Buster would read articles in the farm papers how some new experiment proved something *could* be done with field crops that folks reckoned just couldn't be. Then he would show the article to Tod, and after Tod had read it as best he could the daddy and son would talk it over and figure out how they could put it to advantage on their farm. That Buster was a smart kid.

"He's takin' the ox yoke off me and puttin' me in fast mule harness," Tod once told Faybelle when they got to talking about Buster.

The kid talked to Tod about crop rotation, too; something that Tod's daddy, good farmer though he was, knew nothing about. So Tod rotated his crops.

"We ought to have alfalfa in the rotation because it's a soil builder," said Buster, "but it won't do any good here without irrigation. But beans are legumes, and if we put them in the right order of rotation they will feed the soil, too."

And Tod would say: "Go ahead, son, you-all know more about such things better'n me. You're sure scientific."

So now, on that day when Jay Boy slid down from the tractor seat after listening to Piddle tell of his past doings, and Clydey fed the team in the corral and went in to his own dinner, Tod told them all around the table that he would notify the neighbors that help was needed; for Marvin Smeet to bring his thresher over, old man Mudgett to lend an extra team, and Tennis and Craze Rufe Burge to fix themselves ready to toss bean sacks. Because, Tod wanted it known, the bean harvest could get under way in less than two days.

So after they had all eaten up their vittles they went back to the hard work they had to do for the rest of the day—all except Piddle who went to sleep on his bed, because he was an old man of seventy-one years.

Toward the middle of the afternoon Tod came in where Faybelle was fussing around the kitchen and went over to the water bucket for a drink.

"You-all ain't quittin' for the day, are you?" Faybelle asked.

Tod answered: "No, but I've got things lined up so I can lay off for half an hour."

Then he took Faybelle around the waist—and it wasn't so slim and trim a waist as he knew it years back. "Come on, old sweetheart," he said. "Let's take a walk out to those bean fields of ours, and talk about the harvest to come and them crops we've done gathered."

Faybelle went with him saying nothing, and arm in arm they sauntered out to the fields.

While they walked they looked back now and then, and they saw the house standing where that old tent was pitched thirteen years before—the tent into which the skunk stuck his nose that night and sent them scurrying out like bees from a hive; where they all slept nigh on top of one another, and where Lyndel—their youngest and finest—was born.

Over there the Santa Fe Railway stretched east and west, where the arm of the block signal rose and fell day and night, and where the freights and limiteds got to rolling and rattled up in one direction and down in the other.

Lord, Lord!

It wasn't so *mighty* different.

But that first little forty-acre field had grown to a stretch of bountiful crop a mile long and half a mile wide. Crops the weight of which Tod McClung had never seen before in all his weary life. No such ever before.

"The cleanest crop in the whole country," said Tod, as they came to the edge of the bean field. "Lord, Hon, I've been a lucky cuss!"

"Maybe you had luck comin' to you, Tod. It was as the Lord ordained."

Tod looked like he was studying on something.

"And maybe it was as the Lord ordained we should have a few failures in the crops of humans we raised. Maybe he ordained that—"

"What failures?" asked Faybelle.

"Tewp, for one. He was a tare that had to be rooted out of the land and put where his kind cain't spread the likes among the useful grain. . . . Roddy, for another. Roddy just withered and died."

"And Sudie?"

"Sudie's got her man, and if he's all right she's all right. Just let's hope he's all right."

Neither said anything for a minute but just looked on the fields.

"Lyndel and Buster," said Tod, all of a sudden. "They're like the cleanest crop of bloomin' alfalfa as ever come out of the irrigation on the Rio Grande."

"There's yit Jay Boy," said Faybelle. "You-all 've said naught of Jay Boy."

"When he's reckoned with, the kid harvest will be done."

They looked off to the field on the southwest quarter, the first homestead field, and they saw Clydey fuss about getting a place to set Marvin Smeet's thresher. Tod's Case tractor would twist hell out of that old thresher when the bean harvest got under way.

Then they turned.

They turned because they heard the music of a guitar coming toward them and the pad of feet on the grass. And they saw Jay Boy approach holding and strumming his guitar, and he had a bundle slung over his back. The boy had a smile on his face.

"Goin' somewheres, son?" Tod asked Jay Boy.

"To that old Mississippi River," was the answer.

"It's right smart of a piece away."

"Not too far for ramblin' legs," said Jay Boy.

Tod leaned on the fence and looked the boy straight in the face.

"You've picked a kind of unhandy time to be on your way, son, ain't you?"

"Reckon I'm old enough," said Jay Boy.

"Sure you're old enough," said Tod. "You're sixteen, and sixteen is just right for a boy to start out on the ramble. . . . But you-all cain't go now."

"You-all didn't fuss when Roddy and Tewp took off. You raised nary a kick with them."

"Roddy took off without my knowin', when the bean harvest was done over; and Tewp said 'So long' when the crop was only knee-high to a grasshopper. . . . We didn't miss them the time they chose to ramble, but we *will* miss you, son. There's hard work to be done around here in the next few days."

"And when the harvest is done with?"

"I'm Tod McClung. I don't stop none of my kids when they fix to quit the land and take their own roads, and I don't fret as to where them roads will lead 'em. Go back to your work now, Jay Boy, 'cause we'll need you to handle that old Case tractor. When the last bean is threshed you are free to go your way."

Faybelle said nothing all this while because she knew that Tod was speaking his mind.

They watched Jay Boy walk toward the house. He seemed content with the thought that when the bean harvest was done he would be shed of the land.

Tod left Faybelle leaning on the fence, and he walked to the edge of the bean crop. He grasped a pod in his hand; he mashed it to powder and the beans came out speckled and dry.

"There ain't much difference between you beans in a pod and us folks who walk around on two legs," he said—aloud, as though Faybelle wasn't there and he talked only to the beans. "And there's millions of you-all in this here field like there's billions of us'ns all over the world; us folks ramblin' around or standin' still at home.

"You're all set now to make more of your kind just as we are; the plants that mammied you are matured and ready to rot so you can take their places in the field next year.

"A bean crop, or a half-dozen humans, or a litter of furry things— anything livin' like you and me—cain't foretell the harvest till the crop is past its growin' time. You fight the elements and the tares that creep up on you, and we battle the pitfalls that come our way. It's six and half a dozen with you and me, old mammy and daddy beans. . . . It ain't till maturity that any of us can figure what we raise is a success crop or a failure. I've had my happy moments and my years of grief since the day I started keepin' company with you-all beans. We've had our short and bumper crops together."

Only the wind that brushed the fields talked back to Tod.

"But this year! Lord God! I ain't never seen such a bean crop in all my life!"

He dropped the beans he held in his hand; they fell to the ground and he buried them in the soil with the heel of his shoe. He looked over the fields from east to west and from north to south, and he saw the pod-laden plants all ready to rip from the earth, thresh, and store in the barn.

Then he turned to Faybelle.

"Jay Boy won't have long to wait now, old sweetheart. The bean harvest can git to percolatin' the day after tomorrer."

## Chapter Fourteen

"YOU-ALL boys git up."

That was what Tod called to Jay Boy and Clydey the morning they aimed to start the bean-pulling; called long before daylight had showed its glint in the east, yelled loud because he stood by the kitchen door and the boys were bedded in a shed plumb across the yard.

The air Tod breathed was fresh. It was fall air; nigh cold at that early morning hour—not frosty, but nigh cold.

"She ain't too many days away," Tod said to Faybelle who was fussing over breakfast, fixing biscuits and coffee, milk gravy and eggs.

"What?" she asked.

"The frost. She's on her way."

But Tod hadn't a worry about the frost, for on that very day Marvin Smeet and Luke Flowers were to come over, and together with the McClung folks they would rip the bean plants from the earth and beat old man Winter to the draw. That was all that was needed for Tod to make the bumper crop of his life—to get the beans off the ground and into sacks before the frost hit: the frost that was sure to come—soon—and a killer when it did.

Out in the darkness the bean fields lay: two hundred acres of them, pod-laden and ripe; acres that Tod depended on, a cash crop to get him out of the rut he was in. Lord! Was Tod in debt at the bank after putting all those new improvements on his ranch!

Harvest would see to that, though.

He'd pull the plants and pile them into shocks; after a few days he'd thresh them and sack the beans—send them to the elevator, and, pronto, Tod could say to the banker: "Don't look at me that-a-way, 'cause I don't owe you nothin'."

So because Tod was deep in debt, the frost was on the way, and it would take the bean harvest to get him out of the rut, they all wasted no time in sopping up breakfast and getting outside to pull beans. Marvin and Luke were on the spot when daylight began to peep.

Clydey harnessed up his team, and Jay Boy tinkered about the tractor that was cold and sort of stubborn to start in that early morning chill.

"Twist her tail and git her to movin', son," Tod said. "Crank her up. We cain't dally."

That pesky tractor wouldn't start.

"Here," Tod said impatiently. "Git up on the seat and monkey the throttle, son, and I'll turn the crank. Watch the ignition, or she'll kick like a bay mule."

He took the crank in hand ready to give it a twist, while Jay Boy did this and that to the controls. But Jay Boy's mind wasn't on that ignition. It was rambling somewhere along the Mississippi, in a little canoe in which a guitar made that good old mountain music.

Tod turned the crank; the tractor engine let out a loud cough and then stopped sudden, and when Jay Boy turned to Tod and said "Crank her agin," he saw his daddy sitting on the ground, holding his arm and half whimpering like a kid and half cussing like a he-man.

Jay Boy slid down from the seat and went over to Tod to see how come he cussed so.

"Doggone it, son," moaned Tod. "You-all didn't watch the ignition. She kicked back, and if my arm ain't busted it's the Lord's goodness it ain't."

He sat and groaned, and Jay Boy just stood. Then Faybelle came to the door of the house and yelled: "What's the trouble, Tod? How come you-all cussin' so?"

"Paw's hurt his arm," Jay Boy called to her.

Clydey came from the corral, and Marvin Smeet and Luke Flowers ran like race horses from the shed where they were getting themselves a pitchfork apiece. Faybelle leaned over her husband and cried: "Sweet land of Moab! He's done bust his arm."

"God damn," said Jay Boy.

"Don't cuss afore the preacher, son," Tod managed to say amidst all his groaning. "Git me to the house."

Tod was sickish, but he got to the house on his own power; and all those good folks followed him, wondering what they should do and how they could get Tod in shape for harvesting beans.

They would get the beans in, though. Tod could just sit and rest, and the neighbors would attend the crop. Old daddy Winter wouldn't molest Tod's living while Marvin Smeet and Luke Flowers were around to get it away from his nip. Old man Mudgett would come over and take Tod's place at the pulling. That was a fact.

Piddle was sitting by the fire in the sleeping room, chewing his quid, when Tod and the folks came in the house. He looked up and said, first getting his quid to his back teeth: "You're green around the gills, son. You sick?"

Tod threw himself on the bed, and when his limp arm gave a move he groaned; groaned loud and mournful until it got Faybelle into a worry.

"We'll have to git a doctor to set his arm," said Marvin. "I'll drive into Willard and fetch one. . . . Keep him still and rested till I come back."

Marvin was just about to take off when Faybelle took him by the arm. She just held him and said nothing.

Piddle stood and looked sour.

Marvin saw a worry in Faybelle's face; he didn't know she dreaded to hear what she knew Tod would say next.

"No, you ain't."

That's what Tod said.

Marvin couldn't believe his ears. "But it'll take a doctor to fix your arm so's it'll git to healin'," he said. "That's the sensible thing to do."

"It ain't sensible so long's I've got a wife to do it. She's worth any doctor."

"She ain't medical enough," argued Marvin.

"If a doctor steps in this house he'll git thrown out. I'll git Piddle to he'p me do it."

Tod groaned again, and everybody figured that all this cussedness wasn't helping him a mite.

"It hurts, don't it, Hon?" said Faybelle, tenderly.

Tod sort of moaned.

"We can all take a hand and try to set it," said Marvin to Faybelle, "but I won't guarantee how straight it will turn out to be after we git done. If you-all will git some rags and sticks for a splint, we'll do our best. . . . Sure you don't want a doctor, Tod?"

"Throw him out!" yelled Tod, like as though the doctor was there already.

Faybelle tore up a nice clean house dress she had done up in the wash, and Jay Boy found some good splints out in the scrap lumber pile. So with these to work with they got to doctoring Tod.

Tod threw a spasm as Faybelle washed his arm, and it took Marvin and Luke to hold him down. Then they got to wrapping and splinting and trying to fit Tod's arm back the way it was.

Lord, what a mess! And a good doctor only fifteen miles away rearing for business!

After Piddle had seen what was wrong with Tod he went into the kitchen, sat down by the cookstove handy to the grate, and took up his chewing. When Faybelle came in for some hot water, she said: "I sure wish he'd let us git a doctor."

To that Piddle said nary a word, but he wondered what kind of a ninny this daughter of his had turned out to be anyway.

The morning passed and Faybelle fixed dinner for all, because Marvin and Luke stayed to keep Tod company. Tod wouldn't eat, though; his arm hurt *that* bad, and he was sickish.

"Reckon if you-all can rest here, Tod," said Marvin, "the balance of us 'll git out and pull them beans tomorrer."

To that Tod said: "No. Hold off for a few days and I'll he'p you. I ain't goin' to lay here comf'table and know somebody else is harvestin' my crop for me; me in no fit shape to work. . . . I'll be all right in a day or two."

Everybody thought Tod was talking plumb foolishness.

"Liable to frost any night now, Tod," warned Marvin.

"Let be," sort of half groaned Tod. "I'll harvest my own crop and be ready to he'p you with yours. . . . Let be."

Marvin sat by Tod's bed and talked with him. The splint Faybelle put on Tod's arm wasn't doing a bit of good, for he pained right smart. Mr. Flowers stayed in the kitchen with Faybelle and chatted with her about religion. Piddle went out to sit on the woodpile, to think of way back yonder. Buster had taken off for school when they decided not to harvest that day. Clydey and Jay Boy just lazed around and told each other big windies.

In midafternoon Marvin said to Tod: "I think we should pull them beans tomorrer, Tod; for a fact I do. We'll send Buster in now and then to tell you how things are goin'. . . . Kinda chilly, these nights. The killer is on the way."

All Tod said to that was: "Let be." Then he said "Ouch!" because his arm was that painful.

"Well," said Marvin. "If you-all don't care so much for your own crop I'll take Jay Boy and Clydey and git my own harvested up. I cain't afford to take chances."

Tod said O.K.

Marvin and Luke left before suppertime to do up their chores at home, after telling Jay Boy and Clydey to get over in the morning and help pull beans on the Smeet farm. They also told Faybelle they would send Virgie over to help at doctoring Tod. When Virgie came she was plumb scandalized because Tod wouldn't get a doctor to put himself in shape.

"What-all's the objection?" she asked Faybelle.

"Tod never did have a like for doctors," Faybelle told her. "Sudie had a rising back in Oklahoma once, and Lyndel got down with the measles right here in Mexico. But Tod would rather let 'em die than have a doctor tend 'em. He's just that-away, and Piddle too."

"It don't make sense," said Virgie Smeet.

"The kids got well, though; right on their own power except for the herb potions we soaked 'em in. . . . We gathered the herbs along the Boggy Creek. They was good medicine."

Virgie fussed at Tod, too, and told him he hadn't the common sense of a coon.

"Maybe an infection will set in and you'll die," she said. "You're a strong man, Tod McClung, when you're not carryin' a busted arm, but times like this you're weak and he'pless. . . . And your summer's work liable to ruin, too."

"Shut up," Tod wanted to say; but all Virgie heard was a groan. Tod was a man set in his ways.

It came about that Marvin Smeet wasted no time in getting his own crop in; while Tod McClung lay up with a busted arm and didn't seem to care if the frost nipped and ruined his own year's earnings or not. Clydey and Jay Boy went over and helped Marvin—and on those acres the threshing machine droned while the nice clean pinto beans rolled into the sacks. All through the Estancia Valley—up by Stanley and down by Cedarvale, east to Encino and west to Mountainair—farmers reaped and laughed at the oncoming winter. But Tod McClung groaned and threatened to make hash of any doctor who set foot in his house, and two hundred acres of the finest pinto crop in New Mexico lay out in the weather, still clinging to the earth. And right there in town the banker was sharpening up his pencil, ready to deal Tod McClung misery.

Faybelle tore the September leaf from the calendar—the calendar that had cows on it.

October came.

"If I was a brass monkey," Tod used to say, "I'd git me to hibernatin' on October 10th, 'cause that's about the time the frost hits the valley with a bang. . . . Cain't trust Daddy Winter after October 10th."

But now.

"I'll be up and ready to sack them beans before the 10th," he told Faybelle and Marvin, when those two talked to him anxiously about the crop. "I ain't goin' to lay here and let you-all work for me. . . . That ain't Tod McClung."

Marvin thought Tod was a dad-blamed fool; and Faybelle, because she was a true-loving wife, thought Tod must be ailing right smart or he wouldn't talk that way. He never fussed before when his family got out and worked in the crop.

He ain't no more Tod McClung than the man in the moon, Faybelle thought, as she did this and that around the house.

On the second day of October, Tod was mighty weakly.

Lord! Was he one feeble imitation of a man!

That was the day Faybelle just couldn't understand what had come over him; couldn't tell for herself until that smart boy Buster up and let her know what ailed his daddy.

Because soon after breakfast that morning, just as Buster was washing up ready to go to school, after Clydey and Jay Boy had gone out to putter around the farm now that they had helped Marvin Smeet finish up his harvest, just as Piddle stepped outdoors to sit on the woodpile—Tod called loud and scared-like, and told Faybelle to hurry to him quick.

"What, Hon?" cried Faybelle, worried.

"You-all git 'em off the bean crop," Tod hollered. "They're eatin' it up!"

"Who? What?" asked Faybelle.

Buster came into the sleeping room to see what-all worried his daddy.

"The speckled apes!" yelled Tod. "They're eatin' it up!"

"The speckled apes?"

"Hundreds of 'em. . . . They're gittin' every bean. . . . Do somethin', woman! . . . Pour some high-life on 'em. Git a corncob and turpentine 'em so's they don't come back. . . . They're eatin' up my livin'."

Faybelle turned plumb pale and fluttered about. Tod was craze for sure, she thought. But Buster just stood; he saw what ailed his daddy—he didn't know all those *isms* for nothing.

"Maw," he said, leading Faybelle into the kitchen. "Let me tell you-all somethin' you don't know. Paw's plumb craze from all his sufferin'. He's delirious."

"Delirious?"

"Worse'n that," went on Buster, "he's dyin'—and soon—if you don't act like his wife and git a doctor to him whether he likes it or not. . . . You've got to be boss around here now that Paw's ailin' and ain't got no sense. You've got to boss this outfit, or he'll die and the frost will git the crop, too. . . . Will I call Piddle and the menfolks in?"

Faybelle looked strong, standing there like she meant business now that she'd heard Buster talk.

"Yes."

That's what Faybelle said.

Right then they heard a car drive up in the yard; it was Marvin and Virgie Smeet, Luke Flowers too, come over to say howdy to the McClungs.

"Yes," said Faybelle. "Bring 'em in. Every human bein' of 'em."

From the sleeping room Tod called: "Git 'em off my crop! Turpentine 'em!"

Buster called Marvin, Virgie, and Luke from the car; he hollered at Jay Boy and Clydey in the yard and told them to come a-running; he made Piddle come off the woodpile. When all those folks stood before Faybelle in the kitchen she was ready to speak her mind.

"Listen to him," said Faybelle.

They listened to Tod.

"Shoo! Chase them apes away. They're eatin' my good beans, doggone it!"

That's what they heard.

"He's craze," said Marvin.

"He ain't got a lick of sense," said Virgie.

"He's dyin'," said Faybelle.

Luke Flowers muttered a prayer. He liked to preach, but he didn't hanker to preach Tod's funeral.

Then Faybelle spoke like a she-woman.

"First of all, I'm here to tell you I'm bossin' this ranch now that my man's ravin' like a coot and cain't boss for hisse'f," she said. "I'm here to let you know the only thing that will save Tod McClung and his year's livin' is for you-all folks to do as I say. . . . If you're all willin' to he'p a he'pless man, say 'Yes.' "

"Yes," said everyone but Piddle, who chewed his quid and looked sour.

"All right," cried Faybelle. "You-all git movin'. . . . Buster, Marvin, Luke, Clydey, and Jay Boy—take to the fields and start the bean pullin'. I'll tend my man. You, Virgie Smeet, start your car and head for Willard—and don't come back without a doctor."

Lord!

Then Piddle got rambunctious.

"You're takin' advantage of a he'pless man," he hollered, loud as he could. "You're goin' to let a doctor saw on him and feed him medicine till he dies and you're rid of him! . . . You ain't no lovin' wife or no daughter of mine. You're—"

Faybelle stood firmly on that kitchen floor and was every bit a match for that silly old daddy of hers.

"You-all boys who are goin' to the fields," she said, "take Piddle out as you go and shut him up in the feed shed. . . . Handle him rough, 'cause he's meant to be handled that-a-way."

"The feed shed ain't got no lock," said Jay Boy.

"Then nail it up so's he stays in there and cain't git out. . . . Put a two-by-six across the door. Jail him up, and keep him in there."

Virgie started her car and headed for Willard; Faybelle attended her man who raved about apes in the bean crop; and Marvin, Buster, Luke, Clydey, and Jay Boy each gave a hand to Piddle and boosted him into the feed shed. They set a strong two-by-six plank plumb across the door and spiked it on solid with twenty-penny nails. Piddle hollered and kicked at the door because he couldn't get out—raised a fuss about the doctor—sounded like he was tearing the in'ards of the feed shed to pieces. Then the balance of the menfolks went out and pulled beans.

When Virgie hauled the doctor in the house, Tod was mumbling something and Faybelle sat by his bed and held the hand of his good arm. The doctor took one look at Tod and said: "Wow!"

"Is he dyin'?" asked Faybelle, anxiously.

"No," said the doctor.

So that man who knew all about busted arms took out a little doo-dad with a needle on it—something like they use to vaccinate calves. He gave Tod a poke with it, and soon Faybelle felt her man relax and saw him go to sleep. Then the doctor took off the wrapping and splints.

"Wow!" he said, when he saw Tod's ailing arm.

The doctor had Faybelle fetch him some hot water; he went to his satchel for a big roll of bandage and clean splints; he smeared on Tod's arm a lot of brown stuff that stank. When he finished working Tod's busted arm was a big ball of white cloth.

"He's weak," said the doctor, "and it will be a long time before he can use that arm again. But he'll get well, and except for a crook in his arm, be as good as ever. . . . It will take time. Don't let him work."

"When can he git up and walk about kinda easy?" asked Faybelle.

"In about a week. He mustn't bother that arm, though. . . . I'll have to look at it again; bring him into town."

"Praise the Lord for all his manifold blessin's," said Virgie, who had been there ready to help if the doctor called.

"You've got a strong man for a husband, Mrs. McClung," said the doctor, as he fixed up his satchel.

As he left, ready to climb in Virgie's car and head for town, Faybelle had a thought. She wondered if by chance this man who knew so much about ailments didn't know about other things, too.

"When do you-all reckon it'll freeze, doctor?"

The doctor shrugged his shoulders.

"Hard to say. But not likely for another two weeks or so."

Faybelle returned to the house after Virgie and the doctor drove off. She looked down on Tod, who was sound asleep and seemed not to be hurting a mite. She heard Piddle outside, kicking the feed shed door and hollering like a man in trouble.

"You-all will wake up, Hon, and I'll feed you supper" she said to the sleeping Tod. "You will be up and about in a week. The doctor says so, and he *knows*. The frost is comin', but not so fast we cain't git the crop in. And by the time you go out to the field again, in one short week, the boys should have the beans pulled and shocked. . . . You'll be there to see your livin' fall into the sacks, Tod. Honest to God, you will."

## Chapter Fifteen

Tod McClung sat astraddle his horse watching all that went on before him.

His broken arm was heavily bandaged around the splints and it rested in a sling of clean, white cloth that Faybelle had fixed around his neck. His left hand held the bridle reins. And although Tod was unable to work himself, to give all those folks in the field a hand such as Tod McClung would if he were a well man, he enjoyed watching the business of the harvest and seeing his year's work and earnings fall into the sacks.

Tod McClung was a lucky cuss.

It was a busy day and Tod's horse stood impatiently, nodding his head, scraping the ground with his right forefoot and snorting now and then like he had a hanker to move. But Tod just sat in the saddle and looked ahead of him. He saw plenty going on—plenty to do if he could—but he just sat.

He saw the fields before him; the same fields he had looked on for thirteen years—the field he had watched grow from a quarter mile square to a stretch half a mile wide and a solid mile long.

From his saddle seat he saw the harvest.

The bean harvest.

He saw them reaping the crop he had sown from the seed saved over from the year before—and the seed that produced last year's crop came from this same soil the year before that.

Daddy seed! Granddaddy seed! Great-granddaddy seed!

Lord!

Tod's bean crop had the finest of ancestry—a pedigree which could be traced back to that sack of beans he had bought in Willard thirteen years before. The seed for his first bean crop.

The pinto bean.

Call them what you like. Cowpuncher strawberries, Sheepherder's Delight, and other disrespectable names. Even dirty names.

The Mexicans call them *frijoles*. They love them, and to Mexicans *frijoles* is a loving name. The pinto bean is theirs.

Who brought the first pinto beans to New Mexico? That's what Tod wondered.

Was it Coronado?

Or Oñate?

Lord! That was a long time ago. He must ask Buster, thought Tod, because Buster had told him all about Coronado and Oñate. Nearly four hundred years ago, those boys from Spain first saw the valley—the Estancia valley—the valley of pinto bean makers just like himself.

Tod was a busy man that harvest day for all his broken arm, so he had to ride a saddle pony to get here and there and keep the work moving. But now his horse stood and Tod sat.

Oh, he'd move—Tod didn't sit still very long when there was work going on; if he did, it wasn't Tod. But now he just rested a minute to look.

Ahead of him he saw the field where, only a week before, there had been rows of podded bean plants; but these plants no longer clung to the earth or were fed by it, because they were piled up in neat shocks. Men with pitchforks were loading the wagons, throwing the unthreshed crop up to lanky fellers who tramped it and built the loads on the wagons.

There was old man Mudgett's team, loaned to him by that good neighbor for the harvest, hauling the third wagon down the field. That pair just pulling out toward the thresher—the team with the chestnut mare with her tail shorter than her mate's. That mare's name is Tulip.

Poor Roddy. Roddy just withered and died.

Lord!

Tod wished Tewp was here to help with the harvest. Tewp liked to handle a team and pitch to the thresher. But that boy wrote him that he had a job making bricks at the State Pen along with Cletus and Scatterwhiskers. But five years would pass soon enough. Look how thirteen of them went in such a hurry!

And how neatly the beans were shocked!

Sudie used to like to put the beans in shocks after they were ripped from the ground. She was a handy kid—the oldest of the bunch. Tod remembered how scared she looked that day Lyndel was born—when Faybelle fainted in the bean shock. Lord! She needn't have been scared. Making beans and making kids are six and half a dozen.

There, not more than a hundred feet from where Tod straddled his horse, Marvin Smeet's thresher whined and droned. The dust and chaff rose from it to the sky. There was old Marvin himself up on top feeding the big machine like a regular hand. There on the ground beside it was the Reverend Luke Flowers busy with string and awl sewing up the mouths of the sacks as they filled with beans. There was Craze Rufe and that generally worthless brother of his, Tennis, heaving the sacks up on a stack ready for the wagons to haul off to the barn.

Who was that guy walking over to the water bucket to wet his whistle? That feller all slumped over, chewing and spitting as he went, and not saying a word because he was too doggone busy to talk?

That was Piddle. Faybelle's daddy. The granddaddy of Tod's kids. That's who!

Lord! That ornery old cuss!

There was Buster climbing up on the thresher to have a word with Marvin. He had a pad and pencil in his hand. Some of his doggone arithmetic, by golly. Some of those isms he knew all about.

The old Case tractor roared and sputtered and turned that long belt like a Case tractor should. And right on the seat, tinkering about it as usual, was Jay Boy. Jay Boy who would be off on the ramble when the harvest was over, but right now was making that tractor percolate.

There goes Clydey driving his loaded wagon beside the thresher. Up goes the forkfuls to Marvin who slides them into the feeder—forkfuls of beans still on the plant, still in the pod. And right there to meet the little cleaned and speckled beauties as they fall into the sacks is that old man of God called Luke Flowers.

That was the busiest gathering of human beings in Torrance County.

Was this all the work that was going on, on the Tod McClung ranch?

No, by golly!

Because when the sun reached the noon all these boys would be ready for vittles, and there would be no belt-tightening on Tod's outfit. So Faybelle was over at the house stirring up a mess of chuck big enough to feed the United States Marines.

She had the beef barbecued just as the boys liked it, the meat of that steer calf Tod had Jay Boy butcher the day before. There were pots of this crop's beans, too, boiled down with side meat and red chili. Corn bread and biscuits and cake. And a dishpan full of fried potatoes. Coffee! Buckets full of it. And lots of clabbered milk, because Luke Flowers sure liked corn bread and clabber.

Faybelle didn't have to do all this cooking alone, either, because Virgie Smeet and Earlene Flowers—even Effie Lee Mudgett and the Widow Burge—came over to help her. And while they cooked and got vittles ready for those hungry menfolks they fussed and gassed like women will. And trailing around the kitchen was that three-year-old boy of Earlene's, who didn't look a mite like Preacher Flowers, everybody thought.

And while all this was going on Tod McClung looked to the west and saw the Manzano Mountains ranging along the sky line. And beyond those old hills was the valley of the Rio Grande. And up north along the river, in Albuquerque, his little daughter Lyndel was making herself a lady of the finest kind. A lady fit to come back to the land with maybe a man who would be a gentleman as well.

So Tod sat and looked. Then he figured he had better get on his high horse and lend all those good folks a hand as best he could with a busted arm. So he spurred his pony in the ribs and rode toward the thresher.

Was Tod McClung happy!

Lord, Lord!